quintin jardine
for the death of me

quintin jardine

for the death of me

headline

First published in 2005
by HEADLINE BOOK PUBLISHING

1

Cataloguing in Publication Data is available from the British Library

ISBN 0 7553 2105 7 (hardback)
ISBN 0 7553 2106 5 (trade paperback)

Typeset in Times by Avon DataSet Ltd,
Bidford on Avon, Warwickshire

Printed and bound in Great Britain by
Mackays of Chatham plc, Chatham, Kent

Headline's policy is to use papers that are natural, renewable and
recyclable products and made from wood grown in sustainable forests.
The logging and manufacturing processes are expected to conform to the
environmental regulations of the country of origin.

HEADLINE BOOK PUBLISHING
A division of Hodder Headline
338 Euston Road
London NW1 3BH

www.headline.co.uk
www. hodderheadline.com

A dedication

Most people who know me well believe that I was an only child, but that's not true. There was another, who was born at 2.45 a.m. on 12 January 1949, and who died in the same moment. His passing was certified by the same autocrat who had brushed off our mother's plea for a Caesarean several hours earlier. Our parents were so traumatised by the episode that they never spoke of it to me, and rarely to anyone else. I didn't even know the year of the occurrence, let alone the date, until recently the good people at GRO Scotland helped me find out.

The child wasn't baptised, and his death certificate doesn't even grant him the dignity of a name. To me that's a monstrous wrong, and I propose to exercise my power to put it right, here and now. Since I was named after one of my grandfathers, I'll assume that he would have been named after the other, and I christen him this very day.

Therefore this book is dedicated to the memory of Duncan Jardine, who died because he was too weak to breathe when eventually he struggled from the womb, but who had a soul nonetheless, who was my brother nonetheless, and who has a place of honour on my family tree. Rock on, bro', and I hope that somehow you know how proud I feel as I do this for you, at last.

May 3, 2005

Acknowledgements

To Sharon Hutson, of GRO Scotland, an instrument for good.

To the staff of the Swissôtel Stamford, Fort Siloso, and various other places, in Singapore.

To Aline Lenaz, the Cloak and Dagger bookstore, Princeton NJ, for her help to Oz in his hour of need.

To Martin Fletcher, for believing that I'd deliver this in time, and sticking with the schedule. (It *was* a goal, Martin.)

To the voices in my head.

And with a nod to the fictionally late Kinky Friedman, Benny Luker's near neighbour. May the good people of Texas possess the courage and wisdom to elect him as their governor. Why the hell not?

Just what is it about you?

What the hell gives you the right to intrude on my life, to demand that I should share my innermost secrets with you?

After we were done the last time, I swore to myself that it would be just that: *finis*. 'No more,' I told me. 'From now on your secrets are going to be just that. They'll be shared with nobody. I'll yield to no coercion, no blackmail. Appeals to my good nature will be as fruitful as seed cast upon a black-top highway.'

And now here you are again. What is it, nine times now that you've played on my vanity and lured me into confessing my deeds, and my misdeeds? You've got better at it too. In the early days, maybe the things I told you were as I'd like them to have happened, rather than as they really did, but I can't fool you any more. Now you make sure that what I tell you is the unvarnished truth, and that the man you see is the real me, not the caricature I drew of myself in the early days.

I warn you . . . and, by God, you'd better take me seriously . . . one day you'll push me too far. One day I'll blow the whistle and everyone will know what a sneaky, devious bastard you are, and who you are too.

But for now, okay; I'll go along with your game, I'll indulge you one more time. But I warn you . . . you may not sleep too well afterwards.

1

It was summer, and so it had to be Monaco, because Scotland is too cold and Los Angeles is just too damn hot.

I sat on our hill-top terrace, beneath a sun-blind, gazing out at Roman Abramovich's yacht as it eased towards the harbour. A few feet away, Susie, Janet and Tom were swimming in the pool, all three of them topless. Wee Jonathan was curled up in my lap, having chased himself into a sound sleep.

There was a time when I used to stop and pinch myself, to check that I was solid flesh and blood, that everything was real, and that I wasn't playing the unknowing lead in a sequel to *The Truman Show,* with millions of viewers tuning in every night to update themselves on the soap opera that was my life. Not any more, though. Now I accept the craziness of my existence without question. No longer do I contemplate how it came about or lie awake wondering how long it will last.

I'm Oz Blackstone, A-list movie actor, and I have at least ten years, more if I look after myself, before they start offering me 'old guy' parts. I have a beautiful wife, three beautiful kids and three . . . yes, three . . . homes.

Until around this time last year, Susie and I thought we'd never leave our estate overlooking Loch Lomond. We're both loyal Scots and we'd always insisted that it would always be home base for us, no matter how exotic our lives became. But finally we were worn down by the arguments of agents, of accountants and, crucially, of my dad, who told me that if he'd had the chance at my age he'd have hightailed it out of Scotland as fast as his sturdy legs could have carried him. If there had been any lingering doubt, it was all topped off by the proposal of the Government of the day that people should be locked up without trial on the say-so of a politician rather than a judge. Who'd want to live under a regime that could even contemplate that? They had one in Iraq, and look what happened there.

So, decision finally made, the next step was to decide where we would live. My career makes a place in Los Angeles more or less essential, but our tax people advised us against settling there. They offered us a choice between Ireland and Monaco.

Did I say 'choice'? Hah! 'Nuff respect Dublin, but it took about two seconds to make that one. We went shopping on the Côte d'Azur and found a newly built villa with three public rooms, a study, six bedrooms, a self-contained apartment for Ethel Reid, the kids' nanny, and a small bungalow guarding the entrance to the property, to be occupied by Audrey Kent, our secretary, and her husband Conrad, whose euphemistic job title is 'security manager'.

We didn't sell Loch Lomond, of course. I'll never do that, for all sorts of reasons, some sentimental, others very practical indeed. But we decided that Monaco would be home base, and that Janet, Tom and wee Jonathan would be enrolled in its international school.

Tom is the newest addition to our family. He's my son by my brief second marriage, to Primavera Phillips; he was conceived in its final unhappy moments, but Prim chose not to tell me about him. Indeed, she kept him secret from me until he was three years old, finally leading me to him by way of a merry dance of the kind only she could orchestrate. Not that she meant to: he'd still be unknown to me if she'd had her way. I like to think, though, that whatever had happened I'd have found him eventually. And if I had, whenever it was, wherever it was, I'd have known him straight away. I'll never forget the first time I set eyes on him, in a roadhouse hotel in California, or how it turned my life upside-down.

Funny, my three kids each look completely different. Janet's her mother to the life. Wee Jonathan, the older he grows the more he's looking like my dad. Tom? Well, he's me, no doubt about that, and if you look closely you'll see Primavera's boldness in his eyes. But there's more, there's more, only I'm not ready to deal with that, not yet.

My second marriage, I said. My first, of course, was to the lovely Jan, my soul-mate; but you know about Jan, how we grew up together, then drifted apart, only to be reunited when we realised that we didn't really exist without each other, not properly at any rate. You know how happy we were, living an idyllic, uncomplicated life together in Glasgow, until it became all too complicated, and she and our unborn child were killed, by the intervention of some very bad people. What happened to them? You know that too: they've all gone to hell, and I had the sublime pleasure of sending the biggest and baddest of them there with my own two hands.

'*Oz!*' the girlies yell at premières, award bashes and other movie events. '*Over here, Oz! Give us a wave, Oz! God, isn't he nice, isn't he gorgeous? Did you see that smile?*' The girlies, even one or two of the boysies too, but I don't mind them: I'm a liberal-minded guy. After all, I'm a member of a minority group myself . . . I'm a Fifer. Besides, they're right. I am nice, I am gorgeous and, courtesy of Mac the Dentist, my dad, I do have a pretty dazzling smile. That's what they see and if it makes them happy, well, it makes me happy too. Very few people have seen the other Oz; in fact, I can't think of any who have and are still around to describe him. No, that's not quite true: there's one who's doing thirty years in the USA. He'd be well advised to serve all of them: by that time I might just have forgotten about him.

So, anyway . . . as my mother always chided me for saying . . . there I was, sat in front of our private, well-guarded, multi-million-euro villa, watching the big blue boat and suddenly feeling relatively poor. Only relatively, though: I might not own

5

an oil company, but I'd hit eight figures per movie and there aren't too many of us do that. I'd just finished the third of a trio of projects that Roscoe Brown, my agent, had negotiated for me a year before, and we had reached the stage where we were turning down more work than we were accepting. I'll tell you how big I've become: people are stopping Keanu Reeves in the street and asking if he's me, rather than the other way round. (I believe it pisses him off mightily.)

I'd earned a couple of months' break and I was looking forward to it, to a holiday with the whole family, maybe the last unfettered time we'd have together before Janet started proper school and we were hit by its limitations. My film schedule was fixed for a year ahead, but I wasn't due back in California until mid-September, two months distant. When I went back to work, it would be for Miles Grayson, my mentor and one-time in-law. He had picked up the rights to a boxing movie and wanted me in the lead, opposite his wife, Dawn Phillips, Prim's sister. Miles had decided that he was through with acting: he had recognised what the rest of us in the business had known for a while, that he was much better in the director's chair. The part meant I had to keep myself in good physical condition, but that's part of my normal routine. Every one of my homes has a gym. (Spoiled bastard, eh?)

I looked away from the Big Blue with not a trace of envy . . . Oz is not into boats . . . and laid wee Jonathan gently on the seat next to me, taking care not to wake him as I covered him with a towel. I stepped out into the sun and dived into the sparkling pool, so cleanly that Susie didn't hear me until I surfaced behind her, clamping myself on to her flotation devices.

'G'roff.' She chuckled. 'The kids are watching.'

'No, they're not. They're too busy piloting their big green crocodile. Anyway, it's good for them to see Mummy and Daddy happy.'

'Happy's one thing, Daddy fondling Mummy's tits is something else.' She turned and slipped her arms round my neck. I felt myself harden.

'Let's take it indoors, then.'

She kissed me and I felt her harden too. I love Susie's nipples. They're big and red, like cherries that are trying their best to become strawberries. 'Is this what I'm in for all the next two months?' she murmured.

'If you play your cards right.'

'Excuse me!' A voice came from the doorway, across the terrace.

Having a live-in nanny is one of the privileges of wealth, but I can understand that people might think it brings privacy problems. I suppose it might, but not when the nanny in question is Ethel Reid. She's the soul of discretion, a fountain of wisdom, and a hell of a laugh to boot. She's taken our new lifestyle in her stride, the kids love her, and so do we.

'Lunchtime for the wee ones,' she called out, walking carefully across the tiles to pick up Jonathan, as Janet and Tom scrambled out of the pool. 'The big ones can look after themselves.'

That suited us. Normally we eat as a family whenever we can, but that day Susie and I had a lunchtime appointment. The approach had come out of the blue, when I was in Spain, mid-way through Minghella's *Quixote* movie; it wasn't made via Roscoe, but direct to me, and it was from a novelist. He'd done some on-line research, found out where I was and had got in touch through the production company. The guy's name was Benedict Luker; he sent me a copy of his newly published work, *Blue Star Falling,* and invited me, in a very roundabout way, to read it and tell him what I thought. I get a fair amount of stuff like that and, to be brutal about it, most of it is recycled on the instant, but there was something about this guy's pitch that made me treat it differently. It was probably the letter that did it: I still have it.

Dear Oz
I can't think of a single good reason why you should want to read this escapist crap. If you can come up with one, maybe

7

you can share it with me, so that I can blag some other
unsuspecting bastard.
Yours, not holding my breath,
Benedict Luker
Mysterian.

Yes, it was the letter; after that, how could I not look at it? Whoever this guy was, he'd managed to throw my switch. Besides, I had no scripts to consider, I'd exhausted my reading pile, and it's bloody difficult to find English-language novels in a village in Extremadura that's not all that far from the back of beyond.

It wasn't the longest or most challenging book I'd ever read, but it got me hooked nonetheless. It seemed to be Luker's first novel; it was a fast-action off-beat whodunit, in which the author was, curiously, his own leading character. I'd encountered something like it before, but for the life of me I couldn't remember where. It was the kind of book that looks as if it's meant to be read in bed, just before the light goes out, but if you do, you find yourself awake all night, or at least until it's finished.

When it was, and when Luker the private-eye hero had caught the bad guys, and the Blue Star, which turned out to be a fist-sized diamond, just before it fell into an industrial crusher that would have turned it into a thousand twinkles, I wrote to him, at the New York post-office box address he'd provided. I told him it was the best yarn I'd encountered in a long time and that I couldn't think of a good reason not to read it.

A week later, I received a second letter.

Dear Oz
Thanks. Your opinion matches mine. Now, can you think of
a single good reason why you shouldn't buy the movie
rights?
Yours,
Benedict Luker

8

Actually, I could think of many excellent reasons. I'm an actor, not a producer. I may be a success in the movie business, but I know eff all about virtually all of it. Finding writers, a director, casting, putting a crew together, choosing locations, handling the logistical problems, many of them totally unpredictable: I'd seen it all done, but I hadn't a bloody clue how to do any of it.

But I knew a man who had.

I sent Luker a one-sentence holding reply, 'I'm trying to think of one,' then called my ex in-law and asked him to get hold of a copy of the book. When I told him why I wanted him to read it, Miles questioned my mental condition but said he would. He called me back two days later, all business, and said, 'Okay, here's what you do. I'll come in fifty–fifty on a three-year option and if it gets as far as production we can run it through my company, as long as you agree to play the lead and I get to direct. And don't offer him much money, a hundred thousand dollars tops, and remember, it's an option to produce and the money's an advance against future income.'

I understood most of that, or at least enough to write to Luker and invite him to meet me in Monaco once I was clear of other commitments. He agreed and we set up a lunch meeting in the rooftop grill of the Hôtel de Paris, in Casino Square. I looked down on it as we climbed out of the pool, then checked my watch. 'Christ,' I said to Susie, 'we've only got half an hour.'

She smiled up at me, and those cherries seemed to wink. 'Well, ain't that too damn bad,' she said.

2

We were twenty minutes behind schedule when we set out for the Hôtel de Paris, and even then, Susie's hair was still damp. She had included herself in the meeting because she had read the book and enjoyed it and, as she put it, because there was no way in this lifetime that I was going to lunch in the H de P without her.

We'd only have been fifteen minutes late if the phone hadn't rung, and if Audrey Kent hadn't been in the toilet. But it did, and she was, so I picked it up.

'Oz, it's you.'

I knew that voice; by God, did I know it. 'Last time I looked in the mirror it was,' I told Primavera. 'Which of your diverse personalities is on the other end of the line, and where the hell are you?'

'I'm me,' she replied. 'The concerned mother missing her son.'

'Not the devious tramp on a mission to ruin my life?'

'Not this time.'

Prim and I had had a little difficulty a year or so before. She had been a very silly girl, and had paid various penalties, including a six-month prison term, and loss of custody of our son. I knew which had hurt her the most.

I had seen her once since she'd been inside, when we'd been at Loch Lomond and she'd come to visit Tom. Susie would have been behaving reasonably if she'd raised hell about that, since she'd been as much a potential victim of Prim's failed scam as I had, but she's as generous a woman as I've ever known, and she'd forgiven her. Guilt came into it, maybe: the early stage of our relationship, Susie's and mine, was more than a little adulterous.

'So, I repeat,' I went on, 'where the fuckaya? We're short for time here.'

'I'm in Monte Carlo.' Why was I not surprised by that? Because I knew Prim too well, that's why: she'd lost her ability to set me off balance. 'I've checked into the Columbus, and I'd like to see Tom.'

'A little notice would have been nice.'

'Yes, I know, and I'm sorry.'

Bollocks, I thought. Prim and '*sorry*' were strangers to each other.

'They only gave me my passport back three days ago, after I finished my probation period. I wasn't a hundred per cent certain that they would, and I didn't want to make an arrangement and then have to disappoint him.'

'I can accept that,' I told her. 'But you can't just sweep in unannounced. We agreed that he has to be prepared for each visit. Susie and I are already late for a lunch date; I can't deal with it right now. Tomorrow morning, fine, but not today.'

'Okay,' she conceded, slightly grumpily. 'But what am I going to do in the meantime?'

I glanced at Susie; she shrugged her tanned shoulders. 'Get in a taxi and come to the Hôtel de Paris, Le Grill on the roof. You can have lunch with us, make up a foursome. You might even be amused by it.'

'I can't just drop everything and come.'

'Everything, as in what exactly? You were ready to bomb up here and see Tom. Just get your ass' (*Gone Hollywood: can't help it*) 'in a taxi and don't argue.' I hung up on her.

Conrad was waiting at the front door in the Mercedes. We have two in Monaco, an S-class for posh stuff like being driven to the Hôtel de Paris, and an M-class, which Susie uses for the supermarket trips. (I've never understood the need for off-road capability in the Intermarché car park, but I'm no expert in such matters.) The Merc is the people's car in the principality. You don't see many BMWs there; someone I know told me that it's because they're seen to have Mafia connotations, but I wouldn't know about that.

He's a smooth driver, the boy, as skilled behind the wheel as he is in everything else he does for us. Conrad (woe betide anyone who ever calls him Connie) doesn't have a job description. Some people think he's my minder, but he isn't, not first and foremost at any rate. I can handle such stuff myself and, besides, it doesn't look good for someone like me to have a well-suited heavy on his shoulder all the time. It takes the gloss off the smile, if you understand me. No, he's there to make sure that the intruder protection systems on all our properties are working, all the time, but first and foremost to look after Susie and the kids. Is he good at that? Well, all I'll say is that when we moved to Monaco and Janet and Tom started nursery school, we had a paparazzi problem, guys following them right up to the gate and even inside. We don't, not any more. I don't know how he solved it, because I never asked, but he did.

The traffic was a little bit hairy, so it took fifteen minutes to reach Casino Square. With a clear run you can cross the principality in five. As we pulled up in front of the hotel, its impressive commissionaire stepped forward, ignoring the taxi that followed us as he seized the door handle. He bowed as we stepped out, greeting us by name . . . we weren't regulars, but such courtesies come with the uniform. I bunged him the usual, took Susie's arm and was about to lead her inside when I heard a call from behind.

'Hold on!'

We turned, and there was Prim. She'd had no time to posh up, so I suppose she'd been planning to visit Tom in a close-fitting green satin dress that looked as if it had been cut to make the most of her maternal bosom, and in chosen-to-match shoes with three-inch heels. I suppose the poor wee chap might not have recognised her if she hadn't been wearing a touch of blusher and deep red lipstick. She'd looked a bit scrawny when we'd seen her last,

13

but she'd replaced the few pounds she'd lost in the nick, and the lines around her eyes had vanished.

'Sorry I took so long,' she exclaimed. 'I thought taxis came on demand here, I had to wait almost ten minutes.' She and Susie embraced, briefly, although I could still read a little tension in my wife's body-language. I gave her a small nod, then stood aside for them to lead the way into the hotel's spectacular foyer.

'Who's the fourth member?' Prim asked, as we waited for the lift.

I filled her in quickly on Benedict Luker, his book and the bold and zany approach that had led to our lunch date.

'So you've never met the guy?'

'No,' I agreed, as the elevator arrived and we stepped inside.

'You know how old he is?'

'No. His biog on the book jacket describes him as "an international man of mystery", and that's all.'

'Or what he looks like?'

'There's no photo on the jacket.'

'So how will you know who he is?'

'Well,' I told her as we stepped out and walked towards Le Grill, 'first of all, it's more than likely that he knows what I look like. But if by some tiny chance he doesn't, the fact that he'll be sitting at my table, probably into his third or fourth cocktail by now, should give me a clue.'

His back was towards us as the head waiter led us through the crowded restaurant to the table; the sod had grabbed the best place, facing the sea. He wore a Hawaiian shirt that declared the area to be a taste-free zone, and a cowboy hat . . . yes, a bloody Stetson . . . sat on his head at a jaunty angle. A copy of *USA Today* lay discarded on the floor beside him. As we drew close he heard us, turned and . . .

. . . and that's when the shit hit the fan as spectacularly as I have ever seen, in one of the most prestigious venues in Europe . . . no, make that the world.

Susie let out a scream; her hands flew to her mouth, her knees buckled and she'd have fallen if I hadn't reacted quickly enough to catch her and pull her to me. I let Prim look after her own equilibrium. Fortunately she was up to it. She didn't scream, just stood there staring, like me, and like him. The four of us, indeed probably the whole restaurant, seemed frozen. We had become a diorama, a tableau, a paused DVD, creatures trapped in amber, or any other metaphor that may come to your mind and please you.

I don't know how long we were like that, before Prim broke the spell with a cry of 'Jesus fucking Christ.'

The Archbishop of Monaco was seated at the second table along. I caught the look of outraged horror that crossed his face. At another time I might have apologised for my guest's behaviour, but at that moment, all I cared about was my wife. Plus, Prim had beaten me to the exclamatory punch by about half a second.

Susie was trembling in the crook of my arm, still staring, pop-eyed. I couldn't say anything: I had to let her take it in, let her come to believe what her eyes were telling her, and work out how I was going to tell her what I knew I'd have to.

'Mike?' she said at last. It wasn't at full scream volume, but it wasn't far short of it.

The so-called Benedict Luker stared back at her; as he did, the cowboy hat slid slowly off the back of his head and landed on the floor. He looked to be in his mid forties, although I knew he was younger. He had a lean, weathered face, it had been around the block a few times. One of its more recent features was a scar that started on his right cheek and disappeared into a light, stubbly beard, which, like his hair, was greying. His eyes were the same, though. They'll always give you away.

'Let's go somewhere else,' said Prim, 'somewhere private.'

'No,' I replied, almost before she had finished. 'If we do that I'll probably kill this bastard again, for real this time. Sit down, both of you.'

As I eased my wife into a chair, my guest started to rise from his. Maybe it was courtesy, maybe it was flight; I don't know

15

which and I didn't care. I grabbed hold of his shoulder, doing my best to crush it, and slammed him back down. As I took the seat facing him, my back to the view, his face was twisted in pain, because I really am very strong. I wanted to hurt him more, but with the archbishop still watching it wouldn't have been the thing to do, so I released him.

Susie seemed to have retreated from the edge of hysteria, but she was still stunned; her mouth hung open slightly. Prim had recovered her self-control. 'It really is you, Dylan,' she murmured, 'isn't it?'

He nodded, then looked across at me, into my eyes. 'I didn't mean for this to happen, Oz. You never said you'd bring either of them. If I'd known that . . .'

I've rarely been lost for words.

'You're dead,' said Prim. 'See the man in the red cloak two tables away? We should get him over here to pronounce a fucking miracle. You were a Special Branch cop, you went rogue, and you were shot dead in Amsterdam about six years ago. It was on the telly and everything.'

'True,' he whispered. 'I was shot, but not dead. Everyone thought I was, Oz included. His was the last face I saw before I passed out. But I recovered. They could have let me die, but I had a lot of stuff in my head that they wanted, so they brought me back. Once they'd got it all out, they put me to work . . .'

'Who are they?'

'The drug police, international: a combination of Interpol and the DEA, very serious people. I worked underground for them for a while and helped them bust a very big chain in South East Asia. For that they gave me a new identity, a pay-off, and cut me loose.'

'Benedict Luker was the new identity?' I asked.

'No. I became him a year ago. I wrote the book for fun while I was doing odd jobs in Portugal. I took the pen name off a CD cover. When I sold it, I decided to make another identity change. I pulled a favour from a friend in the DEA, and now Benedict

16

Luker is my official name, although most people call me Benny. Hey, imagine me being called after the Pope, eh?'

'Why didn't you contact me, Your Holiness?' Susie's voice was laced with anger and bitterness. 'We were supposed to be engaged. We were living together.'

He looked at her, and I saw real pain in his eyes once again. 'It was over, Susie, or at least it was on its last legs. I knew it, and so did you.'

'Did I?'

'You didn't say as much, but you did. Remember the time I asked you to set a date for the wedding? You didn't just stall me: you ignored me. You changed the subject. That was a pretty clear message to me. Anyway, I couldn't handle it any more, you rolling in it and me on a copper's pay.'

'So your answer was to turn crook and leave me?'

He winced. 'An opportunity came up; it seemed like a good idea at the time.'

'And if it had worked, if you'd got away with your big score, would I ever have heard from you again?'

'That wasn't my plan.'

'You bastard!' Susie hissed.

I held up a hand, calling a kind of truce. I needed to bring the situation under control, and not just because we were in a public place. I was as shocked as the girls by the reappearance of Michael Dylan. He had always been one for popping up dramatically, but I hadn't expected him to do it again, not because I thought he was dead . . . I'd found out the truth a few years before . . . but because I'd thought he was gone from my life for good. I'd known Dylan for about ten years, since he was a detective inspector in Edinburgh. He'd seen himself as a bit of a high flyer then, but his boss (of whom more later) had left the force under a cloud, and Mike had jumped ship to Glasgow, in the interests of his career. There we had met up again, and he had met up with Susie. The rest of it, Prim had summed up pretty well: he'd gone rogue, and taken a hard, hard fall.

I glanced around: the head waiter had reappeared and was standing behind Prim, looking more uncertain, I suspect, than he'd ever been in his life. I told him to bring us four lobster cocktails, and four medium fillet steaks, with a bottle of 1996 Torres Mas La Plana and some sparkling water. He winced slightly at my choice of a Spanish wine, but gave a tiny bow and disappeared, grateful, I reckoned, that a potential embarrassment seemed to be defusing itself.

'I'm not saying I wouldn't have contacted you,' Dylan resumed, 'if only to let you know I wasn't dead. But then I found out about you and Oz, and the baby, and I reckoned you didn't need that kind of news at that time.'

'And if I hadn't tagged along for lunch, would I ever have been any the wiser?' Susie glared at me. 'You knew, didn't you?'

'That he was Benedict Luker? No way did I know, or I'd have burned his fucking book.'

'But you knew he was alive. Prim and I almost died ourselves when we saw him, but you were only angry. If you were astonished, it was only because he was here. Admit it: you knew and you didn't tell me.'

She had me. 'Yes, I knew, and I kept it from you. But I'm not going to apologise for it. He turned up in Edinburgh just after Janet was born. Did I ever say I thought we might have a stalker? We did, and it was him. I met him, and I told him death became him, and that as far as you were concerned, he should stay that way.' I fixed my eyes on him. 'Incidentally, Benny, I still believe that.'

'But I'm not dead, Oz, and now that Susie and Prim know it, we can't go back there.'

He was kidding himself. I know a man in London, name of Mark Kravitz: if I'd made a single phone call to him and given him instructions . . .

I confess that that dark thought crossed my mind, but I didn't dwell on it. The trouble was that Dylan had been my best friend

18

once. When he was engaged to Susie, I'd been engaged to Prim, and we'd been top of the Glasgow glamour list . . . if you can get such a concept into your head. At the same time, unknown to Susie and me, Dylan and Prim had been a couple too or, rather, were suspected of having coupled on the odd occasion, but we weren't bothered about that any more.

'Okay,' I told him. 'You're still with us, or Benny Luker is. Where's Benny based now? What happened to Portugal? Weren't you supposed to be holed up there?'

'I did my time there, but I moved on when I did the book deal. Nobody watches over me any more. I'm in New York; Benny has an American passport, and a birth certificate.'

'Won't you be a bit visible, as an author?' Prim asked him.

'I'm going to be the reclusive type. Plus, the book's only published in the US, so far at least. I won't have any exposure in Britain. When the movie's made . . . Let's face it, nobody ever cares about the author, do they? Only the director and stars.'

I heard myself gasp. 'Excuse me? The movie? You actually think I'm buying the rights now that I know who you are?'

He smiled, and looked at me the way he used to, out from under his eyebrows. In that moment I recalled what a cheeky, chancing bastard he'd always been.

'Why has it suddenly become a bad deal?' he asked.

The two women frowned in unison and stiffened in their chairs. 'Dylan,' Susie asked, 'were you brain-damaged when that Dutchman shot you?'

He looked at her as if she was. 'No,' he said. 'What's the problem? Oz liked the book well enough to set up this meeting. I could have sent a ringer along, pretending to be Benny Luker, and he'd have been none the wiser. But down the line he'd have had to know, so I decided to face him up now.'

He fell silent as the lobster cocktails were served and as I approved the Mas La Plana, proffered by an unsmiling sommelier . . . I wondered how he'd have reacted if I'd asked for the mighty Yakima Valley red that had sneaked on to his list

19

when nobody was looking . . . but I could tell that it was only a pause.

'If you'd stayed at home with the kids,' he told her, 'and if she,' he jerked his thumb at Primavera, barely glancing at her, 'hadn't turned up . . . and by the way, Oz, what the fuck is she doing here anyway? . . . your old man would have got over his initial shock and we'd have got down to business without interference. Or isn't he allowed to? I remember you saying back in the old days that you reckoned Oz's business brains were hanging behind his cock.'

I couldn't help it, I shot Susie a sharp glance, and saw her turn a nice off-beetroot shade. I also saw her stifle a grin. 'If I did say that,' she shot back, 'I must have been drunk. I was wrong, that's for sure, for I appointed him to the board of the Gantry Group, and he was bloody good. In my least sharp management moments, that's not something I ever dreamed of doing with you.' She drew breath for a moment. 'But the old days really are dead, Mike, so let's not go back there again, ever. Stay at home with the kids, you said. Yes, that's what I do now, and I'm happier doing that than I've ever been in my life. Sure, I was devastated when you went, but you really can't comprehend how big a favour you did me.'

'It wasn't much of a favour for Prim, though.'

I glared at him: that was something that hadn't needed saying, but I needn't have worried.

'Sorry,' Primavera said, with a bitter laugh. 'Susie didn't break Oz and me up. We didn't need any help: we'd have managed that all on our own, given very little time. As for you and me, well, all I can say is that having had some, I can understand why she got over you so easily. You might have been okay for this and that, Mike, but you were no use at the other.' Prim never was one to go for a few simple blood vessels when the jugular is exposed.

The discussion, indeed the situation, was in need of direction. 'That's enough,' I decreed. 'Mike, let's say that you're here impersonating Benny Luker. Agreed?'

20

'Okay,' he said hesitantly.

'In that case, our meeting is postponed. This is now officially a reunion lunch, and you and I will talk business later, somewhere else. Where are you staying?'

'Nowhere. I flew in to Nice a couple of hours ago and took a taxi along here; I expected to be gone by tonight.'

'Then stay over for a day or so. Prim, do you mind if I book him into the Columbus?'

She stared at him, disparagingly. 'As long as you don't give him my room number.'

'Right, I'll call our secretary and have her make the booking.' I looked at Dylan. 'Does Benny have a credit card?'

'Visa and American Express.'

'Give me the Visa details: she'll need them for the reservation.' He drew a wallet from a pocket in the unspeakably gaudy shirt and handed me the plastic. 'Thanks. Once that's done we're going to have a nice civilised lunch, then our driver will take you, me and Prim back to the hotel, and Susie back home. Honey, you'll prepare Tom for a visit from his mum. Prim, you'll change into something casual, and pack a swimsuit if you like, and Conrad will come back for you.'

'Can't I take Tom out?'

'With Conrad, yes, if you insist. But I'd rather you took all three of them, or Janet at least, for Jonathan can be a bit fractious. We've got Tom used to the fact that he's one of a family of three kids, and I don't want anything undermining that.'

'You don't trust me to take him out on my own, do you?'

'Not yet,' I told her, honestly, 'and not for a while. You kept him from me for three years. Maybe in another three I'll be sure you won't run off with him.'

'I won't, but have it your way. It'll be nice taking Janet out for an ice-cream.'

At first Dylan looked puzzled by this conversation, but as it developed, I could see that he was getting the picture.

'Good,' I said. 'Now everybody's as happy as can be

expected.' I made the call to Audrey, then handed the Visa card back to Dylan. 'Michael,' I continued, 'we're all glad you're not dead . . . okay, that's arguable, but let's take it as read for now. Why don't you tell us about a typical day in the life of Benedict Luker, and how you came to write the book? To be honest, old son, I never gave you credit for having that much imagination.'

He did as I asked, and a strange tale it was, if it was to be believed. It seemed that Rob Willis . . . the persona under which he'd settled in Portugal . . . had posed as a former police officer, retired on health grounds after an on-the-job injury. Actually this was an approximation of the truth, but the Iberian peninsula is so crowded with retired British coppers that he was hardly going to be a sore thumb.

It had never occurred to me to doubt Dylan's account of the undercover adventures he had recounted when we had met up in Edinburgh: he'd volunteered it knowing that I had the contacts to check the story out if I chose. Equally, I took this new account at face value.

What he told us was that he had been working in a bar in a town called Tavira when he had been approached by an ex-pat friend of his named Chuck, a retired haulage contractor from the London borough of Walford or somewhere similar. The guy had told him that he had been robbed. His house, a few kilometres in-country, had been burgled while he and his wife had been on the golf course. The thieves had taken the usual, telly, DVD player and all his movies and CDs. Unfortunately, they had also taken his wife's jewel box, which, on that one day, contained a very special rock that she had neglected to put away in the safe. It was a diamond pendant, a stone with a lustrous blue shine that had come into his family about fifteen years earlier, in circumstances that Dylan's confidant thought best to leave vague, but which precluded his reporting the matter to the local police . . . or any other police for that matter.

Chuck's plea to Dylan was simple. 'You were a copper, I know that, but thirty years in the East End sharpens your sense of smell,

22

and I can smell something iffy about you, son. So, how about helping me get my stone back?'

How was he to reward such confidence? By saying no, and maybe start Chuck asking a few questions about his past? No way. So he agreed, and the two of them began their own investigation. Dylan had been a half-decent detective in his time, and the thief had borne no passing resemblance to Raffles, the gentleman burglar, so pretty soon they had a few leads.

'Are you saying,' I asked him, 'that *Blue Star Falling* is based on the truth?'

'Got it in one, Oz,' he replied, with a beam that broke the local smugness record by a mile, and that takes some doing in Monaco. 'It's all tricked up, of course. The locations are changed, the names are changed, and of course the ending was nothing like that.'

'How did it really end, then?'

'I found the diamond with a fence, I got it back off him . . . I threatened him with the police and he believed me . . . and I told Chuck who had stolen it. I didn't want to know any more.'

'What if Chuck reads the book, and recognises the story?'

'Chuck's never read a book in his life, nor has his wife. But even if he did, it's well disguised. I have this really talented editor. She's bloody lovely too; I think I may have some standing there.' He smiled. 'So that's how Benedict Luker, novelist, came to be, and how we all came to be sitting round this table.'

I looked at him with a degree of grudging admiration, something I'd never done in my life before. 'You're a grade-A fucking nutter, Michael.'

He nodded his silver-streaked head. 'Anyone who read my CV would be justified in thinking that. And if they were in any doubt, I can always get you to give them a reference.'

'And me,' Susie exclaimed.

'Don't leave me out,' said Primavera.

3

No question about it, that was the most bizarre and embarrassing lunch of my life. I actually found it necessary to go across to
the archbishop's table and apologise for any offence that my
friends' unguarded tongues might have caused. Untypical
behaviour for Oz, you may think, but my family and I live in the
damn place: the last thing I need is to be denounced from the
high altar.

Nobody wanted dessert . . . well, Prim and Dylan might have,
but I wasn't going to offer it. I knew I had to get Susie out of there
and back home, away from the contrived, artificially civilised
atmosphere, so that she could sit down on her own and come to
terms with the sudden storm that had turned the smooth waters of
her life into a white-capped sea.

I called Conrad as soon as I could and summoned him to the
hotel to pick up Susie; then, in one of those changes of plan which
are my trademark, I summoned a taxi to take Prim, Dylan and me
to the Columbus. In the hotel, I waited by the desk as he checked
in. The receptionist looked more than a little surprised that he had
no luggage, but she didn't query it, maybe because he was with
me. I guess that must have been it, otherwise she'd have taken
one look at that shirt and turned him away. As soon as he had
completed the formalities I walked him the short distance to the
hotel shop and made him buy a couple of polos with the
Columbus logo and its slogan, 'Live Life, Love Life', some
boxers, white socks, a pair of tailored shorts, and a baseball cap.
Cowboy hat, indeed!

'This trip's costing me a fortune,' he grumbled, as he signed the card slip. 'You'd bloody better be prepared to deal.'

'I won't even sit down with you till you look respectable,' I told him cheerfully. 'I've got an image to protect: I can't be seen around town with a fucking tramp.'

He stared at me. 'Is this the same guy who used to chum me to the Horseshoe Bar in Glasgow for a pie and a pint?'

'No, it isn't,' I replied, 'so get used to it.'

Prim was waiting in Reception when we returned: the green number had gone, to be replaced by a sleeveless white shirt, loafers and pedal-pushers. As it always was with her, she managed to look a hell of a lot tastier than in more formal get-up. As Dylan went off to his room to transform himself into something more acceptable, I called Conrad to come and pick her up, then walked her down the steps to the front door to wait for him.

'You all right?' I asked her.

She smiled up at me, almost shyly. 'I'm better now,' she said.

'Have you got over being in the nick?'

A shadow crossed her face. 'You never get over a spell in Cornton Vale. It's not that it's a menacing place, it's just that there's so much sadness there, so much hopelessness. There were no suicides when I was in, but you can understand why there have been.'

'There are suicides everywhere, love, even here.'

'What, as in lose the lot in the Casino then throw yourself in the harbour?'

'I wasn't thinking of that, but it's a possible scenario, I'll grant you.'

'Do you ever go there, you and Susie?'

I laughed. 'That's a good one. In all the time we were together, did you ever know me to gamble on anything other than the lottery?'

'No, but we won the lottery. Didn't that encourage you to risk some more?'

'Hell, no! It encouraged me to quit while I was ahead.

26

Anyway, there are other risks in life than money, and I take plenty of them. Accepting a script that might send your career on to a new level, or set it on irreversible decline: that's a risk. Boarding a plane: that's a risk. Spending ten minutes alone with you: that's a risk.' Hell, where did that one come from, and what did I mean by it?

She didn't ask me either of those questions, though. Instead she smiled, looking at me slightly askance through her Versace shades . . . I always wear Vuarnet myself . . . with the sun glinting off her hair. 'Meeting Mike's a risk too, I suppose.'

I considered that one for a moment. 'No,' I told her, decision made. 'I'm in control there.'

'You think?'

'Sure. As always, Dylan hasn't thought everything through. If I walk away, I lose nothing more than the cost of one posh lunch. He winds up with major financial indigestion.'

'And will you walk away?'

'That won't be my decision, not entirely.'

'You're not going to kick him when he's down, are you?'

I stared at her. 'And if I did? Jesus, you've got a short memory.'

'What? Are you still carrying a grudge because I had a fling with him? I thought you didn't care about that, or about me, any more.'

'I . . .' She'd misunderstood me, but I let it lie. 'Never mind. I'm not going to put the boot in, don't worry.'

'Your choice.' She shrugged, then frowned suddenly. 'Does Tom miss me?'

'I'm sure he does. But he's happy, Prim. He doesn't cry for you, if that's what you mean. Still, I'd like you to see as much of him as you can, within the context of his wider family.'

She wrinkled her nose, and gave me that look again. 'Why don't I just move in with you? Make Ethel redundant and I'll be the nanny.' She laughed as she said it. That made it even more unsettling: over the years I'd found that Prim never said anything

27

casually. Sometimes she'd look me in the eye and tell a flat-out lie, like, 'I don't care about you any more.' Other times she'd say something incredibly flip, like the line about Ethel, but underneath it she'd be saying exactly what was in her mind.

I brushed it off with a laugh of my own, then changed the subject completely. 'Where are you living?' I asked her.

'With Dad, in Auchterarder. I sold my place in London and moved in with him. For the moment at least he needs me: he's been a lost soul since Mum died.'

'I'm not surprised. Elanore left a big space behind her. Is he still working?'

'He is now. He did nothing for a while, but I've managed to nag him into going back to his model-making.'

'So you've got no social life to speak of?'

'In Auchterarder?'

'Okay, it was a daft question. Stay here for a few days, and I'll see if we can introduce you about town.'

She gave me the gauche look again. 'Thanks, but I don't know if I'm ready for that yet. All I really want to do is spend time with Tom, but maybe we'll see.'

Two things happened at once to end our discussion. First, Dylan emerged from the hotel, looking presentable in polo shirt, shorts, and baseball cap, although his legs were obscenely white and his trainers were a disaster. Second, Conrad pulled up in the S-class, bang on cue. For a moment the commissionaire looked annoyed . . . probably by those trainers . . . until I stepped forward and opened the door for Prim, and until I pressed a twenty-euro note into his hand.

We stood and watched her as she waved from the rear window of the departing car.

'Will she ever be seen again?' Dylan asked.

'What?'

'Joking, Oz, joking. It just looked like a movie scene, that's all.'

'You've still got a weird sense of humour, mate. Or you've

been watching too many movies.'

'That's all Benedict Luker has to do in his sad life,' he said, with a bland smile. 'Where are we going?'

'For a walk. You look as if you could use the exercise. Then we'll talk.'

I led him away from the hotel, past the car museum that is Tom's favourite place in the entire charted world, and up an escalator to the road that leads to the rock on which Monaco was founded. It was a steep climb, and by the time we reached the square in front of the Grimaldi Palace, Dylan was breathing hard. (We could have taken a bus, or even a taxi, but I didn't tell him that.)

'This is very nice,' he croaked, as we looked out across the city, 'but it's fucking hot.'

'Appreciate it, Mike,' I told him. 'It's part of the joy of being alive.' To cool him down a little, I walked him through the cathedral . . . hoping that we wouldn't bump into the archbishop . . . pausing for a moment's reflection at Grace Kelly's grave, one movie star paying his respects to another, until finally we turned into the network of narrow old streets and found a shaded bar.

I ordered a couple of bottles of Sol and leaned back in my chair. 'Well, Benny,' I began, 'what do you want for the rights?'

'A million dollars.'

I laughed so hard that the waiter looked hesitant about bringing me the beer.

'A million dollars, just like that. You really have been living in a fantasy world, pal. This isn't *The Horse Whisperer* or *Gone with the Wind* that you're offering me. Let me explain something to you. Every movie project is a risk, and every investor participates in that risk. As the author of the original work, that's what you'd be, an investor just like me. This is the way it plays: I buy an option to develop *Blue Star Falling* as a cinematic work. If it goes all the way, the option price is an advance against a production fee, which is a percentage of the gross budget.'

'What's that likely to be?'

'Which? The percentage or the gross?'

'Both.'

'Okay, let's say two and a half per cent of a budget of thirty million dollars. That's three quarters of a million.'

He gazed at me thoughtfully, as the waiter finally served each of us a beer with a wedge of lime jammed into the neck. 'And that's all I'd get?' he asked, as he pressed it down into the bottle.

I did the same with mine, took a swig, then nodded. 'That's the norm. We might cut you in on a percentage of the DVD profits, though, as an added incentive. If you'd been sensible enough to get yourself an agent, he'd have asked for that.'

'How much?'

'Same percentage, two and a half.'

'What would the likely take be from that?'

'That's impossible to predict.'

Dylan killed most of his beer on one gulp and waved for two more. 'So out with it, what are you going to offer me?'

I glanced at my watch. 'Until about two hours ago, I was going to offer you a hundred thousand US. Now . . . nothing.'

He almost fell out of his chair. 'Nothing? Come on, I'm Benny Luker, author, and I'm letting you in on a book that's doing very nicely in the US. Forget the past, this is a commercial proposition I've got here.'

I sighed and opened the bomb-bay doors, ready to release. 'Benny, I can't forget the past, and you can't wish it away either. I wasn't going into this deal on my own. I'm not a producer, that's not my thing. I've got a partner, who was going to do all the development work, and direct.'

'Who?'

'Miles Grayson.'

He looked at me blankly. 'So?'

'So? So! . . . Like Susie said, are you sure that Dutchman didn't shoot you in the fucking head, Dylan? Remember that scam you and your mate pulled? It involved kidnapping Dawn,

30

Miles's pregnant wife, Prim's sister, and you went along with it. If he had caught up with you, he'd have shot you himself, as often as it took to get the job done. I fancy he still might.'

Comprehension spread across my undead friend's face. 'Shit! I'd forgotten about him.'

'Miles isn't someone you can forget.'

'What if I wrote to him, and to Dawn, apologising for my part in that and saying I'd no idea it was going to get that serious?'

'He'd probably do one of two things: come after you himself, or tell your publisher who you really are, and have your book taken out of print and remaindered. You better believe me, he's got the clout to do that.'

'Then I'm stuffed.'

He was too, or he would have been if I hadn't been overcome by an unprecedented burst of sentimental generosity. 'You're right, though,' I said. 'There is money to be made. Tell you what, I'll give you a fifty-thousand-dollar advance for a three-year option off my own bat. I'll have Roscoe, my agent, draw up a contract and you'll sign it, no questions asked, same terms I've just outlined. There are two people in the world with a chance of persuading Miles to let you live and to go along with this project. I'm one, but it would be a long shot even for me. No, I'll have to get Dawn on-side.'

'Do you think you can?'

'Maybe, if her sister backs me up.'

'Prim. Will she?'

'I reckon. I still have some leverage there. I'd never use it, but she can't be certain of that.'

'Leverage?'

'Our son, Tom. I control her access to him. I love the wee chap, and I'd never cut him off from his mother, but it gives me a hold over her. She'll co-operate with me.'

'If she knows what's best for her?'

'I'd never put it that way, but she needs to stay on my good side and she knows it.'

Dylan stared at me; I think he was a wee bit scared. 'God,' he murmured, 'what a calculating bastard you've become.'

I grinned and gave him the old Jim Holton line. 'Aye, and don't you forget it.'

4

After another beer or two, Dylan agreed to the deal. I arranged to meet him at the Columbus at ten next morning with an agreement for signature, and a cheque for fifty thousand, drawn on my dollar account, then we walked back down the hill and went our separate ways. He set off to look at the boats in the marina, and maybe indulge in a few day-dreams; I grabbed a taxi and went home.

When I got there I went straight to my office and called Roscoe in Los Angeles. I was in luck: he was at his desk. He has all sorts of standard contracts in his files, and knew exactly where to find one to fit the purpose. I gave him the numbers, and asked him to fill them in, then send the finished article to Audrey by e-mail, for her to prepare. He must have been busy, for he didn't bother to ask what the hell I was doing buying movie rights to anything. But if he was, some of that was my doing: Roscoe's star has risen alongside mine in the film world.

That done, I changed into Speedo trunks and went out to the terrace. Prim and Susie were in the pool with the kids, Jonathan included. He can swim almost as well as the other two, but we still make him wear armbands.

I dived in and surfaced beside Tom and Janet. 'Hi, you two. Had a good afternoon?'

'You've been drinking beer,' said my daughter, disapprovingly.

I nodded. 'Yup, and you're just jealous 'cos you're not old enough.'

'Mum took us out,' Tom told me, as if no one else ever did. It's funny: he calls both Prim and Susie 'Mum', but we're never in any doubt which one he's talking about. The wee chap looked as pleased as Punch. For various reasons . . . all of them her own fault . . . Primavera hadn't seen much of him during the previous year, but clearly he didn't hold that against her.

'Let me guess where.' I chuckled.

Prim swam across; like Susie, she did not see the need for a bikini top. Her nipples were different, bigger yet smaller, if you know what I mean. 'The motor museum,' she said. 'I come all this way, and I wind up looking at cars.'

'Those are the rules with our boy,' I told her. 'You can take him anywhere you like in Monaco, as long as it's the motor museum.'

'Can't you wean him off it?'

'Why should I? I like it too.' I grinned at Tom. 'What was your favourite car today, son?'

'The bubble car.'

'Again? That's two days running. Usually he has a different favourite every visit,' I explained.

'Maybe he wants to associate that one with both of us.'

'That's very perceptive: you may well be right,' I granted.

'What's your favourite, Mum?' Tom asked.

'The Cadillac, nineteen sixty-three model,' Prim told him. I stared at her, surprised.

'That's Dad's favourite too,' our son explained. 'Can you buy one, Dad?'

'There would be no point. I'd never drive it; all we'd do is look at it, and we can do that at the museum.'

'Can we get a bubble car, then?'

'I doubt if there's one to be found any more, Tom. Do you know, your Grandpa Blackstone used to have one of those, way back, before your Aunt Ellie and I were born. I've never been able to figure out how he got in and out of it.'

'That's a strange choice of car for a young man,' said Susie,

34

appearing beside us with a furiously paddling Jonathan in tow.

'My mum's parents approved of it,' I said, 'or so she told me, for a reason which probably occurs to you, but which we need not discuss in front of the children.'

'I get the picture. How did your talk with Dylan go? Did you send him off empty-handed?'

'No, tomorrow I'm going to send him off with fifty grand and an option agreement.'

'You're going ahead with it?' Susie looked aghast.

'I'm taking the first step. How many more will I take after that? Depends on one man's attitude, and given things that have happened in the past, it's not going to be easy bringing him on-side.'

'Miles,' Prim exclaimed, getting the point at last.

'The same; we're supposed to be fifty-fifty in the Luker deal.'

'But need Miles ever know who Benny Luker really is?' she asked.

'I've considered that,' I admitted, 'but it would be virtually impossible to keep them apart for ever. Miles likes to eyeball the people he deals with; spinning him a story that Benedict Luker is a hermit in the J. D. Salinger mould wouldn't work for long.'

'It wouldn't be honest either,' Susie remarked, pulling herself out of the pool, then taking Jonathan as I handed the wet, wriggling, rubbery lad up to her.

'There is that, too. Miles has always been straight with me, I couldn't be otherwise with him.'

'I'll speak to Dawn,' Prim declared, to my private satisfaction. Much better that she volunteer than I float the idea.

'If you do,' I warned her, 'be careful what you say, and how you say it. What you're telling her could have an even bigger impact on her than on Miles.'

'No, it won't. Dawn's never associated Mike with the kidnapping. He didn't take her, and he wasn't there at any time. The way she sees it, it was all the other guy's doing. She knew Mike, remember; she cried when she heard he'd died.'

'I bet Miles didn't, though.'

'No,' she conceded.

'If he doesn't go along with it,' Susie ventured, 'what happens?'

'I'll have given Dylan fifty thousand dollars for old times' sake. I'm not going to make the movie without his blessing, even though Roscoe could probably put me together with another producer.'

'Fifty thousand,' she mused. 'I suppose it could have been worse.'

'What do you mean?' Prim asked.

'I could have been married to the bastard.' She chuckled. 'Imagine if I had been, and he'd resurrected himself looking for half my property. He would have, too.'

5

Prim stayed with us until past the kids' bedtime. She wanted to say goodnight to Tom, and that was fine, although I insisted that Ethel should get them all ready as usual, again so that he wouldn't feel different from the others. I like to think that I'm a considerate father; if I am it's because I had a good teacher.

When they were all tucked in, she went to see him and read him a story, probably something from his A. A. Milne collection. When she came back out to the terrace, where Susie and I had supper ready, there was a tear in her eye.

'Is he asleep?' I asked her.

She nodded. 'I barely made it to page two before he was off.'

'It's been an exciting day for him.'

'Are all his days like this?'

'As many as we can manage,' said Susie. 'Oz and I decided long ago to chuck the parenting manual out the window, and spoil them rotten.'

'I've got no problem with that. You don't teach kids proper values by denying them things you can well afford. Making sure they appreciate them, that's the trick.'

We'd invited Ethel, Audrey and Conrad to eat with us. I flashed the terrace lights to let them know we were ready, then opened a bottle of cooking champagne as we waited for them to arrive. That was when my cell-phone started to chirp.

I glanced at the panel; it told me that it was Ellen, my sister. I frowned; we kept in regular touch, but it wasn't like her to call me in the middle of a Wednesday evening. I flipped Mr Moto open.

'Hi, Ellie, what's up? We're just about to sit down to our tea here.'

There was a moment's silence. That was all, but it sent a chill through me. With my Sis, getting a word in is usually an achievement. But it wasn't my Sis. It was Harvey January, my brother-in-law. 'Oz,' he said hesitantly, and I knew for sure it was bad. Harvey is a QC, and not given to stumbling on the phone.

'Who is it?' It wasn't a matter of 'what': I knew that. Something in my tone froze Susie and Prim in their tracks.

'It's your father. Mac's had a heart-attack.'

We all spend some of our adult lives imagining, and dreading, moments like those, but we can't prepare for them. My legs went limp under me, and I sat down hard on the terrace tiles. I didn't want to hear the answer but I had to ask. 'Is he . . .'

'No, but he's very seriously ill. He collapsed at the golf club in Elie this evening; one of his playing partners was a doctor, who resuscitated him and kept him going till the paramedics arrived. They took him to Ninewells, in Dundee. He was unconscious when he arrived, and he's being assessed now. Ellen's on her way there.'

'What are they saying? What's the prognosis?'

'They're not making any promises, Oz.'

'Harvey, I'm on my way.'

'I'll tell Ellen. With luck you should get there around midday tomorrow.'

I glanced at my watch: it was ten past eight. 'Fuck that. I'll be there tonight.'

I snapped the phone closed and picked myself up. Susie took hold of my arms. 'What is it?'

'Dad. Heart-attack.' Just at that moment, Conrad and Audrey walked out on to the terrace. They saw me and their expressions changed.

'Audrey, I want a private jet on the ground at the nearest available airport, ready to take off in half an hour and fly me to Dundee, or as near as they'll let me land. Have an air taxi in position at the heliport right away. Conrad, I want you with me. This will go public and I cannot be fucked about by the media. Susie, drive us to the chopper pad; you can drop Prim back at the Columbus. Prim, find Dylan and tell him to stick around till further notice. I'll cover his hotel tab.'

'I'm coming,' Susie protested.

'No, love, you stay here with the kids for now: it would only alarm them if we both left. If it goes bad, you'll all be over there soon enough.'

She saw the sense of that and nodded. Nobody else questioned anything: that wouldn't have been wise.

6

We were on the road inside fifteen minutes, Conrad driving the off-roader, Susie in the front passenger seat, Prim and I in the back.

'Tell me exactly what Harvey said,' Prim asked quietly. She's a nurse.

I ran through our conversation as closely as I could remember it. 'Does that tell you anything?'

'He survived the trip to hospital; that of itself says something. But any number of things could have happened. He could have had a coronary thrombosis, or an aneurysm. Maybe it's an arterial blockage and they'll be able to fix it with an angioplasty, a device that restores the proper blood flow without a full-scale bypass.'

'Does it sound good or bad?'

'Nothing about this is good, Oz,' she pointed out gently. 'But at least he isn't simply lying on a life-support machine, in a coma, in an IC unit. Mac's a pretty fit man for his age; strong, too. That will improve his chances.'

I took out my cell-phone. 'I'll try calling Ellie. She'll maybe know more by now.'

She put a hand on mine, to stop me. 'Ellen's phone will be switched off in the hospital. She'll get in touch with you if anything changes, I'm sure.'

I had to see the sense of that, but it was bloody difficult. Normally, I'm a patient guy, but crises are something else. My instinct is to solve them there and then, and if I can't I get frustrated. When the solution is out of my hands . . .

You know, physical fear I can handle. I've been in a few tricky situations in my life, including a couple in which it was actually in danger. I've dealt with them all, and it never occurred to me to be scared, not in the heat of the moment, at any rate. There's a big adrenaline rush, sure, but I've always been too caught up in the action to dwell on the consequences of failure. I've got the job done, and dealt with the fear afterwards.

But this was different: this was something that I couldn't handle personally. Other people were doing this job, and I had plenty of time to consider the consequences of their failure. I started to shake; I took a tight grip of my travel bag, trying to control it before anyone saw.

The chopper was waiting for us on the pad at the heliport behind the Columbus. Susie followed me towards it. As Conrad climbed on board, she reached up and touched my cheek. 'Wish I could come,' she whispered.

'So do I, honey, but it's best you stay here, especially with her around.'

'What about Mike? Will he hang around indefinitely?'

'That's up to him, but if he wants to do this precious deal of his, he will. If things . . .' I faltered, then steeled myself. 'If Dad doesn't make it, I'll make other arrangements with him, but I'm refusing to think of that. I'm assuming that he'll come through this and that I'll be back here by the weekend. Don't you get drawn into it, though. Any messages that need to go to Mike, Prim can carry them. I don't want Mike involved with my family, and I don't want him in my house.'

She squeezed my arm, and gave me a half-smile. 'Are you worried about me with my ex?'

I tried to smile back. 'With the size of my ego? You have to be kidding. No, it's just this: he betrayed us all, back then, and you most of all. We might be glad that he's not dead, but it doesn't mask what he did. I'm no moral paragon, but I don't want my kids to have anything to do with him, anything at all.'

She got on her toes and kissed me. 'Don't worry, big guy,' she said, raising her voice above the roar of the helicopter. 'I feel the same way. You be on your way now: when you see Mac, tell him from me that he's not to give us all such a scare again.'

Somehow, I felt better as I ducked the rotors and boarded the Jetcopter, sliding in beside Conrad on the bench seat, and fitting a headset to my ears. 'Buckled in, gentlemen?' the pilot asked.

'We're set,' my assistant replied. 'You know where we're going?'

'General aviation, Cannes-Mandelieu airport, to connect with a Citation jet chartered from Excel Air.'

'Fine. Let's take off.'

'How long will it take?' I asked Conrad, through the headphones. The pilot was connected to the air-traffic system: we couldn't hear him and he couldn't hear us.

'Less than half an hour, sir. Cannes is about fifty kilometres straight line, and this machine can travel. Audrey told the charter company to be ready to take off as soon as we get there, with a flight plan filed to the nearest possible landing point.'

'Do you know where that will be?'

'I'm hoping it'll be Dundee. They normally close at nine p.m. BST, but if staff are available, they can extend that by an hour. The charter company said they'd do their best.'

I nodded and leaned back in my seat, staring out of the window at the coast as we headed west, doing my best not to think the worst, and failing abysmally, until I summoned a picture of Susie's optimistic smile into my mind. That helped, a little.

7

It wasn't hard to find them: Conrad and I walked into the main concourse and there they were, in the cafeteria, each with her hands clasped round a mug of coffee. It was hard to say who looked the more exhausted, Ellen, or Mary, my step-mother. They didn't see me as I approached, trying to read their faces for any signs that might be there.

When I was three or four yards away, Ellie looked up. Her eyes widened and her mouth dropped open; she stood and met me half-way, wrapping me in the sort of hug she used to give me when we were kids. 'God, brother, am I glad to see you,' she exclaimed, as she released me. 'Harvey said you'd be lucky to get here by lunchtime tomorrow. I told him that he can't know you all that well yet. How long did it take you?'

I glanced at my watch: it showed eleven thirty, but it was still on Central European Time, an hour ahead. 'We left Monaco three hours ago,' I told her. 'We were lucky; they kept Dundee airport open for us because it was an emergency.' I gazed around; the place wasn't busy but there were a few people at other tables, most of them looking tired or sombre, in the same situation as us, I guessed.

'What's the score?' I asked.

'He's still under assessment; they haven't really told us anything.'

'Time they did, then. Who's in charge?'

'I don't know.'

Usually it's Ellie who's in charge, but this time she was just another helpless terrified relative, sitting on the sidelines of a loved one's peril.

'Time we found out, then. Where was he admitted?'

'Accident and Emergency.'

'Take me there.' I looked at my assistant. 'Conrad, stay here with Mary for now, and keep an eye out for media. It won't take long for someone to tip the word that I'm here.'

'Yes, sir.' Normally Conrad and I are informal with each other, first-name terms both ways, but he's ex-military and in what he sometimes refers to as 'operational situations' he tends to revert to type.

'Why are you waiting here anyway?' I asked Mary. 'This is hardly private.'

She looked at me, red-eyed. 'There didn't seem to be anywhere else. I tried the chapel, but it's closed.'

Ninewells is a big place; I'd been there before, but I wasn't all that familiar with the layout. Ellie was, though, and she led me through a series of corridors until we spotted a sign announcing the A&E unit. Happily, things were quiet; I dare say it would have been different at the weekend, even in a *douce* city like Dundee, but whatever Wednesday-evening rush there had been seemed to be over.

In a thing that looked like a command unit, we saw a nurse in a dark blue uniform with a tag that gave her name as Sister Kermack. 'She was on duty earlier,' Ellie murmured.

I approached her. 'Are you in charge?' I asked her.

She frowned at me, appraising me, but said nothing.

'Will I speak up a bit?' I snapped. 'Are you in charge here?'

'I'm the senior nurse on duty,' she replied evenly. There might have been a hint of a challenge in her tone: 'and what do you want to make of it?'

'Whatever I have to,' was my unspoken answer. 'Good,' I breezed on. 'We're making progress. My father was admitted here earlier this evening. His name's Macintosh Blackstone.'

46

'Yes, and he was dealt with,' Sister Kermack responded. 'He was sent to the cardio ward.'

She'd probably had a hard day too: no, not probably, certainly. But I'd left my consideration, and my normal good humour, back in Monaco. 'Look,' I said heavily, 'I know I'm being peremptory here, but I want the following, and you're the person best placed to deliver it, or set me on the right track. I'd like to speak to someone who can give me full information on my dad's condition, and I need someone to show me to a place where my step-mother, my sister and I can wait in private, for as long as I have to. I'd also like to speak to your press officer. I don't expect you to do all that stuff yourself, only to direct me to someone who can.'

She looked at me and I could tell that the name had finally clicked. 'You're Oz Blackstone, aren't you?' I nodded, unable to summon up the usual accompanying smile. 'And Mr Blackstone's your father?'

'He always has been.'

'Give me a minute. I'll phone the surgical wards and find out which one he's been referred to, then I'll get the most senior doctor there to talk to you.' She pointed to a door marked 'Staff'. 'That's our quiet room. You can wait in there, if you like.'

'That's okay, you just do what you have to, as quickly as you can.'

We watched her as she turned her back to us and picked up a phone. As she spoke, I couldn't help noticing the back of her neck go pink, then red, then redder. Finally, she hung up and turned back to face us. 'Someone's on his way to speak to you, Mr Blackstone,' she said. I could tell from her face that he would not be bearing good news. So could Ellie: she hugged me, as if for support.

'Is he gone?' I asked her quietly.

'Please,' she begged us, 'wait in the staff room.'

I took pity on her and did as she said. There was a coffee machine, the kind that takes sachets. It's not my favourite, but I switched it on and set it to make a double espresso.

47

I had just handed the end product to Ellie when the door opened and a man in a white coat, with the inevitable stethoscope hanging from his neck, stepped into the room. He looked no more than twenty-five, and he was holding a clip-board as if it was a comforter. Maybe it was. 'Mr Blackstone?' he began. 'I'm Dr Oliphant, senior house officer in the cardio unit.'

I shook his clammy hand. 'This is my sister, Mrs January,' I told him. 'I've just arrived but she and my step-mother have been here for over three hours. What do you have to tell us about our father? Is he in surgery?'

'Well,' the young doctor began. No, he had not brought good news, and he wasn't looking forward to breaking it. 'The thing is . . .'

'Yes?' My patience was totally gone.

'The thing is, he's not here.'

'What?'

'He's been transferred to Edinburgh Royal Infirmary. We don't do the sort of surgery here that he requires.'

'Jesus!' Ellie gasped. I laid a hand on her shoulder to stop her going into orbit.

'I'm terribly sorry that nobody advised you of this, Mrs January, but my colleagues said they couldn't find you. They thought you'd gone home.'

'They thought . . .' She sounded like a volcano, starting to erupt. The lad was in deep trouble, until I decided to rescue him from my sister's wrath.

'Okay,' I said, 'let's not get into a blaming situation. Someone fucked up and that's it. What's our dad's condition? That's all we really care about.'

'He's critical: he's suffered a massive failure of the aortic valve, and he needs replacement surgery or he won't survive.'

'What brought it on?'

'Nothing. We think it's a congenital thing, a defect; the consultant who saw him described it as a time-bomb that could have gone off years ago.'

'When was he transferred?'

'Two hours ago. He could be in surgery in Edinburgh already.'

'How long will the procedure take?'

'Four hours, minimum. At least, that's what I recall from medical-school lectures. I've never seen one done.'

I ruffled Ellie's hair and gave her a hug. He was critical, but he was alive, and they don't make them tougher than Mac Blackstone. 'Come on, sis,' I murmured. 'Let's get down there. We'll get him some bacon rolls on the way; if I know him he'll be hungry when he wakes up.'

8

We didn't burn any rubber on the road to Edinburgh Royal Infirmary; there was no need for we knew he'd be in theatre longer than it would take us to drive there. Before we left, Dr Oliphant phoned and found a colleague there, advising her that we were on our way. She promised to contact her media-relations people. It was necessary: when we rejoined Conrad and Mary we discovered that a Grampian Television crew was camped outside.

We gave them the slip . . . I'm an expert at that, when I want to be . . . and headed off in Ellie's Peugeot towards Perth and the M90.

Conrad drove, with my sister navigating: I chose to sit in the back with Mary.

'I should have known,' she muttered, as we cruised along the A914. 'I should have seen the warning signs.'

I looked at her in profile. It was night, but in Scotland there's always a lighter blue glow in the north at that time of year, so I could see her clearly. 'No, you shouldn't,' I reassured her, 'because there weren't any warning signs. The boy Oliphant said that a consultant cardiologist wouldn't have spotted this before it happened, unless Dad had been hooked up to an ECG machine.'

'I should still have known. I'm his wife.'

'And Ellie's his daughter: she saw him last weekend and she didn't see anything out of the ordinary.'

'Still.'

'Mary,' I said firmly, 'stop blaming yourself. There might have been things in life you should have dealt with better, but not this.'

I don't know what made me say that. Stress, I suppose: it can make your tongue do things you don't mean it to, and I sure as hell didn't want to get into that, not there, not then. I saw her frown, her profile sharp in the gloaming that passes for night in high-summer Scotland, and I looked forward. 'See if you can find some local radio, Ellie,' I called out quickly. 'If someone at the hospital tipped off the telly, they could have it too.'

We had missed the eleven o'clock bulletin on Kingdom Radio by about ten minutes, but we caught up with Radio Forth at midnight as we drove along the Edinburgh bypass. Sure enough, there was a piece at the top of the news, read by a harsh-voiced woman, about 'Scots movie star Oz Blackstone in mercy dash to the bedside of his sick father'.

They were waiting for us at the entrance to the hospital, three television crews, three radio reporters, and the rest of the pack, more than I cared to count. Conrad and I flanked Mary and Ellie, shielding them as best we could. They were reasonably polite and I knew that they were only doing their jobs. It was my fault that they were there, nobody else's. There's a price of fame, but it's not just the famous who have to pay it. Ask the wee boys Beckham if you doubt me.

'How is he, Oz?' one of them called out.

'That's what we're going to find out. I called ahead ten minutes ago and they said that he's still in theatre.' We reached the hospital doors. 'Keep in touch with the PR people,' I told them. 'I'll talk to you again when I have something positive to say, but don't look for it to be tonight.'

The hospital press officer, who introduced herself as Sydney Wavell, met us as soon as we stepped inside: no doubt the poor woman had been summoned from a peaceful evening at home. She took charge of us and led us through several corridors into a small sitting room in what appeared to be the hospital's office area, where we were given coffee and chocolate biscuits. At first I was embarrassed: genuinely, I never feel like a celebrity in Scotland, especially not in Edinburgh, and I try to avoid acting the part, yet here I was getting the full treatment. Still, Ellie and Mary were reaping the benefit, and that was good.

When we were settled in, Ms Wavell left us, returning a few minutes with a doctor. His name was Singh, and he exuded competence and reassurance. He didn't give us any soft soap, but his approach was informed and up-beat. He told us he had just checked with the theatre and that although the operation was in its early stages, Dad was stable and his signs were good. He offered to talk us through the procedure, but I reckoned that was the last thing the girls needed to hear; I didn't fancy it much myself.

We settled to our vigil. Conrad decided that he was going to sit in the corridor outside to guard the door, in case an over-zealous reporter sneaked inside in search of an exclusive. I thought he was suffering from an excess of zeal, until I realised something. He knew my dad, he had played golf with the two of us, and he liked him. He was anxious too, and was simply looking for something to take his mind off it, for a job on which he could focus. So I let him do as he wished.

Behind the closed and guarded door, Ellie curled up in an armchair and took refuge in sleep. She's always been able to do that in a crisis. When our mother was in her last illness, I'd often go into her room at the hospice and find her awake and reading, or listening to music through her headphones, with Ellen counting Zs in a chair by her bedside. Indeed, when I broke my arm as a kid, and they put me under to set it, the first sight I remember as I came to was the top of my sister's head slumped forward on her chest, and the first thing I heard was gentle snoring.

Mary and I aren't blessed in that way. We sat side by side on a small sofa in the glow of the only table-lamp we had left on, staring out of the window towards the city, watching it as it settled down for the night. We sat in silence, and yet both of us knew that there was something occupying the space between us.

I tried to doze off, but there was no hope of that. Instead I tried to occupy myself by thinking of the day that had ended; it had begun as just another summer sunrise, but it had ended with my

53

life changed, profoundly. Mike Dylan's return from his secret exile might have been seen as a shock, but no more than that. I had certainly tried to play it that way, but I couldn't kid myself.

Susie and I had got together in the aftermath of his supposed death; she'd been the emotional equivalent of a sack full of psychotic monkeys, consumed by a cocktail of bereavement, loneliness and betrayal. Me, I'd been easy pickings; in truth, I'd always fancied her and, to be honest, Jan's death had fucked my head up far, far more than I've ever admitted, even to you. Susie might have made the first move, but I made the second, no question about that.

All that apart, though, our relationship, the burgeoning thing we discovered to be love, and finally our marriage had been founded on the premise, in Susie's mind at least, that Dylan was a goner, and that he had indeed died in that shooting in Amsterdam. Now she knew different; she knew what I had known since just after Janet's birth, the truth I had kept from her. We still had to deal with that aspect of it between the two of us: she'd made nothing of it earlier, but I knew it would fester.

Beyond that?

You know me, and you know that if there is one thing the man Oz doesn't suffer from, it's a lack of self-belief. And yet when I thought of the way things had been with Susie and Dylan, how strong and vibrant their relationship had seemed, I found myself worrying about how she'd react to his return, in the longer term, whether she'd look at me differently, whether what she felt would change. There, in the dark, Alanis Morrisette's blistering line came into my head: 'Are you thinking of me when you fuck her?' It stayed there for a while, too, because it touched a nerve and made me face up to another inner truth: after all the years that had gone, sometimes, when I'm with Susie, I think of Jan.

And then there was Primavera. If you really turned up the voltage I'd have to admit that sometimes I think of her too. What she and I had wasn't love, not in the conventional sense: it was pure animal attraction, backed up by two minds that were very far

54

from the norm, and by two generously proportioned egos. When you add mutual self-indulgence to that list, you've got the whole picture of the two of us together. Dylan once said to me that he really belonged with Prim and Susie with me, because they were basically bent, in the non-sexual sense of the word, and we were basically straight. He was right about Susie, but . . .

Now Primavera was back, rehabilitated, evidently remorseful for what she had tried to do to me the previous year, and with a legitimate excuse to claim a permanent role in my life. I wasn't in any doubt that I'd be able to keep her at arm's length, yet she could still throw my switches. It might have seemed weird to you when I told you about the three of us, my wife, my ex-wife and me in the swimming-pool, all of us almost naked, but that didn't do anything to me, especially with the kids around. Yet when I'd seen her earlier, in the Columbus, changed from the more formal dress into her casuals, almost exactly the way she was dressed the first time we ever met, I will admit now that it gave me an instant boner . . . and she had known it.

My dad would live. The longer we sat there the more confident of that I became, the more my faith in Mac Blackstone's immortality restored itself. I had a feeling that I might need him too, most of all for the moral kick up the arse which only he can give me.

I smiled at the thought, and at all the day's drama and ironies. I smiled too because what should have been righteous anger at Dylan's deception and return had been muted by the fact that I actually liked the guy; I'd missed him too.

There were all those things going through my head, but there was something else, something much bigger, something that had been with me for a year. Part of me wanted to let it lie dormant, to push it out of my mind and get on with my life. The trouble was that, however hard I pushed, it wouldn't go away. Maybe I wouldn't have confronted it, but that wasn't my decision alone.

After a while, quite a long while, I glanced at my watch. Being rich, I have a few, but my favourite is a titanium Breitling

55

Aerospace, very light and with a black face and hands and numbers so luminous that they can glow even in daylight. It showed ten past three.

Ellie was still snoozing, slightly audibly, in her chair. I glanced at Mary, just at the moment she turned to look at me. Our eyes met. 'It's taking a long time,' she whispered.

'It's bound to,' I told her. 'They explained all that. This sort of surgery is usually planned, but Dad's in a critical condition. If it takes all night and all day, so be it, as long as it's effective.'

'I suppose so. It's hard, though, the waiting.'

'Tom Petty,' I murmured.

'What?'

'"The Waiting Is The Hardest Part." It's a song by Tom Petty and the Heartbreakers; great band, great lyric.'

'You can be flippant about everything, can't you?'

There was an edge to her voice. Neither of us had ever admitted it, but there had always been a certain tension between Mary and me. It went all the way back to my childhood, when Jan and I were kids together, or, more specifically, to our teenage years. It wasn't that I felt she disliked me, but there was something in the way she looked at me, a wariness that I didn't understand then, and that hurt me a little. It wasn't mutual, that's for sure. For my part, I liked Mary. That *frisson* had carried on into adulthood; then it altered a bit. After Alex More, Mary's husband, left her, and after my mother died, when she and my father grew close, I suppose there was a little private resentment on my part. Yet it didn't overlap the other thing; that was still there, until Prim appeared on the scene.

Mary was pleased. My self-esteem didn't let me deal with it at the time, but she was pleased that somebody had come between me and Jan.

Her pleasure was short-lived, though, for what was between the two of us was too strong; in fact, it was stronger than either of us understood. In the end we simply accepted it and gave in happily to the inevitable. If Mary had been as happy, it would

56

have made my day, but she wasn't. It only showed itself to me, though. As far as I knew, Jan never had a clue.

'A joke? Where's the joke? I don't understand that.'

'You've always been flip, Oz. Your first reaction has always been a throwaway line, a pitch for a quick laugh.'

I felt my eyes narrow. 'Mary, if you think I find anything laughable about my dad lying on that operating slab, you don't know me in the slightest. But you've never really known me, have you?'

'Now it's my turn not to understand,' she shot back. 'What do you mean?'

I gazed at her, rather coldly, I suspect. 'Forget it,' I said. 'We're both tired and under great stress, saying things we'd never normally say. Let's strike everything that's just been said from the record, okay?'

'What did you mean, back in the car, about things I should have handled better?'

'Mary,' I murmured, 'I really don't want to get into this.'

'What did you mean?' she hissed.

I took my wallet from my pocket and opened it. I showed her the photo that's on display there, of Susie and the three kids; the light was good enough for her to see it clearly. Then I slid a finger into the space behind the credit-card slots and drew out another image, of Tom. I'd taken it myself a year earlier, on the day that I'd found him in California, to mark it, but for another reason too.

Before I go any further let me take you back to something I told you in my last confession to you, about the moment in which I saw him for the first time: '*In an instant, I knew everything: there was no thought process involved, I just knew everything.*' That's what I said to you then. I'll bet you thought you knew what I meant; but I'll bet you also, any odds you like, that you didn't.

I showed Mary that photograph, and then I showed her another, a snap of another child, taken thirty-five years earlier. The likeness was incredible: they could have been twins.

Her cheeks seemed to collapse into her face as she sucked in

57

her breath; the gasp was so loud I was afraid she'd waken Ellie, but it would take an earthquake to do that.

'I warned you against this,' I growled quietly, 'but you had to insist. So maybe you'll explain to me why my son, conceived with Primavera and borne by her, should be the living image of my late first wife . . . your daughter. How can that be?'

She shook her head, her mouth set in a tight line.

'It's out of the box now, Mary,' I told her grimly. 'You can't put it back.' I glanced at Ellie, and I feared that there might just be an earthquake in that room if we stayed there. 'Come on,' I whispered. 'Let's take a walk.'

Conrad was sitting in a chair outside the door; he was wide awake. I said we were going for some fresh air, and asked him to sit with Ellie, in case she wakened and our absence made her think the worst.

We couldn't actually go outside, in case we bumped into the press, so I simply turned left at the end of the corridor and tried the first door I saw. It was locked, but the second wasn't, so we stepped inside. When I found the light switch I saw we were in a private office, probably belonging to one of the senior staff.

I took the two photos from my wallet once more, and held them in front of my step-mother until eventually she looked at them again.

'I'm not kidding myself, am I? Those children are almost mirror images. One of them is Tom, and the other's Jan at the same age. We're agreed on that, yes?' I ground the last word out, brutally. She nodded. 'So where does that take us, Mary?'

She tried to turn away, but I grabbed her shoulders and held her, so that she had to look at me. 'Where?' I asked her again, but she stayed silent. I began to wonder whether she had kept her secret for so long that she was unable to give it voice.

So I did it for her. 'Unless there's an ancestral link between the Blackstone and the More family, or the Mores and the Phillipses, that none of us knows about, there are only two possibilities. Either Alex More is my father, or Mac Blackstone is Jan's.'

58

Actually, the first of those had never entered my head until then, the moment when I confronted the truth that had been doing my head in since I first clapped eyes on Tom. I didn't believe it for a second but I found I couldn't avoid it.

'Either way,' I began, then drew a breath to calm me down, for I was in danger of exploding. 'Either way, one thing's for sure: Jan was my half-sister, wasn't she? For me to father a child who's her double, with someone else . . . there can be no other explanation.' And then I found myself voicing the last inevitable question: 'Or are you going to tell me that you didn't know either?'

The last twist, the one my mind hadn't let me consider before, threatened to blow a few circuits in my brain. What if neither Mary nor my dad had known? What if Alex More and my mum . . .

Her silence lasted another ten seconds or so. If I'd thought about it, that last question had offered her an escape route, but if she saw it, she didn't choose to take it. 'No,' she whispered. 'I knew. Alex was sterile. Jan had to be Mac's daughter.'

This is a terrible thing to admit but, although part of me was horrified, the greater part was relieved. I couldn't have handled the discovery that My Dad wasn't really.

It didn't blow away my anger, though: that fell on her, full force. 'And you kept that from the two of us. You let us . . . Christ, Mary, Jan was pregnant when she died!'

'Yes, but . . . Oz, I couldn't.'

'One more thing: does he know? Does my dad know?'

'No, I'm sure he doesn't. It was a one-off: he and Flora had been at a Round Table party in someone's house. Alex was away at a conference so I babysat for Ellen. There was a lot of drink at those Table dos, and that Flora, for the only time in her life, had a right few too many. She was pregnant with you, but I don't think she knew it then. Mac brought her home, and carted her straight upstairs. Then he came back down. He'd had quite a few himself, and I'd sipped my way through the best part of a bottle of wine in the course of the evening. He said something about how nice I looked, I said something similar in return, we got close, there was kissing, and then there was more than kissing. We never mentioned it afterwards . . . I don't know about him, but I was embarrassed, for it was completely untypical behaviour on my part . . . and I think both of us made sure that the same circumstances could never arise again. But I fell pregnant shortly afterwards.'

'So you must have known from the start.'

'No!' Her protest was so spontaneous that I believed her. 'I didn't know about Alex's condition then, neither did he. I didn't know anything about peak fertility times either. We weren't long married and we were trying for a family, trying quite hard if you must know. I admit that when I became pregnant the thought did cross my mind, but I discounted the possibility. Then when Jan was born, she didn't look a bit like Ellen or you . . . You and Jan were babies at the same time, remember.'

'Yes, but Ellie and I both looked like our mum when we were infants; it never occurred to me till I saw Tom, but he's very like my granny Blackstone. So was Jan in the picture I just showed you. When I looked at some older photos, I discovered that they were quite alike as young women too.'

'Mac's never noticed that, I promise you; he certainly never mentioned it to me, and I don't think he'd have been able to keep it to himself if he had noticed it.'

'When did you find out the truth?'

'Years later; when Jan was thirteen, I think. Alex and I had been trying in vain for another baby, and finally we went to see a specialist in Edinburgh. He checked us both out, then said he was very sorry but Alex's sperm count was virtually zero. Alex asked what had brought this on, and the consultant told him he'd always been like that.'

'Jesus, that was tactful of him.'

'Indeed. When I challenged him privately, he tried to claim that the case notes didn't say we already had a child, but he'd examined me pretty carefully so he must have known.'

'Is that why Alex left you?'

'Ultimately, yes. He never asked me who Jan's father was, I never told him, and I'm sure he never guessed. In truth, we barely discussed the matter. We just stumbled on for another four or five years, until he went off with his new love . . . who, ironically, has three children from her first marriage.'

'You never told us, Mary,' I repeated quietly, my calmness restored.

'How could I? Flora was still alive then, and she and your father were blissfully happy. What was I to do? Spill the beans and put that at risk? Make myself the most hated woman in town in the process? I'm sorry, Oz, call me weak, call me a fool, but I kept my mouth shut.'

'But what about Jan and me, when you saw us together as kids?'

'When I found out, you were both in your early teens. You behaved like brother and sister, even if you didn't know you were.'

'Mary,' I told her, 'from the age of . . . fourteen, as I recall . . . Jan and I did not behave exactly as brother and sister should. I'm not saying that she wasn't a good girl, or that I was a bad boy, because we were pretty responsible by contemporary standards, but like any other kids of that age, there was kissing, like you just put it, there was cuddling, there was touching, there was feeling around. The older we got, the more intimate we got.'

'I didn't know that, though. When Jan reached puberty, we had the chat that you're supposed to have. It embarrassed both of us, for she was very much a tomboy at that stage. I never thought of the two of you like that, honestly. When I found out . . . I was shocked, terrified, even, but by then it was too late.'

'When did you find out?'

'I began to worry when I heard a story about you beating up two boys at school, because of something lewd that one of them had said about Jan. Then I found a condom, in its packet, in her room. I didn't need to ask any questions after that.'

'Did you talk to Jan about it?'

'I asked her if she was having sex. I didn't ask her with whom, but there was only one possibility. It's the only time we ever had anything close to an argument. She told me very firmly that we should strike a deal: I wouldn't ask her that question again and she wouldn't ask me either.'

'Even then, couldn't you have told us?'

She reached up and touched my face. 'And if I had, my dear,' she murmured, 'how cruel would that have been? No, I kept it to myself and prayed you'd never find out. And you never would have either, but for Tom.'

'You realised when you saw him, didn't you?'

'How could I not? It was like seeing my own child again. But it didn't occur to Mac at all, I promise you. He said, "He's a real wee Blackstone, isn't he?" but that was all.'

I looked at her. 'Then, Mary,' I said, 'for the love of God, if he comes through tonight, make sure that he never finds out the truth.'

'I'll try.'

I couldn't help it: I felt my eyes harden. 'Trying isn't an option. Make bloody certain that he doesn't.'

9

Maybe I should have blamed my dad. After all, the consequences
of his quick, drink-fuelled, adulterous lapse on the living-room
shag pile would live with me for the rest of my life. But I
couldn't: I'd found out a couple of years before that he isn't
perfect, just as I know I'm not.

When I thought about it some more, I found I didn't blame
Mary either. The same event had doomed her marriage, which
some might see as just, but it had also condemned her to live what
must have been a nightmare. Those who see that as right and
proper retribution are free, as far as I'm concerned, to go and
abuse themselves in some far corner of the planet, for they can
have none of the Christian in their soul. (Unlike Mary, who's
always been a Church member, and who's a true believer. All the
more credit to her, I suppose, that she's come through it as best
she could. Eventually . . . not that night, but on one of only two
other occasions we've ever spoken about the matter ... she
confessed to me that she saw Jan's death as a divine punishment.
I told her that any God who would do a thing like that wasn't
worth an inverted candle, but I don't think she could bring herself
to believe me.)

The surgeon came to see us just before six. It was well daylight
outside, and Ellie was awake. Happily, he was smiling when he
opened the door. Relief came from my sister and my step-mother
in waves, and even from Conrad. I have to confess, for all that I'd
convinced myself that Dad would pull through, a tear came to my
eye when I saw the confirmation in that big, chunky man's face.

I saw something else there too: pure exhaustion. The procedure had taken six hours from start to finish.

He looked at Mary, then Ellie, and finally at me. 'Positive news,' he announced, 'I'm happy to say. We've replaced your father's failed aortic valve with a metal one, and it seems to be functioning well. He's in a recovery room just now; I'm going to keep him heavily sedated for a while, and still on the ventilator, but that's just routine. I'm entirely happy with the way things have gone.'

'Can we see him?' Mary asked.

'From a distance. He's still under, and in theatre conditions. Once you've done that, I recommend that you all go home and get some rest; maybe come back in around twelve hours, if you'd like. Any questions?'

'How close a call was it, Mr . . .?' I asked.

'Blacker,' he replied, 'Cedric Blacker. As close as there can be. If there hadn't been a doctor present when he collapsed, he wouldn't have made it. He can thank his golfing chum for keeping him alive till the ambulance arrived.'

'He'll thank him, don't you worry. So will we all. I know said doctor. He's a gin-swilling old sod normally. Thank God he was on the ball yesterday.'

The four of us were gowned up . . . Conrad held back at first, but I insisted that he join us . . . and shown into the recovery room. As soon as I clapped eyes on him, lying on that bed, zonked out on whatever sedative they'd pumped into him, with a pipe in his mouth and umpteen tubes leading into and out of various parts of his body, all my euphoria disappeared. I'd never imagined seeing him so weak, so old, so vulnerable; the sight filled me with all kinds of dread. He wasn't out of the wood yet. Indeed, looking at him, he seemed to be in the heart of the forest.

The sight of him took me back to my mother's last illness. It took me back to identifying Jan's body in a tiny, impersonal room in a Glasgow hospital: Jan, my lover, my wife, my soul-mate . . . my sister.

It took me forward too: I imagined other people on that bed. Susie, Ellen and Prim. I saw all of them lying under that sheet. And I saw myself too; oh, yes, I saw myself, with a row of gowned people staring misty-eyed at me. Not the kids, though: I couldn't imagine my children in such a situation. What parent can?

Once we had all seen enough . . . most of the time I looked at the monitors, convincing myself that all the peaks were regular and steady . . . and once I had given an update to the small group of diehard journalists who were still standing guard, we took Mr Blacker's advice and headed home. More specifically, we headed for Dad and Mary's, in Anstruther, with me at the wheel, Conrad beside me and the girls sleeping in the back . . . my sister could sleep for Britain. I bought a bag of morning rolls, and the four of us had an old-fashioned Scottish breakfast . . . much the same as a full English breakfast, but heavier on the black pudding and with potato scones thrown in. Then Ellen headed back to St Andrews, to Harvey and my nephews, Jonny and Colin, and I headed for the phone to call Susie.

She was as relieved as the rest of us, and she'd had a sleepless night too. Prim was with her: she had called her an hour before, asking anxiously for any news. I was touched that she'd been as scared as the rest of us, but I was struck too by something else, the ease with which she seemed to have fitted back into our circle, in spite of her efforts to wreck me a year earlier. It spoke volumes about something, but at that moment I was too damn tired to figure out what it was.

I slept for the rest of the morning and into the early afternoon; in fact, it took Conrad's knock at the door to waken me. 'Time to get ready, Oz,' he called, 'if you still want to see your nephews, that is.' I had agreed with Ellie that we would take Mary's car and pick her up from St Andrews. Harvey was in court in Edinburgh that day and she would go home with him. I reckoned that Mary would want to be closer to Dad for the next few days, as, indeed, I did, so I had asked Conrad to book three suites in the Caley Hotel.

It's amazing how much better you look when you're a super-resilient old bastard and you don't have a pipe down your throat and a tube up your knob. I'm not saying that Mac the Dentist looked as if he'd be on the golf course any time soon when we saw him at six that evening, but he was several hundred per cent improved on the version we'd seen in the morning.

We didn't crowd his small room . . . he wasn't given private treatment because of me but because he had health insurance to pick up the tab. Instead I let Mary and Ellie go in first, then followed when they'd had ten minutes.

'You're here, are you?' he croaked. 'I must have been fucking near the wooden waistcoat, then.' There was that old twinkle in his eye, one which, I feared for a while I'd never see again.

'Wouldn't have missed it for the world,' I told him. 'You ever give me another night like that and you'll wish you had pegged it.' I wanted to hug him, but since that was out of the question, I contented myself with sitting by his bedside, taking his hand and holding it against my face. 'How are you feeling?' I asked.

'Damn silly question, son, if you don't mind me saying so. At the moment it's as if somebody's shaved my chest with a chain-saw, but I'm sure it'll get worse in the days to come. I think I preferred it when I was dead.'

'What did you score anyway?'

'Net sixty-nine: I birdied the last two holes. It was probably holing that last putt that did it.'

'That's not what the consultant told me. He said it could have happened at any point of any round you've ever played.'

'You might never have been born in that case.' He looked up at me, suddenly solemn. 'How's Mary handling it?'

'She's fine now.'

'Good, good. Losing her daughter and her husband within the space of a few years wouldn't have been much fun. Tell you something,' he whispered, 'that I hope you'll appreciate. When I was in Never-never Land, I saw Jan. I remember it quite clearly. She was on the other side of a bridge: she waved to me and she called out, "Hello, Uncle Mac," like she used to when she was a kid. I never could work out how Alex More could up and leave a daughter like her and a wife like Mary. Stupid bastard . . . not that I'm complaining, mind.'

'You've done okay out of it. Now shut the fuck up and don't tire yourself out.'

I didn't really need to tell him that: he was so heavily sedated that it wasn't long before he drifted off, back into the curious, wacky, private world of the heroin medicated.

He was better next day, more alert, and as he had predicted, obviously less comfortable as the pain-killing dope was lessened.

The day after that, he was out of bed in a chair.

The third day after his op he was shuffling around in his slippers and we were able to have a longer talk, during which I persuaded him to agree to something I'd been pressing on him for a while. He could have retired years before, and become a full-time golfer. He hadn't, not because he needed extra years on his pension but because, as a dentist in a rural practice, he felt a loyalty to his patients. I'd tried the loyalty-to-Mary gambit often enough before, but he'd pointed out in his inimitable way that she was a patient too, and that my argument had just disappeared up its own arse.

This time, though, I had a stronger hand in the poker game between us. 'You're going to have to get a locum in,' I said casually.

'I know,' he admitted. 'Don't bloody know how I'm going to go about it from here, though.'

'It's done,' I told him. 'A woman called Carol Salt starts tomorrow, that's Monday, if you've lost track of time. She lives in Crail, she's thirty-four, and she's looking to get back into practice now that her second child's going to nursery.'

'How the hell did you . . .?'

'I asked Conrad, a couple of days ago, to speak to the health board. They came up with her name straight away and I gave her a call. I saw her yesterday and we agreed terms. She's coming in on a locum basis initially, with a view to buying the practice.'

He drew me one of the longest looks I've ever had from him. 'I just love it when you get authoritative,' he drawled drily. 'Is that Dallas Salt's daughter?'

'That's her; he practised in Dunfermline, didn't he?'

'Aye, but he'd gone private before he retired. I heard that he offered to hand over to her but she turned him down.'

'That's right. She told me that she believes in the NHS and wants to work in it.'

'Good for her, then. But tell her to forget about buying the practice: if she wants it, once she's seen what fills my waiting room, she can have it. My patients aren't a commodity to be sold. She can pay me a fair rent for the surgery, but that'll be that.'

I grinned at him. He thought it was triumph, but it was pride: I'd known he'd say that, but I hadn't volunteered it to Carol.

'Right,' he said, sipping from a glass of water, 'now you've sorted out my life, it's time you got back to your own.'

'I know. Your surgeon's told me you're now officially on the convalescent list, so I've booked a plane back to Cannes on Tuesday.'

'A plane.' He shook his head, then winced. 'My son, hiring bloody planes. Why don't you just buy one?'

'Not one, a fleet, actually; Susie and I have been thinking about buying an air-charter company. There's money to be made there.'

'Get away with you. You don't know what to get up to next, you two.' He frowned. 'Have you heard from Tom's mum lately?' The question took me by surprise but he's always been good at that. My dad's always had a fondness for Primavera; he didn't know the whole story of what happened last year, only that she was a bit silly and got banged up for deception, but even if he had, he wouldn't have shut her out. Like son, like father, I suppose.

'Last Wednesday, as it happens. She came out to Monaco to visit him. She was as cut up as the rest of us when she heard what happened; she sends her love.'

'You give her mine too, when Susie's not listening.' He winked. 'You got the rest of the summer off?'

'Yes, just like you. Once you're out of here, by the way, I want you and Mary, and Jonny and Colin, through at Loch Lomond. There's a pool to swim in and plenty of ground to walk around. It'll be good for your recovery.'

'We'll see.'

'You will, for sure. I've told Mary and Jonny to make sure it happens.'

'Ah,' he said, 'if my oldest grandchild's on-side, I'd better go along with it. He's grown into a formidable young man.'

'That he has. He has a formidable girl-friend too; his mum's a bit worried about that, if you know what I mean.'

'Tell her not to, will you? I remember when you and Jan turned sixteen, I decided that my prime responsibility as a father was to make damn sure you knew about the importance of contributing to the profits of London Rubber, then put my trust in your good sense. Christ, what else was I to do? Throw buckets of water over the pair of you?'

I smiled, although he didn't fully understand why. 'That wouldn't have done a hell of a lot of good,' I confessed. 'Don't worry, I've already had that discussion with Jonny. Told him to buy in bulk, to cut down the chances of being spotted in Boots by some loose-tongued friend of Ellie's or of his girl's mum. I reckoned that Harvey was a bit new on the scene to be expected to handle that one.'

'Harvey will never be able to handle that one. Nice guy when you get to know him, but I don't think he was ever sixteen.' He paused. 'You know, you're a bloody good uncle; make sure you're as good a dad.'

'Susie says I'm doing all right.' I changed the subject. 'Speaking of my brother-in-law, he's invited me to lunch tomorrow, in the New Club.'

'That's a bit daring on his part. I didn't think they let actors in there. What's that about?'

'I don't think it's about anything other than being friendly.'

'Nah, son, Harvey being friendly is him taking you for a pint or, rather, you taking him but him insisting on buying. When he invited me to the New Club it was to ask me if it was okay to marry Ellie.'

I raised an eyebrow. 'A major-occasion venue, is it? What could that be? You don't think my sister's up the duff, do you?'

'What was that?' Ellie barked, from the doorway.

10

Happily she found the idea laughable. It was also inconceivable (a nice play on words, if I may say so): I had forgotten that after Colin's birth her marriage had been in such a sad and sorry state that she had decided to have herself sterilised. She had suggested to Alan Sinclair, her first husband, that he might have a vasectomy but he had chickened out.

When she developed an infection after the procedure and became pretty seriously ill, I offered to vasectomise him myself, with the garden shears. I'd never liked Alan, but that incident pretty much put an end to our relationship. When Ellie decided to bin the tosser, I couldn't have been happier.

Harvey January was a different sort altogether. My dad and I had raised four eyebrows between us when he first appeared on the scene. He's a lawyer, and not just any old lawyer but a Queen's Counsel, so we were concerned that she had picked on another work-obsessed, boring stuffed shirt just like Mr Sinclair. When we spent some time getting to know him, we found we were wrong. Harvey's actually a shy bloke for a lawyer. (I know, I didn't think it was possible, either.) But he's in no way boring, and his shirt doesn't have anything in it but himself; he wears tee-shirts on Sundays just like the rest of us. Learning to play golf, on my advice (or at last taking the game up: it will be a long learning curve for him) was the clincher. My dad takes the view that all golfers are inherently okay; I don't agree with that, but it got Harvey's feet well under Mac the Dentist's table. It worked with his potential step-sons too: Jonny takes a certain unspoken, pleasure from giving a QC a shot a hole ... including the par threes ... and still taking a golf ball a round off him, while Colin's chuffed that he doesn't get any shots when they play. (That won't last long, though: Colin's an improver and he's passing him by.) To top it all off, he loves my sister and lavishes attention, and as much money as she will allow, upon her.

My dad was right about the New Club invitation, though: very strange that he should choose to take me, an actor, of all people, brother-in-law or not, to one of the most formal settings in Edinburgh. I'd been there once before, a guest at a reception organised by Clark Gow: no, that's not a person, it's an accountancy firm. They're our tax advisers, Susie's and mine, and one of their Scottish partners is a member. It's located in a reasonably modern, if formidably ugly, building on Princes Street, but that has nothing to do with the name. That goes back, I suppose, to the days in the eighteenth century when it really was new. Most of contemporary Edinburgh doesn't know that it's there, but that doesn't matter, because most of contemporary Edinburgh wouldn't aspire to membership. (To be honest, my impression is that if they did, they wouldn't have a cat's chance in hell.)

At the appointed hour, twelve thirty, I pressed the buzzer at the anonymous, unimpressive door (it cost me a quid, dropped in the can of the beggar over whom I had to step to reach it), announced myself as a guest of Mr January, and was admitted. (Actually it had cost me more than that quid. When I had left Monaco I'd travelled light, so I'd had to visit Edinburgh's other Harvey, Nichols, to pick up some appropriate clothing. It wouldn't have done for me to embarrass my brother-in-law.)

He was waiting for me in the foyer when I reached the top of the stair, in the three-piece outfit that is the advocate's uniform. He wore a striped shirt, his badge of professional rank. It's true: in that historic but strange institution, the Faculty of Advocates, junior counsel traditionally have worn plain shirts while seniors have always worn stripes. It's all changing, of course, as more and more women reach QC status. (Those who swore that such a thing would only happen over their dead bodies have all now passed on to that state. I wonder if they look up as the black high heels step over them: bet they do, the dirty old sods.)

He walked me through to the lounge for a pre-lunch drink, which in my case was a John Panton . . . ginger beer and lime with a dash of angostura, named after the famous golfer who's credited with inventing it. Harvey had a La Ina sherry, chilled.

We made small-talk for a while as we looked out of the picture window, across Princes Street to the castle, its skyline altered by the scaffolding stands that would seat the crowds at the following month's military tattoo. Harvey was as relieved as the rest of us at my dad's progress, and as pleased when I told him about Carol Salt's installation as locum, and about Mac the Dentist's agreement to become just plain Mac for the rest of his days.

I found myself asking him how he was settling into fatherhood or, at least, the step variety.

'I'm astonished,' he confessed, 'how much I'm enjoying it. There was never any prospect of children in my first marriage. I was too busy, and my wife had other priorities in her life. I know I've missed a large chunk of it, the early years, but at any stage it's great to watch children and become a part of their lives.'

'Better not let Jonny hear you call him a child,' I advised him. 'He thinks of himself as an adult, these days.'

'He's starting to behave like it too. Between you and me, his mother's becoming a bit concerned that he should be properly prepared for manhood, and the responsibility that it brings with it: duty of care and all that, you know what I mean. With his girlfriend being seventeen, Ellen thinks I should . . .'

I had to laugh. 'Harvey, all due respect, but I can't think of anyone less qualified for that task. Tell Ellie not to worry, the job's done.'

He looked at me gratefully. 'Thanks, Oz. I should have known, for that lad worships the ground you walk on.'

It's true that there's a special bond between Jonny and me, but I try to discourage worship. After all, I'm a bit of a false god, as you know. 'Don't underrate your own influence on him, Harvey. He asked me what I think of the law as a profession.'

'I know. We've discussed it: he told me that you approve of the idea.'

I shrugged and grinned at him. 'I don't like to lie to my nephew, but in the circumstances . . .' Harvey's face fell. 'Joke!' I called out. I like him, but I'll never take him to a stand-up comedy club.

'Good,' he said, rising to his feet, 'because I've spoken to a couple of friends of mine at Edinburgh University, and to the director of training at the Faculty of Advocates. They've all agreed to give him a preview of what it will involve.'

'Fine, but just remember, he is only sixteen, so don't be too disappointed if he turns round next year and says he wants to be a zoologist, or a golf pro or something equally bizarre.'

'Or an actor?'

'That's an ambition I will definitely not encourage. My business is full of crazy people.'

Harvey chuckled as he led me into the dining room. 'So's mine: usually we call them clients.' I began to rethink the idea of a night at the stand-up club.

The lunch wasn't *nouvelle cuisine,* but that was okay with me: I was brought up on Scotch broth and haddock fried in bread-crumbs, the more chips the better. It wasn't until the cheeseboard had arrived that my brother-in-law-proved my dad right by getting down to the real business of the day.

'I've got something on my mind, Oz,' he said, 'and I'd like your advice.'

'Plead guilty and throw yourself on the mercy of the judge.'

He smiled weakly, as befitted a pretty weak wisecrack. 'I might need a mirror to do that soon,' he replied. 'What I'm going to tell you has to remain confidential, until an announcement is made.' He glanced around. 'Half the members of this place might know about it, but they're within the institution, as it were, and it's important that it doesn't leak outside. The fact is, I'm going to be elevated to the Bench: a vacancy's arisen, I've been proposed and the Judicial Appointments Board has nodded its head. My installation will take place within the next three weeks.'

'Supreme Court?' I asked.

'Of course. If they'd offered me a Sheriff's position I'd have turned it down flat.'

'Well, congratulations. I knew you were headed there some day, but I thought you were still too young.'

He shook his head. 'In the old days I would have been, but things have changed. The new system isn't afraid to trust a forty-three-year-old to produce sensible judgments.'

'Quite bloody right too,' I told him. 'I have to say that I'm more than a little chuffed that you chose to confide in me, but what the hell do you need my advice for? Is Ellie giving you grief about it?'

'Not at all. I wouldn't have gone for it without her full support. No, it's my first wife who's the problem.'

I frowned: I know more than most about troublesome ex-wives. 'Why should that be?' I asked. 'She's been off the pitch for over ten years now, hasn't she?'

He pursed his lips. 'Pitches, as you put it, mean nothing to Madeleine. I haven't seen her in over five years . . . and then it was by accident . . . but I'm quite certain she still takes an interest in my career.'

'What makes you certain?'

'When our decree was granted, she promised me that she would. She didn't take the civilised option when it came to ending the marriage. I had to sue for divorce on the ground of adultery: her counsel rather foolishly tried to nail me for a ridiculous sum as aliment. I had the Dean of Faculty in my corner. The judge listened to him, as he would, and she was awarded one pound a year. My costs were awarded against her too, but I didn't pursue her for those.'

'Bloody generous of you.'

'That's exactly what the Dean said: in the circumstances, he had to waive his fee as a courtesy to a fellow silk, even though I was still a fairly junior QC in those days.'

'Remind me never to sue a lawyer.'

'The odds would be against you, I concede. Maddy should have known that too, but you couldn't tell her anything. She was livid with the judgment: she talked about appealing it, but her solicitor point-blank refused to help her. Finally she went off, clutching her pound, throwing me many a withering glance, and promising to take a special interest in my career.'

'Has she remarried?'

'No, and she still calls herself Madeleine January.'

'When did you last hear from her?'

'When Ellen and I were married: Maddy sent her a sympathy card.'

'Jesus!' I spluttered, then glanced around to make sure there were no clergymen in the room this time. 'How did my sister react to that?'

'She set a new world record for tearing a greetings card into small pieces. It looked like confetti when she was finished. She was all for posting it back to her with a note saying that she'd do the same to her next time, but I headed her off that. She couldn't have anyway: I don't know where Maddy is.'

'Is that part of the problem?' I asked him.

'Very perceptive, Oz: I fear I may be about to come under attack, but I don't know from which direction.'

'But, Harvey, how could she possibly attack you? You're a pillar of the community, one of the most respected figures in your profession, and you don't have an enemy in the world . . . apart from her, it seems. She, on the other hand, ran off with a bloody actor, not even a movie star like me, but a bit player.'

He raised an eyebrow. 'How did you know he was an actor,' he asked, 'far less have his credits list in your head?'

I'd put my size ten in it, hadn't I? There was nothing to do but own up. 'When you started going out with Ellie,' I confessed, 'I

76

had you checked out by an ex-copper friend of mine, a guy called Ricky Ross.'

He beamed. 'Ex-Superintendent Ross,' he exclaimed. 'I've had him in the witness box many a time. He's very good: I'm not surprised your information's accurate.'

'Sorry, mate,' I muttered lamely.

'Don't be. I'd have done the same to you in the circumstances.'

'That's good to know, but let's go back to the original question. How could this Madeleine woman possibly attack someone like you?'

'Well . . .' he began. As wells go, this one was pretty deep. 'There are a couple of photographs, which would embarrass me, and everyone associated with me, if their very existence was ever known. If they were ever published . . .' He shuddered. 'God forbid that they ever should be.'

'But Maddy's capable?'

'Yes, I fear so.'

'And she has them?'

'I fear that also. Let me fill you in on the background. Madeleine Raymond . . . her maiden name . . . and I met when I was at Oxford, doing my BA. We shared a couple of classes. When I came back to Edinburgh to do my law degree, she followed me up here. Looking back, she probably reckoned that I was some sort of a catch. I fell for her, no doubt about it, and we were married as soon as I'd graduated and obtained my practising certificate. Big mistake on my part: I should have stalled her, maybe suggested living together for a while. But I didn't and pretty much as soon as the knot was tied, I began to regret it. Maddy liked to party: so did I, to an extent, but I was career-minded and determined to get to the Bar as soon as I could. There was also the question of money. My family's well fixed, as Ricky Ross will have told you, but I wasn't prepared to let my folks pick up the tab any more than was necessary. So, like all young advocates, I went through a period where my income was pretty limited. She didn't like that at all.'

77

'Didn't she work?'

'She temped on occasion, to make ends meet, when she had to, but she hated it, and she let me know.'

'How long did the marriage last?'

'Seven years, though God knows how.'

'How did it come to an end?'

'I found out about her fling with the actor chap, Rory Roseberry. I learned later that he wasn't the first. I was in the Crown Office at the time and she'd been playing numerous games while I was away prosecuting on the High Court circuit. Finally a brother advocate tipped me off. I decided to take action so I hired a private investigator.' He grinned. 'Believe it or not, I actually considered approaching you, but I was told that you didn't do divorce work.'

'Looking back,' I told him, 'I wish I had. The stuff I did was usually balls-achingly boring.'

'I don't believe that you mean that. You're not the window-peeping type, Oz. I employed those chaps because I had to, but I detested them and what they did, not least because they seemed to enjoy it. They were good, though. They produced all the evidence I needed very quickly.'

'How did you handle it?'

'Brutally, I have to admit. I threw her out: we were living in my father's Edinburgh flat at the time, since he'd retired to Florida by then. I changed the locks, and rented a small place for her.'

'And the photographs?'

He sighed. 'Yes, the photographs. Remember I said I wasn't a regular party animal? Well, there was one time. We'd had some people in for dinner one Saturday night, at a period when things were okay, and we'd all had rather a lot to drink. The morning after I must still have been pissed, because when I got up . . .' He paused. 'You know my old man was a judge too, don't you?'

I nodded. 'The first Lord January.'

'That's right. Well, thing is, he shouldn't have done so, but he'd a set of Supreme Court robes in the wardrobe at home, and a wig. So I got up, then, in a mad whim, put the robes on as a dressing-gown, stuck the wig on my head, and lurched off for a pee. When I came back to the bedroom, Maddy yelled at me to stop, framed in the doorway, and fired off a couple of snaps. I laughed about it, I bloody laughed, but the thing was I was bollock-naked underneath. Worse than that, I had an . . .'

'Enough said. I take it that you're entirely recognisable in the photos.'

'Oh, yes. Photography was Madeleine's principal hobby, apart from actors. She was rather good at it, I'm afraid.'

My devious mind was working fast, considering all the options. 'Leave her aside for a moment,' I told him. 'What about the possibility that when the film was developed, a technician might have ripped off a couple of extra prints, and that they'll show up in the *News of the World* the weekend before your installation?'

'That's highly unlikely. We went on holiday to Mauritius the following week. The film was finished off and developed out there. No, my fear is that Maddy still has the bloody things; in fact, I'm certain she has. You see when I chucked her out, I gathered all her possessions together and boxed them. That included her photographic collection, and rather obviously, the first thing I did was look for those two prints. I found them, all right, and reduced them to ashes, but when I looked through the negatives, I discovered that the vital strip was missing.'

'Maybe she burned it herself.'

He shot me a look that made me fear for all the poor buggers who'd soon be appearing before him in the dock. 'No chance,' he murmured grimly.

'Has she ever threatened you with them, specifically? Surely, if your divorce was hostile, she'd have been tempted to use them then?'

'That would have been foolish, and foolish she certainly is not. Showing me up in the media wouldn't have affected the outcome, and any attempt at blackmail would have landed her in the clink. At that time I'd have reported her to the police and taken out a fearsome interdict prohibiting publication in any form.'

'Can't you do that now?'

'I could, but I'd have to establish a likelihood of publication, and I'd have to know who to interdict. Then there's the Internet: it's impossible to prevent something appearing on a rogue website. Besides, if I took pre-emptive action, the very fact would stir up the hornets.'

'Look, are you sure you're not exaggerating this?'

'I'm sure. When Ellen and I were married, that card wasn't the only thing she sent. I received an e-mail. No message, just two photographic attachments.'

'I see.' We were the only people left in the dining room. I looked at him. 'You said you wanted my advice, Harvey.'

He seemed lost, more vulnerable than I could ever have imagined. 'What should I do, Oz?' he whispered. 'I'm kicking myself for allowing my name to go forward with this problem unresolved. I'm kicking myself for not getting hold of those negatives, one way or another, and destroying them. I'm kicking myself for letting the bloody situation arise in the first place.'

'Enough with the kicking, for Christ's sake,' I protested, 'otherwise you'll have me putting the boot into you too. What are your options?'

'The way I see it, I don't have any. I must withdraw. I can't embarrass the Bench, but most of all I can't embarrass Ellen, the boys, you, Mac. I can't shame the family.'

I felt heart-sorry for him. I had grown to be very fond of my brother-in-law; it hurt me to see him so distraught, and when I get hurt, often I get angry. At that moment, Madeleine January moved right to the top of my get-even list.

'That's rubbish,' I told him. 'For a start, don't worry about the Bench: I don't need to remind you that it has a fairly recent history of embarrassing itself. As for the family . . . I speak for it, for every single member, and I'm telling you that if you decline this honour, our disappointment in you would be far greater than any awkwardness caused by a bloody silly snapshot. You're going to be installed, and you're going to become as great a judge as everybody's been predicting. Okay, what's the worst case? Someone runs the picture with a large black stripe obscuring your dick. At least you were pointing it at a female at the time. That'll probably come as a welcome relief to your fellow judges.'

He managed a weak grin at that one.

'Harvey,' I went on, 'you might think you're asking for my advice, but you're not. What you really want is my help, and you're going to get it.'

'Oz, I couldn't possibly ask you to involve yourself in this sordid business.'

'You don't have to. You're my sister's husband. What affects you affects her, even if she is likely to greet the news with a roar of laughter that would knock you over when you tell her . . . as you must.'

'But what can you do?'

'As much as I can. For openers, I'm going to ask a woman named Alison Goodchild to call you. She's the best media-relations consultant in town. You'll brief her and she'll put together a response for you, in the event that this nonsense does go public. It'll be full and frank: I know from experience that you never gain by being evasive in circumstances like these. Once that's under way, I'm going to find this ex of yours and I'm going to get those negatives from her.'

'How?'

'Quietly, very quietly, and very discreetly.'

'But legally, Oz, it has to be legally.'

'Harvey, I'm not going to steal the damn things, but if you're worried about my methods, I'll simply find the woman, then sit you and her down at the same table and let the pair of you sort it out.'

'That wouldn't work. I can't tell you how vindictive Maddy can be: the very sight of me would trigger her off.'

'Sounds like she's well named.'

'You could be right: there's always been a crazy streak about her. That's what attracted me in the first place.' He glanced at me. 'Maybe you can understand that.'

He didn't have to explain. 'As with me and Primavera? You may have a point there, but which of us is crazy? There are differing views on that.'

'I know which one of you I'd rely on in a crisis. I'm demonstrating that right now. If you want me to see this Goodchild woman, I will, even though it runs against all my instincts.'

'Don't worry about it: Alison's ethics are as sound as yours. You tell her something in confidence and she'll never repeat it, not even if she was under oath . . . not even if it was you on the Bench demanding an answer.'

'I'm not enjoying these images, Oz. How will you find Madeleine? You're a busy man, and when you're between films there's Susie and the kids.'

'It won't be difficult,' I assured him. 'And besides, I know the very bloke who can help me.'

11

I still look up to Ewan Capperauld; it seems like no time at all since we met at a cast gathering in Edinburgh before we started to shoot *Skinner's Rules,* which turned out to be my breakthrough movie, the one in which I realised I knew what I was doing.

Indeed, to normal people it would be no time at all, but guys like us aren't normal. A lot has happened to both of us since then, in career terms. Mine has rocketed, while Ewan's seems to have settled on a plateau. He's still A list, no doubt about that, but I've overtaken him in every respect, choice of parts, billing and inevitably, because everything is interlinked, money. He isn't jealous, though: he knows there's no logic to our business. The first time we met, his luvvie side got a bit out of control, but since then he's treated me as a friend and a professional colleague, and I'm proud of that.

I hadn't expected him to be in Edinburgh when I phoned Alison Goodchild to arrange for her to call Harvey . . . he has an interest in her business, so I asked her if she knew his whereabouts, and was surprised when she told me that he was in town visiting his parents.

He was there when I called their number, and more than happy to meet me in the Caley Hotel for a drink. In days gone by we'd have been more at home in somewhere like Whigham's, but honestly, if we're after privacy, places like that are no longer an option, even in a city which knows that both of us are no better than we should be.

'Good to see you, Oz,' he began, as we settled down at a small corner table. 'The more I see of your career, the more gob-smacked I get.'

'It's 'ard to stay 'umble,' I replied. 'So I've given up trying. Seriously, though, it's all down to Miles for giving me a start and to Roscoe Brown, my agent, for building on it.'

'I wish he was mine,' Ewan murmured. 'I feel I could use a little . . . added impetus, let's say.'

'Why shouldn't he be?'

'Would he take me on? I've never found a satisfactory replacement for Margaret, you know.' His ex-wife had been his agent, until she had gone rather spectacularly off the rails.

'Of course he would. He's still growing, and on the look-out for top talent. Want me to get him to call you?'

He scratched his stubbled chin, then made a decision. 'Yes. Why not? No harm done in talking to him. Thanks for that, Oz. Anything I can do for you in return?'

I grinned, a little embarrassed at having to admit that there had been an ulterior motive for my call. 'As it happens there is. I'm trying to trace an actor named Rory Roseberry. He's not in our league, but you've been around longer than I have so I wondered if you might have run into him way back.'

'You don't have a part for him, do you?'

'Not as far as I know. No, I'm trying to trace somebody through him.'

'It wouldn't be Mad Maddy January, would it?'

I should have expected him to make a connection, yet I was taken by surprise. 'As a matter of fact it is. How did you guess?'

'I read the *Scotsman,* old son. I know that your sister married her ex last year.'

'You know Madeleine?'

'Past tense, Oz. Let's say I knew her fleetingly, and biblically, I should be ashamed to say, about fifteen years ago. I wasn't alone in having that distinction: she had a thing about actors. My shame comes from being aware at the time that there was a husband in her background, and from the fact that there was a wife in mine.'

'What was she like?'

'Wild, and captivating; bloody gorgeous. The sort of girl you just know, if you meet her early enough, is going to make some poor sod a terrible wife some day. I bumped into your in-law once, a few years later at a civic reception in the City Chambers that I attended with Margaret. She was with him, and yet not, if you know what I mean. She was chatting up some bloke on the far side of the room. I felt sorry for Harvey: I could see that he'd given up trying to cope with her. When my path crossed hers that evening, I tried to blank her, but she gave me a wink that would really have shopped me to my wife, had she seen it. Dangerous woman; it wasn't long after that that she was caught *in flagrante* with Rosebud.'

'Rosebud? Is that Roseberry's nickname?'

Ewan chuckled. 'Old son, it's his real fucking name: he was christened Roderick Rosebud. His nickname is "Sledge". How could it be anything else?'

'That must have ruined *Citizen Kane* for a lot of people who hadn't seen it before they met him. What do you know about him? Is Maddy still with him?'

'I don't know if she ever really was, or if it was just another fling. You'll need to speak to him about that.'

'Is he still around?'

'Sure. I saw a mention of his name last week, in a review of *Death of a Salesman* at Pitlochry Festival Theatre.'

'Do you know if it's still running?'

'I'm not sure. Why don't you call the theatre?'

I dug out my mobile, called the network directory to retrieve the number, and called the box office. I was in luck: Rory Roseberry was still playing Willy Loman. (A little young for the part, I thought, assuming that he was in the same age ball-park as Madeleine. I hoped the makeup department was up to it.)

'Fancy a night in Pitlochry?' I asked Ewan.

'Why not?' he exclaimed. 'Arthur Miller is one of my gods, and I still have a taste for the exotic.'

I booked two tickets and pre-show dinner, then told Conrad that I was borrowing Mary's car for the night.

Dinner at Pitlochry was excellent, better than I'd expected. Even on a Monday the restaurant was busy, and Ewan and I were aware of more than a few glances in our direction. Eventually, once we'd finished eating, a middle-aged bloke sidled over to us and asked us, diffidently, if we'd sign his menu. We did, and that kicked it off: we wound up touring all the tables and signing every menu in the place, including four for the staff.

The play was okay, but I'd been right in my guess about the casting. In a less taxing role, Rory 'Sledge' Roseberry would have been a capable actor, but he wasn't up to playing a man in his mid-sixties, for all the efforts of the people who'd applied the slap. He looked as if he'd been embalmed, rather than made up. Ewan was more critical that I was: he sighed when Rosebud first appeared and I heard several tuts and soft moans escape him during the performance. The supporting cast were good, and probably saved the day, although an extra, playing one of two women picked up in a restaurant by Willy's sons, kept peering into the audience as if she was looking for someone. I guessed that word of our presence had spread backstage.

When the curtain fell we stood and everyone else took our lead. I wondered how many standing ovations they'd had during the run.

As the auditorium cleared, we jumped on to the stage and found the manager, who was happy to show us to Roseberry's dressing room. He greeted us, still in his slap, the lines etched on his forehead looking even more grotesque close up. 'Good to see you again, Ewan,' he exclaimed, a little too heartily. 'It must be, what, ten years? Remember, I had a part in that highland epic of Miles Grayson's. We didn't have any scenes together, though, did we?'

Mr Capperauld had snapped into luvvie mode. 'No, dear chap,' he purred, 'sadly we did not. It would have been a pleasure for me, and instructive, I'm sure.' He moved on before Sledge could begin to ponder on whether the piss was being taken. 'Do you know Oz Blackstone?' he asked.

'Oh, yes,' Roseberry replied. 'I was in *Skinner's Rules*. Remember, Oz? I played Haggerty, the gruff Glaswegian copper.'

He took me completely off guard, for I'd had no recollection of the fact. I did my best to cover up, though. 'That's right,' I replied. 'You had a great line: "Aw, yis're all fuckin' heart and generosity through here in Edinburgh, are yis no'?" Something like that, wasn't it?'

'I'm impressed.' He shouldn't have been. I remembered it because I'd heard it so often: we'd got to take seven before Miles Grayson had been happy with his delivery, and he is not a man who appreciates wasting film stock. 'To what do I owe the honour? Were you simply passing through or is this a special trip?'

'The latter,' I told him, watching his little chest swell with pride. 'I need to ask you about someone.'

The greasepaint seemed to crack a little as he deflated. 'Who would that be?'

'My brother-in-law's ex-wife, Madeleine January.'

'Aaah!' The sound was part exclamation, part sigh. 'The dear Maddy. She did not do me any favours, that one. Do you know, after my fling with her turned awkward, I went for four years before I landed another part in Edinburgh? Four fucking years without a Festival appearance, just when I was beginning to be someone. I won't say that it ruined my career but it didn't do it any good. Your brother-in-law carries a grudge, I'm afraid, Oz,' he said bitterly.

I couldn't let that go. 'I've got to tell you, Rory, that Harvey's never carried a grudge in his life. If you were turned down for parts, it's because the directors didn't fancy you for them, end of story. But suppose he had marked a few cards, you could hardly have blamed him. If I caught anyone around my wife, I'd pound seven different shades of shite out of him.'

He raised a haughty eyebrow. 'You think you're up to that? You may have played a couple of tough guys, but you are only a film actor. Anyway, if a woman's not getting enough at home, she's fair game. You should bear that in mind: complacency is our enemy, and all that.'

I don't think he even saw the punch, a quick straight right hand. He'd pushed my angry button and no mistake. It nailed him square on the chin, lifted him off his feet and dumped him in an armchair that was positioned conveniently behind him. Ewan didn't react at all, other than to give a quiet wince. He'd had a go at the woman as well, so maybe he was wondering if he'd be next.

I waited until the glaze had gone out of Rosebud's eyes, and until they were focused on me again. They were filled with fear: he had no thoughts of getting back to his feet. 'Harvey should have done that ten years ago,' I told him, 'but, like I say, he isn't that sort of guy. Now, I don't have all night. Where is Maddy?'

'I don't know,' he muttered. 'I haven't seen her for over five years.'

'But you hear things, don't you?'

'Yes, occasionally. The last word I had of her she was with an Australian.'

'Another actor?'

'Not so much. This one was a singer, mostly, although he'd done some straight work on Aussie television. He had a part in the *Cats* revival in the Playhouse a couple of years back. That's when they met. Maddy was doing local PR for the company.'

'Name?'

'Wilde, Sandy Wilde.'

It meant nothing to me. 'Are they still in Edinburgh?'

'No. When the run ended, she went with him. She could be anywhere now.'

12

When I started out at the bottom of the ladder of the business that's made me rich and famous, I had a London agent. We parted company after I made the switch to movies from voice-overs for TV ads, but there were no hard feelings on either side. Sylvester 'Sly' Burr got me good money for the sort of work I was doing, but when the time came he had the sense to recognise his limits, and the integrity to admit to them. Nowadays the very fact that I used to be a client of his is worth a large mention on his website.

I called him early doors the next morning: I knew he'd be there, for his office is above his flat in Earls Court and he likes to be at his desk for eight, to deal with the morning mail, read the red-tops for headlines . . . the more salacious the better . . . involving his artist roster, and escape from Mrs Burr.

'Oz, my boy!' I could almost see him beam. Sly's a bit of a caricature (if I was making a film of his life, I'd probably cast Ron Moody in the lead) and that includes an avuncular fondness for his clients, present and past. I've never heard him badmouth anyone, even though he exists in a world where figurative stilettos in the back are considered normal behaviour. He might be a sharp guy around a pound coin, but he made me plenty of them.

I'd have liked to chat for a bit, but I didn't have time, so I got straight down to business. 'I need to trace someone, Sly,' I told him.

'One of mine?'

'Not as far as I know. I don't know who his agent is, but you're the best search engine I know, so I thought I'd run the name past you. Sandy Wilde: he's Australian, described to me as a singer rather than an actor, with credits on television down under and in musicals in the UK.'

I waited as his brain clicked into gear. Sly never forgets a name and he has a terrific showbiz database, much of which he carries in his head. 'Wilde, Wilde, Sandy, not Marty, not Kim,' he muttered to himself. 'Yes, yes, yes, I've got him. Big geezer, good voice, good dancer; bats for both teams.' That took me a little by surprise: it was Sly's way of saying that Wilde was bisexual. 'I can't remember who he's with, though. You got a part for him in something you're doing?'

'No, I'm more concerned with something he's got a part in. I want to trace someone through him.'

'Male or female?'

'Female.'

'In the business?'

'Not as such; this lady seems to collect actors.'

'What's her name?'

'Madeleine January.'

'January, January. Mmm.' Sly went back to pondering. 'I know 'er,' he exclaimed, with a small cry of triumph. 'She works for the Billy Dorset Agency. A year or so back she tried to poach one of my lads, Barton Mawhinney. He was giving her one and she thought he'd follow her across the street when she asked him, but he stayed loyal. When he told me about it, I had a word with Billy. He wasn't too pleased; there's still some honour in our business, Oz.'

'I'm glad to hear it: there's less in Hollywood, I can tell you.'

He chuckled. 'Hollywood, eh? Who'd 'ave thought it? Good for you, son, I'm really pleased, the way you've made it. How are things panning out with your new guy? You still happy with him?'

'Look at my credits, Sly. What do you think?'

'Yeah, of course you are. Look, leave this with me, I'll have a word with Barton and with Billy Dorset, see if he's still seeing her, and if she still works there.'

'Thanks.' I'd been hoping he'd offer to do that. 'When you do, though, don't let slip to anyone that it's me who's looking for her.'

'Worry not, my son.' He paused. 'But what will I say? I'll need some kind of story.'

'Don't say anything unless you're asked. But if you are, tell her that Ewan Capperauld asked if you knew where to find her. Tell her that a journalist's been looking all over Edinburgh for her.'

'A journalist? Is that true?'

I smiled. 'It is, Sly, in a manner of speaking.'

13

The real truth was that I hadn't given any thought to the central question of how I'd approach Harvey's ex-wife. But as Sly Burr forced me to think about it, a rudimentary and very simple plan began to form in my mind.

There would be a 'journalist': Conrad Kent.

I didn't say anything to him, though, as we checked out of the hotel. I was still fine-tuning the approach in my mind.

I said farewell to Mary in a corner of the foyer: she'd decided to stay in Edinburgh for another day, then go back to Anstruther to adapt the house so that my dad could live on the ground floor for a while. Walking would be part of his recovery regime, but it would be on the level, for a while at least.

We hadn't spoken about Jan since that long night in the hospital, but I couldn't let it go at that. 'You're not going to let anything slip, are you?' I asked her. 'You sure you'll be strong enough to keep the secret?'

'I've kept it this long, haven't I? Don't worry, Oz, it'll die with me. Your father will never know he was Jan's father too.'

'With respect, Mary, the truth won't die with you ... unless you outlive me, that is. I'll have to carry it with me.'

She looked up at me. 'How do you feel about Jan now?' she asked me.

I felt my forehead knot. 'I don't know. How am I supposed to feel?'

'Before you knew the truth, what was she to you?'

'She was the one, the one above all others.'

'Then let her still be that.'

'She was my half-sister, Mary.'

'That's not what it says on her birth certificate, or on your marriage certificate, or on her gravestone.'

'I know, but now I feel as if I loved her under false pretences, somehow. It's doing my head in. If she'd known the truth, it wouldn't have been that way . . . we wouldn't have been that way.'

'That's where you're wrong. She did, and it was; you were.'

I felt myself sway; I glanced at Conrad in case he'd noticed, but he had his back to us. 'Jan knew?' I whispered, incredulous.

She nodded. 'I didn't tell you the whole truth at the hospital. She guessed; I don't know how, but she guessed. Sometimes I think she had special gifts.'

I'm in no doubt about that: I've seen Jan a couple of times since she died. Before, I didn't believe in the transcendence of the human spirit beyond this plane of existence; I do now.

'When did she find out?'

'When you were in your mid-twenties; she came to me and asked point-blank if you were her brother. She told me she'd had a weird experience. She'd been washing one day when she looked in the mirror and saw your face; quite clearly, she said. She stared for a while, until you winked at her, then altered, but only slightly, and she was herself again. I couldn't lie to her: her insight was too strong.'

'What did she say?'

'Nothing. I told her and she turned and walked away. We only discussed it once more after that.'

'Mid-twenties,' I murmured, 'just when we drifted apart for a while.'

'That was why. She was very clever: she made you think it was mostly your idea, but if you think about it, I'm sure you'll realise that it was hers. She kept you at a distance, but not too far away. House-sharing with the woman Turkel was a kind of screen she built between the two of you.'

I thought back to those days and I smiled. 'It didn't stop her ringing my door at midnight a few times.'

'I know; she couldn't really live without you.'

'What made her stop trying?'

'Isn't it obvious? Primavera. All your other flings she regarded as harmless, but when you met her, Jan saw that it was different. When you went off to Spain with her, she came to me; that was the only time I ever saw her cry as an adult. She said to me, "I don't care, Mum. I don't really care about anyone or anything but Oz." And so I told her, "Then get him back." And she did. And she was happy again, until the day she died.'

She reached up once more, and touched my face, as she'd done in the hospital. 'Let it rest, Oz. You were very special together, you two; you should be proud of that. Bloodlines aren't everything: it's love that counts. Cling on to that thought, and enjoy what's left of your life: there's at least half of it in front of you, with luck.'

'Susie?' I asked. 'Did she ever tell you what she really thought of Susie?'

Mary laughed lightly. 'As a matter of fact she did. She said she thought of her as the other side of Primavera; that they were much the same person, only one was a cherub and the other was an imp.'

'No prizes for guessing which was which. She was pretty generous, though, describing Primavera as a mere imp. Horns, pitchfork and a tail fit her better when she goes off the rails.'

'In that case you can be sure that Jan's glad you've wound up with the right one.'

I squeezed her hand. 'Look after my dad,' I said. 'Get him through to Loch Lomond as soon as he's ready for it.'

'I will, I promise. Go and catch your plane now.'

Actually it wasn't a matter of catching it: the aircraft was at our disposal. Nevertheless I wanted to see Susie and the kids again, and I had to catch up with old Benny Luker, who was, no doubt, running up a monster tab in the Columbus at my expense.

In the taxi to the terminal and eventually on the flight itself, my mind turned back to my mission for Harvey and to Madeleine January. I looked at Conrad, and imagined him trying to pretend to be a journalist. The more I did, the more trouble I had with the notion. My security manager is a very straight guy; there's no duplicity about him.

Fortunately, I had a ready alternative, someone who was absolutely full of it.

14

I'd been phoning Susie several times every day, of course, so I knew that there were no crises at home. Prim was still there; she said that she had intended to leave the previous Sunday, but she had agreed to stay on until I got back. Susie hadn't seen Dylan since I'd been away. I was glad to hear it, but I never doubted that I'd find him in the hotel. He had fifty thousand green-backed reasons not to leave the principality.

The flight was as uneventful as the first, but this time Conrad and I were in a mood to enjoy the personal service that came with the charter deal. As soon as we landed in Cannes, I switched on my cell-phone; the Citation was still taxiing to the terminal building when it rang.

'Oz, where you been, son?' Sly Burr exclaimed in my ear. 'I been trying to get you.'

'I've been a bit up in the air. What is it, Sly?'

'I asked around about your lady,' he said. 'She ain't with Billy Dorset any more, or with Bart Mawhinney. Billy fired her last year, and she dumped Bart after I shopped her for trying to poach him.'

'What about Sandy Wilde? Are you sure he's out of the picture?'

'As far out as you can get without being dead: he met up with another Aussie, a dancer in a TV show they worked on together. They went back down under together; last I heard Sandy had a part in another soap, and the other fella . . .'

'Fella?'

'Sandy's a switch-hitter, I told you. His pal's dancing in another show.'

'So the trail's cold.'

'Did I say that? Billy told me that he sacked her because he had another complaint from an agent, Renée Danziger, about her having it off with her talent, an actor called Lee Kan Tong. That's his real name, by the way: professionally, he's Tony Lee. A lot of these Orientals anglicise their names. This time, Madeleine didn't try to talk the guy away from Renée, but she had a reputation for it and that was enough. Billy decided she was a liability.'

'Liability? She sounds like the ideal business-development exec.'

Sly sighed. 'I told you, son, we don't work that way. The big agencies might not be as scrupulous, but us small people, we all know each other, like colleagues.'

'So is that what she's doing now? "Developing" potential new clients for a big agency?'

'Nah. I called Renée and asked if Tony Lee was still seeing her. Apparently he is.'

I smiled. Trust my man Sly to come up with the goods. 'Great. Where can I track her down?'

There was a pause, too long to be anything but significant. 'Ah, well, son, that's the thing, ain't it? This Tony, he was offered a job, wasn't he? With an outfit called the Heritage Theatre Company as director. So he took it, and Madeleine went with him.'

'Went? Went where?'

'Singapore, mate, that's where she is.'

The smile turned into a sigh: my mission had just taken on another dimension. 'Singapore?'

'Yes, it's in the Far East.'

'I know where it is, Sly. It's a fucking long way, that's where it is. You're sure about this?'

'Dead certain. Renée had an e-mail from him last week. He mentioned Maddy, said that she was coping with the heat, no problem.'

'Okay, thanks for that, Sly.'

'That's no problem either. Any time, son.' There was another pause. 'Say, you wouldn't put a word in for me with Ewan Capperauld, would you? I hear he's not too chuffed with his new agency.'

I couldn't help but laugh. 'What happened to scruples?'

'Ah, but he's with one of the big outfits; fuck them and all who sail in them.'

'Ewan's not for you, Sly, you know that as well as I do. I'll introduce you to Roscoe Brown, though: he's looking for an associate in London.'

'Thanks, son. That'll be appreciated. Is he Jewish?'

I was still chuckling as I hung up on him, unclipped my seatbelt and climbed out of the Citation into a blazing Mediterranean afternoon. I wondered how much hotter it was in Singapore.

15

The kids were all over me when I made it back home. Even Tom, who's normally a quiet lad, yelled with delight when he saw me and came charging up to me, almost elbowing his half-sister out of the way. Half-sister: I looked at him and Janet and thought again of myself, and Jan. When I did so I realised, to my surprise, that the turmoil had gone. Mary was right: love really does conquer all. The thing that cracked it, that gave me peace, was the disclosure that Jan had known all along, and that she had decided that nothing, least of all an accident of birth for which neither of us had been responsible, was going to keep us apart.

I played with Janet, Tom and wee Jonathan for the rest of the afternoon, around the house and in the pool, until finally we were all knackered. When Ethel arrived to take them for their evening meal, I collapsed on to a lounger next to Susie and Prim; she had been there when I'd got back. I looked at the two of them, and thought of Jan again, and what she'd said about them. I confess that when I considered the generosity with which the good side had allowed the repentant bad side back into our circle, I began to worry. I hoped it wouldn't backfire.

'Is Mac really going to be all right?' Susie asked me. I glanced to my right and saw two faces each one waiting for my answer with the same concern. My dad inspires that in people.

'He really is,' I promised them both. 'He might well have died, there in the golf club, but he didn't, and when they kept him alive long enough to get him into theatre . . . well, it hasn't exactly been plain sailing from then on, but it's been okay. Once he recovers fully from the surgery and the new valve gets bedded in, he'll be as fit as any other sixty-six-year-old retired dentist, and a bloody sight fitter than most.'

'He's retiring?' Prim exclaimed. I'd told Susie about Carol Salt, clearly she hadn't passed it on.

I nodded. 'Finally, he is. He's decided, having nearly done it once, that dying on the golf course is a hell of a lot better than dying in harness. I've found someone to take on his practice and the deal's done.'

Prim grinned. 'What a pity. I need a filling replaced and I was hoping that Mac would do it.'

'The world is still full of expensive dentists,' I told her, 'and you can afford it.'

She left at seven. She said that she'd finally agreed to have dinner with Dylan in the Columbus. While I was away, they'd shared a few Bellinis in the cocktail bar of an evening, but that had been all.

'How is Benny?' I asked, as I walked her to the door, where Conrad was waiting with the car.

'Bored. He says he's memorised the model and year of every car in the motor museum, and he's, here I quote, "on first-name terms with every fucking fish in the fucking aquarium". However, he also said that he's ahead in the casino.'

'I'm going to cure his boredom, and give him more funds to gamble with. Tell him to be waiting for me in the lobby at noon tomorrow; we'll go for a spot of lunch and I'll brighten his day.' That reminded me. 'Have you had a chance to speak to Dawn yet?'

'No: I'm not going to break that news over the phone. I'll see her on Thursday: she and Miles are bringing Bruce to visit Dad in Auchterarder. Oh, yes, Miles did ask how you'd got on with Mr Luker. I stalled him; told him that Mac's illness had put things on hold, but that you'd pick it up again when you got back.'

'Good girl. I still think he'll go ape-shit, but you never know.'

I kissed her cheek, bade her farewell, then went back to Susie, who was in our bedroom showering off the pool water.

I hadn't seen her for almost a week, so it was a while before we were ready for dinner. When we were, we decided that we'd go out to Le Café de la Mer, in the Grand Hotel for a bite of steak and a sea view.

Once we'd reached the coffee stage, I told her about my lunch with Harvey. When she'd picked herself off the floor and stopped laughing about the thought of him and his hard-on in a judge's robes and wig, she became suitably outraged at the thought of Madeleine being out there and in a position to ruin his career.

'You've got to help him, Oz,' she said. 'Harvey's really nice; he and Ellie don't deserve that. Find the woman and get the negatives back.'

'I've had another thought.' I chuckled casually. 'I'll find her and lock her in a small room with my sister.'

'Steady on, now,' Susie protested. 'There's a UN convention against that sort of thing.' She winked at me. 'It's a good idea, though. Still, finding her's the first priority. Any ideas?'

'I know where she is.' I explained the detective work that Sly Burr had done on my behalf.

'Well done, Mr Burr,' she said. 'Singapore? That's a long way off; maybe she won't hear about Harvey going on the Bench.'

'She'll hear about it, love. Unless she's cut herself off from every friend and relative she ever had in Britain, she's going to find out . . . or at least we have to assume that she will. The crossed-fingers option isn't open to us.'

'What is, then? What can we do?'

I gazed across the table at her. 'Well, I do have an idea, but it involves a trip out there, to Singapore. Do you fancy coming? You and the kids, that is.'

'Have you ever been there?' she asked.

'No.'

'In that case you don't have any idea how humid it can be. I know: I was there when I was eighteen and I still haven't forgotten. I can't take the children out there, especially not wee Jonathan: we'd have to paint him in sun-block. Plus I don't fancy explaining to Janet and Tom that they can't go in the pool when it's sunny, in case they come out parboiled. Plus they have earthquakes out there and tsunamis and stuff.'

She had a valid point, a whole list of them in fact. Neither Susie nor I is the timid type, until it comes to our children. Then our protection instinct clicks in, quick time.

'Could we send a detective?' she asked me.

'To do what, exactly? Harvey insisted that any steps I take have to be within the law. That being the case, we can hardly brief him not to take "fuck off" for an answer, can we?'

'Then you've got to go, Oz.'

I nodded. 'You're right, but I'm not going alone. If I turn up on Maddy's doorstep and ask her for those photos, one, she's going to know who I am and how I relate to Harvey, two, no way will she hand them over in a month of February twenty-ninths. She'll twig and she'll send an image straight to the tabloid of her choice. But worry not, I've thought it through and I have a plan, a most ingenious plan.'

'What's that?'

'She's not going to send them an image. She's going to hand it over.'

16

Dylan had done some more clothes shopping since I'd seen him last. He turned up for our meeting in a pale blue Columbus polo shirt and a pair of light tan slacks, with a pair of French-made Vuarnet sunglasses, the brand I'd advised him to buy, perched back on his head. He'd trimmed the beard until it looked more like designer stubble; for the first time since that day he'd been shot in Amsterdam, he seemed pretty much like the guy I'd known so well in Scotland.

'Nice get-up,' I remarked, as we stepped outside to a waiting taxi.

'Glad you like it,' he replied. 'Most of it went on your tab in the hotel. Not the shades, though: couldn't get them here.' Christ, he was even sounding like the old Dylan.

'How did you last so long in the police force?' I asked him. 'How come nobody saw through you long before they did?'

'I was never bent, Oz, not until I got involved with that bloke, and in the kidnap. And they never saw through me then either. It took you, you clever shit, to figure out that I was in on the operation. I was on my way to Bali, and to a pile of money, until you stepped in.'

I looked at him as the taxi drove off, heading for L'Intempo, in Le Meridien. 'Mike, you'd never have seen any of that money. You'd have wound up buried under a banyan tree or some such.'

He glanced at me slightly scornfully. 'You think?'

'I know. There was someone else involved in your plot: they were pulling your string all along. You were expendable, mate, and once you were well away, you'd have been expended. Your function was simply to disappear, and to carry the can, all of it and everything in it.'

'How do you know all that?'

'I traced the third person; she told me all about it.'

'I don't believe you.'

'Look me in the eye,' I challenged, 'then say that.'

He didn't need to: he knew me well enough to know that I was telling it as it was, or had been. 'Who was she?' he asked quietly.

'Your pal's sister.'

'He never had a sister.'

'That shows how much you knew. Smart copper, eh?'

I'd knocked some of the rediscovered brashness out of him; that pleased me, quietly.

'What happened to her?'

'Much the same as was going to happen to you. She's no longer with us.'

'Jesus.'

I smiled. 'And here you were thinking you'd been a criminal mastermind. Pinocchio, pal, that's who you were, but now you can go back to being a real boy again. Be careful telling lies, though: your nose couldn't do with being any longer than it is. I tell you, the Dutchman who shot you, de Witt, he really did save your life.'

'Maybe I should go to Holland and thank him,' Dylan murmured, unsmiling, as he rubbed the side of his chest.

'Best not, Benny,' I said. 'Best not.'

We sat in silence until the taxi arrived at the hotel. I paid off the driver and led the way inside: L'Intempo was quiet, since it was still not long after midday, but as I glanced around I saw a tennis player, a French singer and two racing drivers, one of whom I know since he's a fellow Scot. I gave him a wave as we were shown to a table with a sea view.

'Let's get the business over with,' I said. I opened my document case and took out the contract that Roscoe had supplied and that Audrey had produced. It was drawn up in the name of Elmer Productions, a company I'd set up with a view to getting involved in deals like this one. This was its first venture. The name? That's a play on Mrs Susie Blackstone's maiden surname, Gantry, and the 1960 movie that won Burt Lancaster an Oscar.

'Read that,' I told him. 'It sets out the deal we discussed, on the basis of the offer I made, more or less.'

'More or less?'

'Just more, actually. I've put you in for three per cent of budget and DVD sales, and for two per cent of net profits once the film's recovered its costs, and is in profit by twenty million dollars.'

'Who gets the rest?'

'I do, and Miles, and any investors we bring in. Don't quibble about it: it's what Roscoe Brown would have got you if he'd been negotiating for you. I know this because I asked him.'

'What if I'd had someone better than him?'

'That person doesn't exist ... although, come to think of it, neither does Benedict Luker, so maybe that idea isn't so far-fetched. No, read it, then sign it, Mike. It's a good deal. That and the added value in book sales will make you a millionaire.'

He signed it without reading it. I took that as a sign of friendship, and wished that I hadn't upped the advance to the full hundred thousand, taking a chance that eventually I'd get Miles's half back. His eyes widened when he looked at the cheque I pushed across the table, and then he did look at the contract. 'It's only an advance,' I reminded him. 'Mind you, when you tell your publisher that I've optioned it, your sales will go up straight away, and you'll get a UK distribution deal.'

'You're beginning to sound like my guardian angel. *Blue Star Falling* hasn't even earned out its advance in the US yet.'

'I know: I checked with the publisher. I know what your advance was, but it'll be bigger on your next one.'

'That's good to hear. You've helped me in another way this morning, although you don't even know it. My next book: it's a version of another true story; my own, the kidnap, me getting shot

107

and everything. What you said about there being a third person involved, it's got me thinking. I knew there was something lacking and that . . . It's the missing ingredient, isn't it? It makes it all hang together. Thanks, Oz.'

I stared at him, and had to make an effort to keep my voice down. 'Mike, Benny, cool it,' I hissed at him. 'Are you seriously saying that you're going to write a book about you kidnapping Dawn Phillips?'

'Sure. You'll be in it too, and Miles. But don't worry, you'll all be so heavily disguised that you'll be undetectable as real people.'

'But we'll know, Mike, we'll know.'

He stared at me dead-pan, and then his face cracked into a smile. 'Gotcha!' he exclaimed.

'You bastard. You're buying the lunch for that.'

'It was worth it, just to see your face. Don't worry, Oz, I'm not that crazy. My next book's almost finished, in fact. It's based on some of the stuff I did when I was under cover, and it's going to be good.'

'What will the DEA and the like say about that?'

'They won't give a shit, as long as it makes them look like the good guys.'

'Let me see a manuscript when you get it finished.'

He grinned again. 'Okay, but it'll cost you more than a hundred thousand.'

We settled down to lunch, a salad, followed by sea bream. I'd given myself a hard workout in the gym that morning, so I'd earned it. As we finished a bottle of El Preludi, I turned to the next item on my agenda.

'A friend of mine's in trouble,' I told him. 'And I'm going to help him.'

I explained Harvey's predicament, without naming him, but I could tell early on that Dylan had guessed who he was. It wouldn't have been like him not to have got himself up to date with my life before our meeting.

'Sounds like your friend's in for an embarrassing time,' he said, when I had finished. 'The woman's already dropped a broad hint that she has this time-bomb waiting for him and that she's waiting to pick her moment. As soon as she gets a whiff that you're on her trail, she's going to let it off.'

'Exactly. So she must never suspect that I'm after her.'

'Then how are you going to get these negatives off her?'

'I'm going to buy them . . . or, at least, someone is, on my behalf. Maddy, the woman, is going to have a visit from a tabloid journalist, looking to dig the dirt on her ex, who's about to get a very big appointment. He's going to offer her money for everything she's got on him, and if she has photos to back it, so much the better. She'll produce the goods.'

'What if she only produces prints?'

'Then it's no deal. The tabloid's paying for an exclusive. It can't take the chance she'll flog them somewhere else. The money will be for everything she's got.'

'How much?'

'A hundred thou, sterling.'

'That should get her attention.'

'I reckon.'

'So who're you going to get to play the part of the journo? If it's an actor, it can't be anyone she's likely to have seen on telly, or in the movies. And if she's a serial actor shagger, like you say, that makes it even more difficult.'

'As always, Mike, you get straight to the heart of the problem.' I leaned across the table. 'Tell me, since you didn't make it to Bali, how do you fancy a trip to Singapore?'

17

I hadn't been certain that he'd agree. He'd done more role-playing in the five years gone by than all but a few people do in a lifetime, and some of it had been downright dangerous, especially the stuff he'd done after his near-death experience in Amsterdam. If he'd said, 'No, thank you very much, I have a nice uneventful life in New York now, and I'd like it to stay that way,' I wouldn't have blamed him. I'd have been disappointed, though, because it would have forced me to revert to Plan B, Primavera as the journalist, and I'm sure Susie would have balked at that, however cosily they seemed to be getting along.

But he didn't let me down. He grinned, and it was like being back in the Horseshoe bar. 'I'll call it a research trip,' he said. 'You never know, there might be a book comes out of all this.'

I shrugged my shoulders. 'As long as the names and circumstances are changed to protect the guilty, I don't care.'

'Only one condition,' he added. 'We don't go anywhere near Thailand. I was there under cover, and it would be dangerous for me to go back.'

I accepted that: if events took us in that direction, I'd hire local talent and leave him behind in Singapore.

The trip was taking shape, but I wanted to go out there with as much information as I could, no loose ends untied. Madeleine had moved on from Harvey to Rory Roseberry, having done a quick low-flying mission over Ewan Capperauld. Rosebud had been chopped in favour of Sandy Wilde, from whom she had moved to Barton Mawhinney, dumped in turn when he shopped her to Sly.

Her last known sighting since then had been with Tony Lee.

Her sexual itinerary was pretty much mapped out, but I wondered whether there had been any other detours along the way. There was no more I could get from Ewan, Rory or Bart, but Sandy Wilde was a source of information as yet untapped.

As soon as I got back to my office from lunch with Dylan, I called Sly Burr. He didn't know who Wilde's agent was, but he undertook to find out. It took him less than an hour. 'He's with Porter and Green,' he told me. 'They're international: they got offices in London, New York, LA and Sydney. Big outfit, too big for the likes of Sandy, I'd 'ave thought, but people are always surprising you.' He gave me their London number, and filled me in on their top people.

I called it straight away, and asked to be put through to the executive who handled Sandy Wilde's account. The receptionist was efficient: she took less than two seconds to tell me that he had gone back to Australia. 'I know that,' I replied. 'But that wasn't what I asked you. It's midnight in Sydney: I want information now.'

'What's your interest in Mr Wilde?' she asked.

'I'm a producer, Elmer Productions. I'm starting to cast a movie project and he's been suggested for a part.'

'I see.' It sounded as if she was deciding whether or not to brush me off: I decided to push her.

'Tell you what,' I said, 'put me through to Jez Green. I don't have time to be fannied about.'

I'd given her my icy, authoritative voice, the one I'd developed playing Douglas Jardine in *Red Leather:* it worked as well on her as it had on his team. 'Sorry, sir,' she said. 'I was just checking our files. Mr Wilde's account executive was Alanah Day. I'll put you through to her, Mr . . . er?'

'Gantry.'

I held the line, listening to Sir Elton singing about a porch swing in Tupelo, and wondering if he was being paid for it, until he was cut off in mid-chorus (pity, I like that song; I reckon

Peachtree Road is his strongest album in years) and replaced by a slightly tired female voice, so languid that I wondered if she'd had a liquid lunch. 'Mr Gantry,' she drawled, 'Aimée says you have a part for Sandy Wilde.'

'He's been put in the frame,' I replied obliquely. Unusually for someone whose fortune is built on pretence, I try to avoid telling flat-out lies.

'You'll have to go a long way to audition him, darling. He's gone back to Oz.' I said nothing. 'You know Oz, as in Oz Blackstone. Down under.' She gave a small squealing laugh. 'Oz Blackstone, down under,' she exclaimed, awake all of a sudden. 'I should be so lucky.'

'Don't hold your breath,' I said. 'Can you put me in touch with him?'

'Afraid not,' she replied, the drawl returned. 'We've dropped him.'

Bugger it! I thought. 'Why?' I asked.

'I'm not at liberty to say.' She fell silent. I thought she was waiting for me to come back, but I was wrong. 'Listen,' she murmured confidentially, 'I shouldn't do this, but Sandy's an all-right guy and if you've got something for him, I'm not going to stand in his way. This is the last personal number I had for him.' She recited a phone number with an Australian prefix. 'It's a mobile. He may still have it, he may not; it's all I can do for you.'

'Thanks, Alanah,' I told her. 'I appreciate it. A tip in return: don't waste your time having wet dreams about Oz. He's no use in the sack . . . or so his wife told me.'

I thought about waiting until next morning, Australian time, before calling Wilde, but I decided that if one of us was going to be disturbed at midnight, it might as well be him, so I dialled the number. It took around fifteen seconds to connect, but only five to produce an answer.

'Sandy,' a voice snapped. 'Who the fuck is this?'

I switched identities. 'My name's Dylan,' I lied. (Okay, sometimes I can't avoid it.) 'I'm calling from Monaco.'

'Monaco?'

'Yes, it's where I'm based. I'm doing a background report on someone, and your name's come up.'

'Who?'

'A woman named January, Madeleine January.'

I heard an intake of breath on the other side of the world. 'You want good stuff, or do you want bad stuff?'

'Bad stuff will do?'

'That's fine, 'cos there ain't any other kind with that . . .' (I have to tell you that here Sandy used the C-word.) 'I used to have a career. Now I don't and it's her fucking fault.'

I hadn't been expecting this. 'How come?'

'I met the . . .' (He used that word again.) '. . . in Edinburgh. She was with some small-time Scots bit player with a spot in the show I was in. She worked on the PR side. She made a play for me; all over me, she was. She told me she was hacked off with the other guy, but that she fancied me rotten. Normally, I don't pitch for women, but this one really turned me on. I took her back to London with me, she got a job with an agency and everything was great for a while. Then it started to stall. She started staying out nights; I got suspicious, but she laughed it off. Finally I started staying out nights; I got close to a guy on my show, got back to my old style. I didn't tell her, though: I wasn't sure how she'd react, but I knew it wouldn't be good. She's a strong woman and I didn't fancy losing any important bits. So I decided that the only way was for me and Byron to come back down here. I left her, just like that. My agency played ball, they came up with a great part in a TV show, and Byron got a gig in *Les Mis* too, out front of the chorus, billing, everything. We were top of the world, man, like Cagney, and then it all went up in flames, just like him.'

'How?'

'The part I had in the show, I played an outback hunk, a real stud. I was a big hit, and I'd just signed a recording deal, the kind I've been after all my life. Then some pictures appeared in a scandal sheet down here. No warning, no nothing. I woke up one morning and there they were. Me and Byron, naked, nothing left to even an Aussie's imagination. That was that. The show dropped me, the record contract was torn up, my agency blew me out and, to top it off, Byron got fired too. You know where I am right now, mate? I'm between shows in a fuckin' gay club. That's all the work I can get.'

'That's a sad story, but how does it relate to Madeleine January?'

'Are you fucking thick?' No, I'm not, but I wanted him to tell me the whole story, for the tape on which I record all my phone conversations. 'I don't know how she got those pictures, but she got them. Maybe she snooped on us herself, for she was a good photographer, or maybe she paid someone to do it, but she was behind it, no question.'

'How do you know that?'

'I know, because after it's all done, and Byron and I are sitting at his place . . . we were discreet, Mr Dylan, we didn't live together . . . still in shock, I had a call, on the very fucking phone I'm talking to you now on. It was Maddy, and you know what she said? She said, "Gotcha!" in the most vicious, scary voice I ever heard, and then she hung up.'

'Jesus!' I whispered, and not for Sandy's benefit.

'This report you're doing?' he asked. 'Who's it for?'

'I can't tell you that,' I replied, very sincerely.

'Well, whoever it is, you tell him that if he's crossed Maddy in any way, he should be in fear of his life, or at least of the bits of it that he loves.'

I thanked Sandy and wished him well. Before I hung up I had him give me all his contact details; I told him it was in case I needed a formal statement from him, but the truth was that I felt sorry for him and intended to do what I could to revive his career. I was pretty sure that when Miles Grayson heard the story, he'd want to help him too, and a good word from Miles is the Aussie equivalent of a papal blessing.

I decided I had to call my brother-in-law to give him an update on my progress. When I told him where Dylan and I were going he announced that he would be picking up our costs . . . as if I'd have allowed it. When I told him what Maddy had done to Sandy Wilde he fell silent for a while.

'I may not be able to sort this by being nice, Harvey,' I said. 'In fact, I really don't want to. I promise you that I will protect and preserve your reputation, but after what I've learned about this lady, my strong inclination is to crush her like a nut.'

18

We left on Friday morning. I didn't enjoy it, but I knew I couldn't just send Dylan out there alone and hope. I didn't trust him that much; in fact, I barely trusted him at all. I tried again to talk Susie into coming with us, and leaving the kids with Ethel, Audrey and Conrad, but she still wouldn't have it.

'I'll trust you not to make another drama out of it,' she said. 'Your idea's sound, and Mike's the ideal guy to play the part of a duplicitous sleazeball. Get the business done and get home as quick as you can.'

Audrey had booked us on Lufthansa; we could have gone KLM, through Amsterdam, but I didn't even suggest that to Mike. Officially he might be dead, but in my experience the security guys there are real sharp bastards, and I didn't fancy taking even the outside chance that one of them might recall a face from the past, especially if he saw it alongside mine.

There's no quick flight to Singapore, even in first class. When we took off, I popped a couple of melatonin pills, not just to help me sleep on the flight but to minimise the jetlag when we got there. For some reason, melatonin isn't encouraged in the UK, but you can buy it everywhere else in the world.

Even with a couple of hours' sleep I had time to watch three movies, before the information system told us that we were flying down the Malaysian coast and beginning our descent towards Changi Airport. It was mid-afternoon when we touched down and began the long taxi to the gate. I looked out and saw blue skies, acres of grey tarmac and some very modern terminal buildings.

When we disembarked, the interior lived up to the promise of the rest. I've been in more than a few international airports in my time, but I have never arrived in more pleasant surroundings than Singapore. The whole atmosphere was welcoming, from the helpful guys who directed us to the carousel, and through to the immigration process, where we were greeted with a smile and a welcome, in complete contrast to the grim-faced people who guard the gates of the USA and appraise you on the basis that you, and everyone else on the flight you've just come off, are a terrorist until they say that you're not.

I've often wondered why Americans are surprised that they're unpopular abroad when their immigration officials show such open hostility towards every other nationality on the surface of the planet . . . and sometimes their own, if they happen to be black or Hispanic. I thought this aspect was exaggerated until Roscoe Brown explained to me what 'DWB' means. It stands for Driving While Black, and it's a common reason to be pulled over in the US, if your face fits, so to speak.

There's none of that in Singapore.

We stepped out into the airport concourse and straight into a big mistake. A limo driver stood there, in lightweight grey suit and peaked cap, holding up a sign that read 'Mr Os Blackstone'. It hadn't occurred to me until that minute, but I'm a pretty big name internationally these days (misspelled or not) and the last thing I needed at that time was to advertise my presence in Singapore, or to have someone else do it in a public place.

I stepped up to the guy, said, 'That's me,' and quietly but firmly took the card from him. He smiled nonetheless, bowed and took charge of our baggage trolley. We followed him outside, into an afternoon temperature that wasn't much different from what we'd left in Monaco. I looked around as the driver opened the door of the limo, and loaded our cases: the place was much greener than I'd expected and more breezy. I got the sense that without the wind we'd be experiencing the humidity as Susie had described it.

I asked the driver to show us something of the island before taking us to the hotel. A licence posted on the glass divider told me that his name was Mr Goh. 'My pleasure, sir,' he said, with a trace of American in his accent. 'That's part of our service.'

He took us along a broad highway, heading west, I judged, which he told us was the Pan Island Expressway. He talked us through the trip as we passed through the northern suburbs, skirted the nature reserve, then swung round past something he called Mount Faber, although I confess I saw only a hill, with a cable car leading up to the summit. As we passed the port, I realised we were heading into the heart of the city, and that it boasted some pretty impressive buildings. Finally he swung off the main highway, and drove towards Raffles Hotel, then past it and swung round until he stopped in front of the big impressive foyer of the Swissôtel Stamford.

Dylan stared up as we stepped out; our hotel looked as if it was the tallest building in Singapore. We soon found out how tall: when we checked in we were allocated adjoining suites on the sixty-fourth floor, with killer views across the city. Dylan suggested a trip to the complimentary cocktail bar, but I put that on hold and headed instead for the eighth-floor gym to work off some of the after-effects of the flight. As I ran on one of half a dozen treadmills, I had my choice of eight different television channels including BBC World, CNN and CNBC. I saw our Prime Minister on all three at different times; there really is no escape, you know.

The melatonin was working. I'd insisted that Mike take some, and he seemed to be okay too, so much so that after we'd eaten enough of the complimentary nosh in the executive club, we decided to head out for a beer, rather than drink in one of the umpteen restaurants in the hotel, or in our rooms, for all the view to end all views. We asked the concierge to mark our card: he did more than that. He pulled over a taxi and instructed him to take us to Clarke Quay, and then gave us detailed instructions on how to find a place called the Crazy Elephant.

It wasn't difficult: even if he hadn't mentioned the tethered bungee ride machine next door, or the cage in which some poor idiot volunteer was dropped into the Singapore river, we'd have found it by the noise. Wherever you go, Saturday night is the same. (Okay, maybe Vatican City doesn't quite rock like the Kasbah, but you know what I mean.)

The Elephant turned out to be the best blues bar in Singapore, with live music on stage and beer on draught. My Scots instincts will live as long as I do: I'd been in Sing for about five hours and already I'd spotted a fundamental truth about the place. Wherever you go, the booze is always more expensive than the food. That doesn't mean they don't drink there, though.

We found space at a high table on the quayside by the river. As Dylan ordered two pints of Tiger from a Filipina waitress, I glanced into the bar and did a double-take when a guy who looked very like Eric Burdon jumped up on to the stage at the back. There was nothing for it, we left the table and drifted to another indoors, braving the heat to get closer to the action.

And then it bloody happened, didn't it? I got clocked again.

I hate to say it, but it's sadly true. Wherever you go in this world there's always some drunk Jock who thinks that because you were born north of Hadrian's Wall, like him, you and he have a special relationship . . . unless you're wearing a blue replica shirt, that is, and his has green and white hoops, or vice versa. (No, come to think of it, especially vice versa.) I suppose in those circumstances the relationship can still be special, but in a different way altogether.

Happily I wasn't wearing my East Fife replica shirt that night, but I might as well have been. The stare usually registers first: it draws me to it, like a fucking magnet. I turn my head and it locks on to me. Then the eyes widen. Then the jaw drops slightly and the grin widens. Then comes the 'Hey!' And finally, 'Hey! It's the boy himself, it's the boy Oz Blackstone, is it no'? What brings you tae a place like this Oz, big star like you?'

That's how it all came off. By that time the whole fucking

place was looking at me, Eric Burdon, or his double, was seriously pissed off because it was meant to be looking at him, and I was trying to work out what lunacy had brought me there. I had it in mind also to have a serious word with the concierge when we got back to the hotel for sending us to a zoo like this one. (I know, he was only doing his job as best he could. My mum raised me better than that, so I didn't actually say anything to him, other than 'Thanks for the advice,' but, still, it was what went through my mind at the time.)

The geezer left the bar and lurched towards me, clutching a pint bottle of Heineken; he was in his late twenties, I'd have said. He wore a black silk shirt covered with dragon images, light tan slacks, and his fair hair was mussed up. I know from experience that all you can do at such times is let it happen for a while, but somewhere deep inside Dylan, his copper reflexes kicked in. He stood, and I knew that he was going to have the guy's arm up his back and huckle him outside, maybe accidentally drop him in the river. That I needed even less than the unwelcome local publicity, for it might have attracted the attention of the real police, so I reached out, caught his belt and jerked him back down on to his seat. 'No,' I said quietly, as the triumphant Glaswegian reached us. Had I forgotten to mention the unmistakable accent? Sorry.

'Hey, therr!' he breathed in my ear, as his arm went around my shoulders. I flexed them very slightly, but very quickly, letting him feel the sudden bunching of the muscles under my shirt: it's my patented invisible warning signal and it always works. The arm was withdrawn, and the guy straightened up. 'It is you, isn't it?' he asked, a little more circumspectly.

'Yes, it's me,' I confessed. 'Now, do me a favour and shut the fuck up. I don't like being embarrassed in public.' I nodded at the stone-faced Dylan. 'My pal here likes it even less.'

The man noticed my companion for the first time. 'Is this your minder, like?'

'No. Like I say, he's my pal. Mostly, I do my own minding.' I shouldn't have answered him; when I did it was like an invitation to take a seat, which he did. I glanced around: a few people were still staring at me, but mostly they had gone back to looking at the stage. 'Eric' caught my eye: he'd recognised me too. I gave him a nod and mouthed a quick 'Sorry', half-way through the chorus of 'We got to get out of this place'. That didn't seem to be a bad idea, but I reckoned we were stuck with our new pal for a while wherever we went.

'So, what's your name?' I asked him. 'You know me,' I nodded to Dylan, 'and this is Benny.'

'Sammy,' he announced. 'Sammy Grant, frae Maryhill . . . or East Bearsden, as my maw prefers tae call it.' He frowned suddenly, and I saw that he was looking at my left ear, where it's a bit chewed up. 'What happened tae that?' he asked, pointing indelicately, as if I was a zoo monkey with the power of speech.

'I took a gun off a guy last year in San Francisco . . . not quite quickly enough.'

The Weegie laughed. 'Aye, sure. You're takin' the pish, right?'

'No, it's true. He was a bag-snatcher, I chased him and when I caught him he pulled a gun on me.'

'What happened to him?'

I smiled cheerfully at the memory. 'After he'd recovered from a bad case of concussion, he did a plea bargain that got him off with only ten to fifteen years.'

Sammy was impressed. 'Ooyah!' He whistled. 'Ma man Oz.'

So was Dylan: he glanced at me as if to make quite certain I wasn't kidding. I gave him a quick nod.

'What's it like, getting shot?' our gallus friend asked.

'It's not something you want to try,' Mike murmured.

Sammy looked at him, at the supporting cast. 'Are you tellin' me you've been shot an all, Benny? That'll be right.'

'I'm telling you it's much better to be the one doing the shooting.'

'What, are you a hitman, like? Aye, you really are kidding me now, eh?'

'He's a writer,' I said, to steer him away from the topic. 'He's always doing research into stuff like that. That's what we're doing here, planning a new movie. Isn't that right, Benny?'

Dylan nodded dutifully.

'Hey, that's great,' said Sammy.

'So, what's your story?' I asked him. 'What brings you here? Holiday? A stag trip with your mates?' I nodded towards the guys he seemed to have been with, who had decided to ignore him, and us.

He shook his tousled head. 'No, I work here,' he said, 'for the DRZ Bank, over in Change Alley. I'm a dealer; I specialise in Japanese stocks.' All of a sudden he looked a lot more sober, and a little embarrassed. It occurred to me that the spectre of Nick Leeson might be taking some time to blow away.

'I've got some of them,' I said, to put him at his ease. 'My wife and I have an offshore investment portfolio; it's spread around the world, but quite a chunk's in Far East markets. We're thinking about backing off a bit, though: it's just a wee bit unstable politically for our liking.'

'That might not be a daft move,' Sammy suggested. I made a mental note to talk it through with Susie and our broker when I got back.

'So what's to do in Singapore?' I asked. 'We've only just got here.'

'Ah could tell by the eyes. Guys that have just got here all look a wee bit like it's still yesterday. First time here?' We both nodded. 'Well, you're pretty much doin' what there is tae do in Sing, partyin'. No' that this bar here is the end-all. It depends what you're lookin' for. If it's women, no problem here: there's a hell of a lot of them pass through this place.'

'That's not on my agenda, thanks. How big is the city in population terms?'

'Four million plus, they reckon, and growin'. The island's probably smaller than Glasgow, but it'll soon have more people than Scotland. That doesnae count the tourists either. Ah reckon there's more of them, especially Aussies, since the Bali bomb and the tsunami. If the casino happens, Christ knows how many there'll be.'

'Casino?'

'Aye, the Yanks want to build one, if they can persuade the government to let them.'

'And will they?'

'Hard to say. There's resistance, but they're talking about three billion US. It's hard to turn that doon, even here, in the richest place in South East Asia.'

'What's the cultural side like? I'm an actor, remember, so how's the theatre side of things?'

'Loads of it. There's big visitin' shows, like *The Sound of Music,* and there's local outfits that are producing here all the time, mostly in English but sometimes in Chinese. This place is Chinese, Ah mean the whole culture is Chinese, don't make any mistake about it; that's why it's no' in Malaysia.'

Sammy seemed to be an interesting guy, now that we'd got over the initial nonsense, and not nearly as pissed as I'd thought at first. I've observed that sometimes the Jock abroad feels he has to act out the stereotype.

'Ever heard of an outfit called the Heritage Theatre Company?' I asked him.

'Heritage? Heritage? Heritage?' He scratched his head hard, as if he was shaking up its contents. 'The name's familiar. I've seen it on posters advertising things on the Esplanade, I'm sure.'

'The Esplanade?'

'Big new complex down on Marina Bay, across frae where Ah work. They have all sorts of venues there.'

'Mmm, I must check it out.' I waved at a waitress. 'Eric' (or maybe it really was him: the voice said it might be) was taking a break and glasses were being refilled all over the place. 'Two more pints of Tiger, please. Sammy, want another Heineken?'

He beamed. 'Aye, thanks, Oz.' You'd have thought I'd offered him another Rolex.

I gave the girl fifty dollars. She came back two minutes later with three beers and not a lot of change, then she asked for my autograph. Great, I thought, as I signed. Word will get around: not what I wanted.

'Are there many of us here, Sammy?' I asked.

'Us?'

'British people.'

'Not just Jocks, you mean? Aye, lots. Most of that crowd at the bar for a start. Half the guys Ah work wi' are Brits, and there's others in advertising and construction. The truth is they need us to make this place tick. It's a good deal for us: the money's good and the tax is a lot less than in Britain. Then there's the weather.'

The humidity had kicked in with nightfall, even on the riverfront. 'Does it ever change?'

'Oh, aye,' said Sammy. 'Sometimes we get monsoons.'

19

We chucked it after another couple of beers; Sammy insisted on getting another round in so he could tell his pals at the office that he'd bought Oz Blackstone and his mate a Tiger.

Before we gave in to the need for sleep and went off to kidnap a taxi, we arranged to meet Sammy next day, for a walking tour of the city centre. He suggested the Long Bar in Raffles, but I reckoned it would be a lot harder to get out of there than to get in, so I told him instead to meet us in the foyer of the Stamford. That prompted him to suggest that, there and then, we should all go to the New Asia disco on the seventieth floor, but I got out of that one by telling him that it sounded like no place for a thirty-eight-year-old father of three to be found.

(We didn't tell Sammy afterwards, but we did sneak a look when we got back to the hotel. I left quickly, though: all we could see were long legs in black dresses, and I realised straight away that I could have got into serious trouble there. Normally that wouldn't have stopped Dylan, but by then he was too dazed and confused to remember which name he was using, so he bailed out too.)

The melatonin did its stuff: I popped another couple and was asleep by one and awake by eight. The hotel gym opened early, so I went down there again and did a quick aerobic circuit topped off by some sets of serious weights, then swam a few widths of the circular pool, which was deserted, save for a couple of British Airways flight attendants in bikinis. I had just come out of the water and was towelling myself down when one of them came over and asked me to sign her trip schedule. I might as well have issued a press release, I thought.

It got worse. I was barely back in my room before the phone rang: a programme assistant from a local television station was put straight through by the hotel operator to ask me if I'd do a drop-in on a chat show at seven that evening. I lied again (I was becoming uncomfortably good at that) and told her I couldn't be certain that I'd be in Singapore by then. She sounded so crestfallen that I gave in and agreed to do it. I figured that if it was general knowledge that I was on the island there was no point in trying to hide.

When I hung up, I noticed that a red light was flashing on the phone, signifying a message. I called it up, and heard Primavera; she'd phoned the night before when Dylan and I were out on the town.

'Oz,' she began, 'I hope to God they've put me through to the right room. I'm at Dad's and I've spoken to my sister and brother-in-law about the surprising development with Mr Luker. As you can imagine it came as a hell of a shock to them both, but I've managed to persuade him that Benny wasn't personally involved in the difficulty they had and that the other man was almost completely responsible. They're okay to go on with the project, on the basis that they don't have to see Mr Luker at any time. Give me a call to confirm that you've received this, and get in touch with them whenever you can.'

It was better than I'd expected: I'd envisaged having to weigh in with Miles myself at the end of the day, to win him over. Prim had done a good job. I called her mobile to tell her as much. It was the middle of the night in Auchterarder, and it was switched off, so I left her a voice message saying, 'Well done, Benny owes you one,' and hung up. Then I rang Mike's room to give him the good news, but when he answered he sounded like a Martian, so I told him I'd see him downstairs at midday, and went off to the club room for breakfast.

Once I had eaten, I picked up a map of the city centre. It told me that the Esplanade theatre complex was located in two hedgehog-shaped buildings I could see from the club windows. I asked the concierge, a pleasant girl whose name-tag said she was called Polly, whether they were easy to reach. She told me that there was a walkway which led straight there from more or less under the hotel.

I found it easily enough, at the foot of the escalator leading to the City Hall MRT station. (The MRT is Singapore's subway; it is to the London Underground as the classic Cadillac in the Monaco motor museum is to the nearby East German Trabant.) The walkway turned out to be a shopping mall. I hadn't sussed this out at that time, but Sing is a very, very serious retail place. Eventually I was glad that Susie didn't make the trip, because there wouldn't have been enough suitcases on the island to carry back the stuff she'd have bought.

It took me ten leisurely minutes to reach the Esplanade, and when I did I found that the walkway led me into an underground car park from which another escalator raised me up into a vast modern marble foyer.

Bear in mind that it was still well short of eleven on a Sunday morning, but there were other visitors, sightseers in the place, and there were two blue-suited receptionists on duty. One of them looked like an even further upmarket version of one of the tall Chinese waitresses we had seen briefly (at least I had seen them: Dylan's eyes had been crossing by that time) in the New Asia the night before.

She approached me and welcomed me, with a smile that said she meant it, to the Theatres on the Bay. She gave me a rundown on some of their recent performances, including the Sadlers Wells ballet (Ali, my irreverent grocer pal in Edinburgh, used to call ballet 'poofs' football', and may well still do so) and on some of their forthcoming attractions. She told me that the following night there would be a performance by the University of Florida Wind Symphony. You know me well enough by now to read my mind: I tried to keep the smile off my face, but I failed. We both wound up laughing; I liked this girl.

The burst of early visitors had come to an end, so we were able to talk. She told me that her name was Marie Lin, and that she was an actress, supplementing her income by doing shifts in the complex. She was Singapore-born, but she had the ambition to leave the island and work either in Britain or America.

'Not Australia?' I asked her.

'Fewer opportunities for Chinese people,' she replied.

She hadn't appeared to recognise me, so I told her that I was an actor too. She asked my name, and I gave her one of the cards I carry, with my personal contact details. She was a little embarrassed when she read it, but in an attractive way. 'I'm sorry, Mr Blackstone,' she said. 'I should have . . .'

'I've had a long flight and a hard night in the Crazy Elephant,' I replied. 'My wife wouldn't have recognised me this morning.'

I handed her another card and told her to note her mobile number on the back, then I had her write down Roscoe Brown's address and invited her to drop him a line with my endorsement; I gave her another card to include with it as proof we'd actually met, to make sure that Roscoe's secretary didn't bin it.

I'm sure she must have wondered whether there would be strings attached. There weren't, as it happened, and even if there had been, Marie Lin seemed like the sort of girl who'd have cut them off with a very sharp knife. In fact, I was thinking ahead: *Blue Star Falling* had a part for a Chinese girl and she looked as if she'd be perfect for it.

I reckoned that I could rely on her. 'While I'm here,' I said, 'I'm trying to track someone down. Are you familiar with a theatre group called Heritage?'

'I've worked with them,' she told me, 'not recently, but last year I had a part in one of their productions.'

Direct hit: well done, Oz. 'Do you know the director, Tony Lee?'

'No, I don't. The man who was there then, he left or, rather, was fired by the Arts Ministry. But his replacement's name is Lee Kan Tong.'

'Yeah, but he was Tony Lee in London.'

'That doesn't surprise me. It's quite usual for young Singaporeans to adopt English names; not just actors, all people. Me, I am Lin May Wee; you see why I change it for the stage.'

I smiled at her. 'Nice one. Do you know where I could find Lee Kan Tong?'

'I'm sorry, Mr Blackstone.'

'Oz.'

She gave a little bow of acknowledgement. God, but she was attractive; I made a mental note not to tell Dylan about her. 'I'm sorry, Oz. The Heritage Theatre Company had an office behind Boat Quay, but they moved early this year. I think it's in Riverside Point now. It won't be open today, though.' That was a bit of a bugger: I wanted to pin down Maddy January as quickly as I could, and preferably that day.

'I don't suppose it will, Marie,' I agreed. 'Still, I can always take a run out there just to check where it is.'

'Take a water taxi,' she suggested.

'What?'

'A water taxi. You go out to the front of the building, past the open-air theatre and you'll find a jetty. You talk to the man there and he'll call you a boat.' She paused. 'Wait,' she said, then turned to her colleague. I heard them speaking quietly in Chinese, then the other woman glanced at me and her brown eyes widened; she smiled and nodded.

'I'll take you there,' Marie announced. 'Anna says you're a VIP, so we have to look after you. She's the front-of-house manager, so if she says it's okay, it's okay. Come on.'

She went behind her counter and picked something up. I assumed it was a handbag, but when I looked I saw that it was a collapsible umbrella. 'Are we due a storm?' I asked.

She smiled. 'We don't use umbrellas for rain here: usually it goes straight through them. This is for the sun.'

131

As it transpired, when we went outside, she found she didn't need it. A layer of light cloud hung over the city, killing the glare that had welcomed the day: the humidity was full blast, though. There were several people waiting at the jetty on the esplanade, but Marie had a word with the man, I gave him ten dollars and, as if by magic, within three minutes a boat cruised towards us.

It was a long wooden craft, one of many on the river, with an open-sided cabin hung with red lights. The night before, from Clarke Quay, they'd all looked like floating brothels, but by day, this one at least was revealed as an ancient craft that must have seen and survived invasion, restoration and a million tourist bums in the sixty years since. Marie gave me the river tour as we went, past the statue of the Merlion, a mythical beast (which I suspect, although I can't prove it, was invented by an advertising agency), the former GPO building, which is now the Fullerton Hotel, the bars and restaurants of old Boat Quay, bustling as they got ready to open for the day, and Clarke Quay itself, which, by the light of day, I saw was much newer and purpose-built.

Finally we pulled up at the Riverside Point jetty. The boatman had a simple approach: he didn't tie up, he simply jammed the prow of the vessel into the landing-stage, and revved the engine to keep it steady as we jumped off.

We didn't have far to walk. Riverside Point was a complex of offices and restaurants, which also seemed to be the temporary home of the Singapore History Museum. (It wasn't very big, but I don't suppose Singapore's had a hell of a lot of history.) One of the restaurants included a micro-brewery . . . something else Dylan would be avoiding; we stepped past it and into the foyer, looking for the usual list of tenants.

The Heritage Theatre Company was there, all right, one floor up. 'Wait here, Marie,' I told my escort. 'I'll go up, on the off-chance that there is somebody there.' I confess that I hadn't thought this through properly. I was supposed to be the guiding genius in the background with Mike doing the legwork, so what was I doing heading for an office where my presence might have tipped off Maddy, through her boyfriend, that I was looking for her? God knows, but I did it.

The office was in a narrow corridor lined with glass-walled suites. It was distinguishable from the rest by the posters which were plastered all over it, advertising performances past and some that were still to come. I couldn't see inside, for the glass was opaque, but it appeared that Heritage had all the space on the left of the corridor as I walked down it.

A Chinese face beamed at me from the entrance door; it was on yet another poster, but this one carried only that smile and the name, 'Lee Kan Tong, Director'. Other than that there was nothing, no list of office hours to say whether they were open or closed. What the hell? I thought, and turned the handle.

The door opened. Marie was right, nobody was there . . . but somebody had been. The lay-out was simple: there were open-plan areas on either side of a single private office. Its door was gaping wide, and the room had been trashed. The place had been turned upside-down: desk drawers and filing cabinets lay open and their contents were all over the floor. The chair behind the desk was upside-down, as if someone had thrown it aside. Lee Kan Tong was either a very untidy human being, or he had a big problem. Whatever it was, I knew I shouldn't be witnessing it.

'Fuck!' I whispered, and then I started behaving sensibly. I took off my T-shirt, used it to wipe the door handle very thoroughly after I'd closed it behind me, then put it back on and got the hell out of there.

Marie was waiting in the foyer, as I'd asked. 'You're right,' I told her. 'Office closed on Sundays.'

20

We walked out to Merchant Road, where I stopped a taxi, one with wheels this time. I dropped Marie back at the Esplanade, then told the driver to take me to the Stamford. I still had fifteen minutes before I was due to meet Sammy and Dylan, and I figured that a fresh shirt might be in order.

I was heading for the lift when the foyer concierge called out. 'Excuse me, Mr Blackstone, I have a message for you, sir.'

As I walked over to him, I guessed it might be from Dylan, telling me that he was crashing out for the rest of the day. Could I have been more wrong? No.

'A lady called, sir,' he told me. 'She asked to speak to you. I told her you were out, but that she could leave voicemail. She said she had to speak with you in person, and she left this number, asking if you would call her back.'

He handed me a notelet bearing the hotel crest and a number; I glanced at it and saw it was local. 'Did she say anything else?'

'No, sir, only that it was urgent.'

Many things in my life seem urgent to the other people involved, but not to me. I thanked him and headed liftward. On the way up, I found myself wondering who it might be. Probably the girl from the television station; but she had left a message before, no problem, so why not this time? A journalist? Maybe, but wouldn't she have left a name, or more likely called back every half-hour till she got a result?

I was still pondering when I got to my suite. I chose a Coke from the mini-bar, popped it and took it into the bathroom, where

I had a quick shower. By that time I had almost forgotten about the call: my mind was back at Riverside Point, wondering who had given Lee Kan Tong's office such a duffing up. My best guess was a theatre rival, looking to blag a copy of a script that Heritage held; these things happen in the arts world, although we'd never admit it to outsiders.

The note was still on my table as I pulled on a dry T-shirt, this one advertising Jimmy Buffet's Margaritaville in Las Vegas. I had half a mind not to bother about the woman, just to head downstairs and out with the lads. Fortunately, or not (you decide later), the other half made me pick it up and dial the number.

'Yes? Who's speaking?' The voice on the other end was female all right, but not Singaporean . . . at least, not Asian. It was mature, not a youngster, but not old either; my age maybe. It was also clearly agitated.

'This is Oz Blackstone. I have a message asking me to call you. Assuming I have the right number, who are you?'

The woman sighed, and I could have sworn it was with relief. 'Oz,' she exclaimed. 'I'm so glad you called me back. God, you don't know how glad.'

'I'm glad you're glad, but who the hell are you?'

'We've never met,' she replied, seemingly determined not to answer my straight question, 'but we have something in common. My ex-husband is your brother-in-law. My name's Madeleine January, and I need to see you.'

Everywhere's a village, I thought. Four million inhabitants or not it's still a fucking village. I paused, just to give myself some thinking time. 'Are you, indeed?' I replied at last. 'How did you know I was here?'

'I heard a trailer for tonight's *Mai Bong Show* on local telly. They said you were on it.'

'No, I meant how did you know I was in this hotel?' My master plan had been hit right on the head. I decided to stall her until I could come up with another.

'I called around. You weren't in Raffles, and you weren't in the Fullerton; this was third choice.'

'Remind me to chastise my secretary for booking me in downmarket,' I murmured. I had Plan B: it was, let her make the running. 'Since you know I'm on air this evening, you must realise that I'm pretty busy.'

'I appreciate that, but this really is very urgent. Can we meet?'

'When?'

'Two o'clock.'

I let her hang on for a few seconds. Finally I sighed. 'Okay, if you insist; but be clear, I'm only doing this because of the Harvey connection. Where?'

'There's an island called Sentosa, near the port, with lots of attractions on it. One of them's a place called Fort Siloso. Go there and then follow the yellow route till you get to the children's playground at the top. I'll be there. Make sure you get there just after two. I want to be sure I'm there before you.'

'Okay, but why the drama? I'm on holiday, remember.'

'I'll explain later. Just be there, Oz. It'll be worth it to Harvey in the long run, I assure you.' She hung up.

21

I stood in the window for a while, staring out at Singapore and thinking as I sipped my can of warm Coke. Maybe, just maybe, there wasn't going to be a need for all the subterfuge I'd planned; maybe Mike's air fare had been a waste of money.

I called his suite, but there was no answer. I checked my watch; it was ten past midday.

He and Sammy Grant were waiting for me. They were sitting in the foyer bar; each of them looked the worse for wear, and they appeared to be chewing, rather than drinking, two Corona beers.

'Where have you been?' Dylan moaned. 'Pumping iron in that fucking gym again?'

'That was a while ago. I've been on the river since then.'

'Have a beer, then, and work it off.'

'Don't be disgusting, Benny.' I thought it politic to remind him that we were travelling under his new name, just in case he had forgotten; I had also decided to keep him in the dark about Prim's good news. That could wait for a while. 'You know I never drink before lunch.' I clapped my hands together and looked enthusiastic.

Sammy jumped to his feet; Dylan seemed to slither to his. That's the only way I can describe it. 'Okay,' our new friend began, 'I thought I'd take us to Orchard Road. Ah know you guys won't usually do the shops on a stag trip, but there's a place up there called the Lucky Plaza. It's just fuckin' magic; you'll get every sort of fake you can imagine. There's even a wee tailor's shop there called Armani.'

'That's a nice idea, Sam,' I said, 'but you're right. We're not going to the shops. I've been reading up and I want to go to a place called Sentosa.'

'Sentosa?' he exclaimed. 'But it's Sunday. It'll be fuckin' heavin'; it's a family day.'

'Nonetheless, it's where I want to go, and I am the Mighty Oz. Besides, we might not get another chance.'

Remember I told you about that cable car we saw when the limo driver gave us what passes for the grand tour? That's how most people get to Sentosa. You can board it at Mount Faber, but Sammy reckoned it would be quieter at the ferry terminal, so we taxied there.

There weren't too many people around, but we still had to queue for a while as all of the punters were tourists and all of them had to have the various day-trip packages explained to them. Not us, though: Sammy simply walked up to the window and asked for three returns. The man behind the counter gazed at us gratefully as I paid; he looked knackered, even in his air-conditioned booth.

We took the lift up to the boarding platform, showed our tickets to the attendant and jumped on to the first empty slow-moving car that came along. It swung us out into space and over two cruise liners, moored side by side. 'I can never work out why people would want to pay money to get into a boat and sail round in circles,' Dylan muttered; the Corona had not improved his mood.

'I used to say that too,' I shot back. 'Now that I can afford it, and I've had a chance to cruise the Great Barrier Reef on Miles Grayson's yacht, I'm not quite so sure. You can afford it now, Benny. Maybe your view will change.'

He gave me a sour look. 'Does having money cure sea-sickness?' he asked.

I smiled at him, a little wickedly, I must confess. 'If you get seasick how do you feel about cable cars swinging in the wind?'

'Bastard! Do you think you could get on your mobile and ask the driver to hurry up?'

Happily, we made it to the other side before the boy threw up, although Sammy didn't take his eyes off him for the rest of the journey. He was first off, holding on to the guardrail to steady himself as he hit solid ground. The way out led us through a gift shop. Sammy, having started on the road that leads to male-pattern baldness, headed for the part that sold sun-hats. Mike was going to follow him, until I caught his sleeve.

'I'm meeting someone here,' I murmured in his ear. 'Whatever I do, play along with it, and when we get to a certain point, steer our boy off to one side. You'll know when we get there.'

The prospect of doing something with a purpose seemed to sharpen him up in an instant. 'Okay, but who are you meeting?'

'Maddy January: she called me this morning. I'll tell you more later, when I know myself. For now, follow my lead.'

Sammy was back in only a minute, wearing a pale green hat with a Merlion crest. It matched Dylan's complexion; if I had seen any Irn Bru on sale I'd have bought him a can. (For those of you who do not know, Irn Bru is one of two traditional Scottish hangover remedies. The other is more bevvy, but Mike had tried that and it didn't seem to have done much good.)

'Right, gentlemen,' said our guide, with the air of a man who was beginning to wish he hadn't talked himself into whatever he had talked himself into. 'Where will it be? The aquarium?'

Dylan glared at him. 'They've got a big one in Monaco,' I said. 'Benny's got fish up his arse.'

'Did you ken that there's a fish that does that? It swims up your arse, or even up your dick,' Sammy volunteered, bewilderingly. 'South American it is, called the canduri.'

'I feel no better for knowing that,' I told him sincerely.

He chuckled. 'Maybe no', right enough, but don't pish in the Amazon, that's all Ah'm saying. How about lookin' at Volcano World, then?'

'I live a few hundred miles from a couple of real ones. No, Sam, when I was out on the river I met a girl who told me about a place called Fort Siloso. She said that anybody who comes to Singapore should see it.'

'Siloso? Aye, okay. We'll need to take the bus, though.'

I bought a couple of Subways for the boys . . . it occurred to me that a large sandwich might do both of them more good than harm . . . and three bottles of water, then, when they had eaten, followed Sammy over to the stop. He led us on to a Blue Line bus, which dropped us close to the entrance to the fort, and the aquarium.

It was crowded with kids as we walked past; from out of nowhere a sudden pang hit me. I wondered what Susie, Janet, Tom and Jonathan were doing at that moment. I realised at once that they'd be sleeping, but it didn't help. I wanted to be home with them, and the thought made me determined that I was not going to let the first Mrs January jerk me around. I was ready to scare those pictures out of her, and I reckoned I could do that too, if it came to it.

As Sammy bought three tickets with the fifty-dollar note I gave him, I glanced at my watch: it showed that it had gone quarter to two. The norm of the place seemed to be that we waited for a tram to take us up what looked like a fairly steep hill . . . not unnatural: you'd expect a fort to be on a hill-top. The attendant told us that one had just left and that we'd have to wait fifteen minutes. I thanked him for the tip and started walking. Sammy and Dylan both looked slightly aghast, but they fell in behind me.

Yellow footsteps showed the way: they led us to the guard-house, with uniformed wax figures . . . and, for some reason, a wax whippet . . . and the first of what turned out to be a series of voice presentations, then up a twisting path towards a gun emplacement, and a progression of displays, in which a character called Sergeant Major Cooper talked us through the perils of life as a nineteenth-century soldier, cook, tailor and coolie. (I don't know why they gave the poor sods that name, they must have been anything but.)

By the time we'd come through it all, it was five past two. We stepped into the open air, past a mock-up of a cannon being fired. We were near the top of the hill; I looked ahead and saw a child's swing, and a play suspension bridge.

'I'm going for a seat over there,' I announced. 'You guys go on, and I'll catch you up later.'

'We'll wait wi' you,' said Sammy.

'No, just do like I say. I want to phone my wife: my dad's been ill, and I need to check on him.'

'Come on,' Benny barked. 'It's fucking baking out here. There's buildings over there and I want to get under cover.' He headed off in that direction, our friend slouching along behind him.

I mounted the last slope and stepped out on to the flat area of the playground. I saw a bench, but no sign of a woman, or anyone else for that matter. I wondered if I had been set up; if so, there was nothing I could do but sit it out and see what happened.

I had barely lowered myself on to the bench when I heard a sound, a creaking from the play bridge. I turned: it was swaying from side to side under the weight of a woman who was walking across it, clutching the guardrope in one hand and a small bag in the other. Not a great weight, I guessed. She was tall and slim, with shoulder-length auburn hair that shone and shimmered as she moved; her crowning glory and no mistake. She looked to be around forty, but she had kept her figure. I could tell that because it was on show, in close-fitting pedal-pushers and a sleeveless shirt, tailored to hold her breasts high. Twenty years on, it wasn't hard to understand what Harvey, and all those guys since, had seen in her.

She skipped off the bridge walked the few steps across to my bench and sat beside me. 'Oz,' she murmured.

'That's who you asked for, Madeleine.'

'You're alone?'

'I have a couple of mates with me, but I've got rid of them.'

'Good. I'm very sensitive about who sees me just now.'

'Makes a change, from what Harvey told me.'

'I'm sure. I'm sorry, Oz, but that man was the biggest disappointment of my life. A typical career-driven Edinburgh lawyer, and I was fool enough to think I could make him interesting. When I finally gave up, and looked elsewhere, he treated me like shit.'

'You went off with another bloke, then tried to take him to the cleaners. He didn't let you. You should have done your homework, Maddy, before you took him on like that, in his home city, in his home courts. You were fucked from all directions, from the off.'

'Maybe that's so, but I didn't leave myself entirely unprotected. I had intended to get even with the smug bastard, at a time when it would do him most harm.'

'Had?'

'My plans have changed. I need money, Oz, rather urgently. My partner and I have to leave Singapore.'

'Who have you fucked this time?'

'You don't want to know that.'

'Too right I do.'

'Look, we're in trouble, it doesn't matter what sort, but it's bad. We need cash, in a hurry. That's why I'm prepared to sell Harvey the thing he knows I've been holding over him.'

Things were changing fast. It looked as if the goods I'd come to get were being delivered into my hands. The only question seemed to be price. I decided to haggle. 'Let me tell you something, some truth. I know what you're talking about. That's why I'm here. Harvey sent me to find you and get those negatives back. He asked me to be all nice and legal about it, as he would, since he's a nice and legal guy. But the thing is, I'm not. Understand this; my sister's involved in the situation, and if you do what you're planning to Harvey, just like you did to that poor

144

bastard Wilde in Australia, she and her boys will be badly hurt too. Washing on from that, so will the rest of my family, my dad, even my kids. There's no way I'm going to let that happen, especially now that I've got you sitting here beside me. I'll do anything to protect them, and if that means eliminating you, so be it. From the sound of things there's a queue of volunteers for the job.'

I glanced at her: her tan had turned a very unhealthy colour. I grabbed the bag from her hand, resisting her feeble effort to prevent me, and opened it. Inside I found a purse, and one other item, an automatic pistol, a small-calibre, palm-size lady's weapon, but no joke at close quarters. There was nothing in the purse other than three hundred and ten Sing dollars and a Visa card, but there was a full magazine in the gun. I gave her the purse back and pocketed the pistol. 'Oz,' she protested, 'I need that.'

'No, you don't. If a hard lady like you has been scared as badly as this, it's going to be no use to you against the people who have done it.'

Women always take me by surprise: my stepmother had done it big time a few days before, and my brother-in-law's ex did it again. She buried her face in her hands and began to cry. 'In that case,' she sobbed, 'do me a favour and shoot me now, because those people will probably do a lot worse.'

I said nothing for a while. I looked around, but we were still alone. I was pretty sure that Dylan would be watching us; suddenly I was glad of it.

'What do you want?' I asked her.

She let out another couple of sobs, then pulled herself together. She whispered something, so quietly that I couldn't hear her. I told her so. 'Fifty thousand US,' she repeated, a little louder.

'And you give me?'

'The negatives, and every print I have.'

'You'd get ten thousand sterling, tops, from a Scottish tabloid,' I pointed out.

145

'Money's never been my motivation, until now. But, like you said, it's not just Harvey who's involved.'

'When?'

'Tonight. It has to be tonight.'

'Jesus, how am I going to get hold of fifty grand on a Sunday?'

She looked at me, with a tiny smile that I found amusing. 'Oz, people like you can get hold of fifty grand any time.'

'You have to believe that if you cross me on this I will help these people find you.'

'Having listened to you, I do believe it. You really don't live up to your image, do you?'

'Not a bit. Where do we complete?'

'I'll come to your hotel.'

'No fucking way, paparazzi hang around there. Pick somewhere less obvious.'

She frowned. 'There's a place called the Next Page on Mohamed Sultan; it's a pub where the actors hang out. It would be natural for you to go there, and it'll be safe for me because there are plenty of people around. I'll be in one of the private booths at the back. Be there at seven.'

'I can't: I'm on telly, remember.'

'Damn! So you are. Make it nine, in that case. It'll still be busy then.'

'Okay, but, Maddy, I repeat, don't even think of pulling a fast one on me.'

'Don't worry. I won't.'

I gave her a last stare, to make her a true believer. She made as if to stand, but I put a hand on her thigh to stop her. 'Tell me, in case I have to explain it to Harvey. What the fuck have you done to get in trouble this bad?'

'I told you, you don't want to know.'

'I bloody do: now tell me.'

'I've been stupid, more stupid than I've ever been in all my stupid life. I've been hoist by my own thingie . . .'

'Sounds agonising.'

'You know, by my own whatchacallit.'

'Petard?'

'That's the word. It all began when Tony and I had been here for a few months. I began to notice gaps in his diary, periods when I didn't know where he was. I'm a bit of a control freak where my men are concerned, so I asked him. He got evasive, gave me general answers about business. I'd been down that road with Sandy, so I decided to deal with it the same way.'

'You mean . . .'

She was hurried, anxious: she cut me off. 'I followed him, with my camera. I've studied photography, and I'm very good at it, as Harvey will have told you. I trailed him to an address in Chinatown, just off Pagoda Street, a first-floor flat. I found a vantage-point across the road, I used a telephoto lens and I saw him in a room, in his shirt, with another man. I thought, Fuck me, this one's gay too! and I hit the motor drive.' She chewed her lip.

'Let me guess,' I said. 'You tried to put the black on Tony and he's turned very nasty.'

'No, not like you mean anyway. He found out, but not that way. I made a huge mistake. To get best quality I use film, not digital, for serious stuff. I hadn't set up my own darkroom facilities here, so I had it developed commercially, in a shop right there in Chinatown. Oz, those Triads are everywhere. The guy who developed the film must have run off another set of prints, and handed them on to the man Tony met.'

In a flash, I saw why she was scared. 'You mean the other man was a Triad?' I asked her.

'Not any old gangster: he's the leader of the whole Singapore organisation. And there's more. I never suspected it for a moment, but Tony's a Triad member himself. A couple of days ago, he came home and he went berserk; he'd been shown the photographs, and told me he knew everything, that the film had been handed in for processing by a dark-haired Western woman, and where. Well, he went crazy at me. He told me he's been in the organisation since he was in his teens. He went to London

147

because of it, and his move back to Singapore was engineered by them as a sort of promotion. He didn't tell me how they work, only that they're an old-established network, and that you'll find them in Chinese communities across the world. Tony says that the Triads as a society are compulsively secretive, and so brutal they make the Mafia look like Amnesty International. In their areas they control everything, drugs, protection, prostitution, you name it. The Singapore government's been at war with them for decades. They've hanged some of them, they've caned others half to death, but they still haven't won. The organisation's still there.'

Nothing she said surprised me. I'd heard of the Triads; many a film production company's had to buy their co-operation, especially in Canada. 'Yes,' I murmured. 'You really are in the shit.'

'And how! The man at the top has decided I'm a government spy: he's ordered Tony to kill me.'

'And does Tony plan to? Are you hiding from him?'

'No. He loves me; we're getting off the island together, as fast as we can. That's why we need the money. Tony's playing for time. He has me hiding out with a friend in the theatre company, and he's told the leader that he's carried out his orders and that I'm dead.'

'Does the guy believe him?'

'We don't know for sure. He said that he did, but that others might not, so he wants to see my head. Tony told him that he'd buried my body out on the nature reserve. He told him, tough, to dig me up.'

'I don't think he's convinced anybody,' I told her. 'I went to Tony's office this morning; it had been turned upside-down. Would you bet that whoever did it wasn't looking for your film?'

Jesus, this woman: the thought ran through my mind that maybe I should just shoot her. Easier all round. 'So,' I hissed at her furiously, 'this deadly, ruthless international terror organisation thinks you're a government spy, and you've set up a meeting with me, in a public place. Thanks a fucking bunch. Why didn't you just put a chip in a fucking android or something and send it to my hotel? "Help me, Obi-Wan Blackstone. Only you can save me!" Come to think of it, you even look a bit like Carrie Fisher, minus the daft hairstyle. Well, I have news for you, dear, I'm not Obi-Wan, I'm Darth Vader. Now, please, fuck off. I'll see you at nine tonight.'

22

When I thought about it, I realised that if these Triads had followed Maddy to our meeting-place, I'd have found her on the other side of the bridge, minus her head. Not that that improved my mood a hell of a lot.

Even Sammy could see that something was wrong when I caught up with him and Mike, although he said nothing. We saw it through to the end of the Siloso tour, then caught the cable car back to the mainland. We picked up a taxi at the terminal and headed back to the hotel, where I left the other two with the excuse that I had to speak to the telly people about the night's events.

In reality, I went to my room to speak to a man about fifty thousand US dollars. Maddy had been right: people like me can always get their hands on cash at any time. I called American Express, found someone senior enough to make big decisions and told him what I wanted. He guaranteed that the money would be at the Stamford by five o'clock.

After that I really did have to speak to the television people; the show's assistant producer told me that they would send a limo for me at six, and that I had been slotted in as the first item, after the presenter Mai Bong's warm-up. He said that the questioning wouldn't be difficult, 'just the usual stuff'. I grimaced at that: the day I'd had . . . so far . . . and here I was, giving some interviewer I didn't know a blank cheque.

In my experience there are two kinds of talk-show host, those who ask intelligent questions and convey an interest in their guests, and those who see them as a wall off which they can bounce their own sparkling personalities. I hoped that Mai Bong wasn't one of those, otherwise it might be an interesting ride.

I checked my watch for the umpteenth time that day. I had one and a half hours to wait until the money arrived, but at least it was late enough to call home without having Susie slaughter me.

She sounded so pleased to hear me that it moved my homesickness up several notches. 'How's the quest?' she asked.

'With a bit of luck, it'll be over tonight. I've located the woman, and she's willing to deal: the pics for fifty thousand US.'

'That's not too bad: Harvey can afford that, no problem.'

'Not as well as I can, though. It'll be a present for my sister.'

She laughed. 'Sometimes you can be too nice for your own good.'

'That's not what Maddy January thinks: she's had to choose whether I'm bluffing or whether she should be really scared of me. Happily she's made the right choice.'

'What's she like? A bit of a bitch, like Harvey says?'

'No, that's probably an understatement. She's a thoroughly dangerous woman, but this time she's bitten off way too big a mouthful. Shit!' I had just remembered that I still had her gun in my pocket. I didn't need to read the tourist guide to know that the locals would take a pretty dim view if they found it.

'What?' Susie asked.

'Nothing. I nearly dropped a drink, that's all.'

'Speaking of drink,' she retorted, 'how's that long glass of water you're travelling with?'

'Better now than he was this morning. We had a couple last night. I worked them off; he didn't.'

'What are you doing tonight?'

I told her about the short-notice television show. 'After that I'm meeting Maddy to close on our deal. All being well, we're on the first available plane out of here, and home on Tuesday.'

'All had better be well. Oz, once you've paid her off, is there any chance Harvey will ever hear from her again?'

'Very little, I would say. She'll probably be off the island before we are.' I asked her about my dad; she said that he was doing so well they were letting him home the following day, with nursing support from his local medical practice. It was the first good news I'd had in Singapore. I told my wife I loved her and hung up, then helped myself to that drink I'd pretended to spill, a half-bottle of a pretty decent Aussie chardonnay.

As I sipped it, I thought about what I had got myself into or, rather, what Harvey had got me into. Time to report back, I decided, so I called him. He was astonished when I told him that Maddy had contacted me. I didn't go into detail, just said that things had gone sour for her in Singapore and she needed to raise cash to do a runner. We had a discussion about whose cash it was going to be, Harvey insisting that it would be his, but we left that issue unresolved … or, at least, I let him think we had.

Finally, I called Semple House, Auchterarder. I was after Miles, but it was Prim who answered. 'They left last night: I told you it was only a flying visit.'

'I didn't think it was that short. How's your dad?'

'Fine. How's yours?'

'Getting finer by the day. He's getting home tomorrow.'

'That's great. Would you mind if I went to see him?'

'I wouldn't, but you'd better phone Mary first to make sure he's receiving, so to speak.'

'Will do.' There followed one of those Prim pauses, where you could hear her mind work, and her curiosity get the better of her. 'Oz,' she asked at last, 'what the hell are you doing in Singapore? There was no mention of it when I was with you in Monaco.'

'Family business. There's a situation involving Harvey and his former wife; I'm sorting it out for him and she's out here.'

'Maddy January?' she exclaimed.

'You know her?'

'I've met her, yes.'

'You never told me that.'

'The subject never came up; I didn't see the need to.'

153

'I suppose not,' I conceded. 'Where did you come across her?'

'In Edinburgh, before I met you. It was when Dawn was trying to get her career under way, working in the Lyceum theatre company. I was home on leave from my nursing job in Africa; I hung around with Dawn's crowd, and so did she. As I recall it, she was screwing an actor at the time; an insipid jerk he was. I'm sure she was still married to Harvey, but that issue was never raised. There was a rumour that she'd had a fling with Ewan Capperauld before that . . . Well, actually, now that I recall it, it wasn't a rumour: she was quite open about it. I assumed that she was bullshitting, though.'

'No, she wasn't; I have that from the man himself, but let it not pass your lips.'

'His secret's safe with me.' She chuckled. 'No chance of an introduction to said man, is there?'

'Maybe, if the opportunity arises. I'll warn him first, though. Come to think of it, you almost did meet him, that day on the set in Edinburgh when Miles poleaxed your boyfriend.'

'Nicky was never really my boyfriend, you know that. That was all to get at you.'

'You succeeded: there was such a fucking row that Ewan locked himself in his trailer and didn't come out for an hour.'

'He'd have been better locking himself away from Maddy January: gorgeous though she was, that woman struck me as big trouble waiting to happen.'

'And it has, my dear, it has.'

'I can just imagine her first line when she sees you, you being an actor an all: is that a gun in your pocket or are you just pleased to see me?'

'Actually, it's a gun, but it's so small I'd be offended if she asked that.'

I had hung up on her, called Susie again just so I could hear her say, 'Hello,' for a second time that morning, and was half-way through the chardonnay, when Dylan knocked at my door. I let him in; he let himself into the mini-bar and grabbed a bottle of

Corona. There was a fruit bowl on the table; he complained that it didn't contain any limes, then cut himself a slice of lemon instead and shoved it into the neck of the bottle. No class; the boy never had any class.

'So,' he said, when he'd stopped spluttering from the foam that had surged up the neck of the bottle when he took his first swig, a problem when you substitute lemon for lime, 'what's the fucking story?'

'Very interesting,' I assured him. 'I want you to do something for me.' I took the pistol from my pocket and handed it to him.

He almost jumped from his chair. 'Jesus Christ, Oz! Where did you get that?'

'It's Maddy's. I took it from her for everyone's safety, although hers is in very short supply at the moment. Dump it for me when I'm at the TV studio. Don't mess about: go down to the river and chuck it in. And make fucking sure you're not seen.'

'Teach your granny. Do you think I've never lost a hot gun before? But why the hell is she walking around with it? The Singaporeans cane you for that sort of thing, woman or not, plus they bang you inside for a while.'

I told him Madeleine's whole sorry tale, watching, as I did, his eyebrows rise higher and higher. 'She's photographed a Triad chief?' he gasped. 'They think she's a spy? Oz, don't go near this woman again. I'll make the trade, and I'm keeping the fucking gun until I do.'

'Wrong on both counts. She'll run a mile if she sees anyone but me. And the gun goes in the river.'

'You're mad, you know that? Barking fucking mad. I can just hear the TV interview.

'"And why are you in Singapore, Mr Blackstone?"

'"I'm here to pay off a blackmailer so she can escape the Triads before they cut her fucking head off."

'Jesus, their ratings will go sky-high.'

23

The cash arrived on time, delivered to the hotel by courier. I signed for it then took it upstairs to the safe in my room.

To set the scene for what I'm about to tell you, I hope you'll understand that, with all the day's events, I was not in the best frame of mind to be appearing on a live television show. I thought about pulling out, using delayed jetlag as an excuse, but that might have drawn more headlines, so I decided I wouldn't disappoint my Singaporean fans. The cricket movie *Red Leather* was a huge success on the island when it was released, and the DVD has been number one in the charts all this year, so I'm not bragging: there really are quite a few of them.

The production assistant who'd booked me in for the show was in the limo when it came to collect me. It was a stretch Honda, with a bar in the back. My enthusiastic escort offered me champagne, enthusiastically, but I declined. The last thing I needed was a loosened tongue, and that seemed to be the idea; get the guest a little pissed, but not too much, and see what happens.

I'd done no real homework on the show; if Susie had been there, or Roscoe, I'd have had a bollocking for that, but they weren't, so my omissions went unchecked. One of the things I didn't find out until I arrived at the studio was that there would be a studio audience, and that they wouldn't just be there to laugh and clap on cue, they'd be chipping into the discussion. The producer explained all this in the green room . . . they'd taken the term literally: almost everything in it was green, even some of the dim sum things on the buffet table. The other guest was there too;

I'd always wanted to meet Eric Cantona, but he didn't seem all that bothered about me, although he was very polite.

I'd expected our host to come in at some point, to say hello and put us at our ease. That was what had happened on every other talk-show I've ever done, but clearly they didn't go in for such a courtesy on that particular production. It wasn't the most professional thing I've ever encountered, before or since, and I wasn't too impressed.

You know me well enough by now, I hope, to appreciate that I'm rarely bothered by trivia; it takes something big to blow my fuses. They started to overheat, though, when I walked on set and under the hot lights towards the seat that was waiting for me, and discovered for the first time that Mai Bong wasn't the attractive Chinese lady I'd been expecting, but a man, a smarmy wee geezer with greased-up black hair and heavy makeup. I expected him to stand, to welcome me to his show and offer a handshake … Parky always does that … but, no, he just sat there, beaming like a small round fifty-year-old cat, and, for some reason, winking at the studio audience.

I glanced at them too, as I settled, as best I could, into the uncomfortable plastic bucket they'd provided for me; it had been designed for an arse slightly smaller than mine, deliberate no doubt, to put the guest at a disadvantage from the off, and maybe even get the occasional cheap laugh, if he reacted to it.

Two faces jumped out at me from the crowd, one beaming, the other smiling shyly. There were three rows, and Sammy Grant was at the back, looking as chuffed with himself as Mai Bong did. Marie Lin was front and centre: she'd changed out of the blue uniform into a long black dress with a slit in the side that showed something I hadn't noticed before. She had great legs.

'Okay-lah!' Mr Mai squealed, in a high-pitched voice. 'Welcome to Singapore, Mr Jardine. First visit?'

The guy had just opened his mouth and he was annoying me even more. 'You've obviously invited the wrong bloke,' I told him, being careful to smile as if I meant it. 'Douglas Jardine, the guy you're talking about, was a part I played. Look,' I rubbed a finger across my freshly shaved top lip, 'the silly little moustache has gone, plus I'm not wearing whites and a cap.' I was actually wearing a Siegfried and Roy T-shirt that I'd bought in Las Vegas, with a big white tiger on the front. 'Please, Bong, let's not confuse the people at home and in the studio, especially the lovely Marie there in the front row, who took me for a river-ride this morning, and my fellow Jock, Sammy, at the back, who tried to get me hammered in the Crazy Elephant last night, then gave up his hung-over Sunday to show me Sentosa. My name's Oz Blackstone, okay-lah.'

I turned back to the audience. 'Hey, Sammy, pal,' I called out. 'How did you get in here? Did you just walk in off the street?'

'Aye,' he replied, his voice amplified by one of the live mikes that hung above the seating. 'That's how it works. You just queue up, like. Ah've never done it before, but it's dead easy.'

'It can't be all that big a show if you can do that,' I fired back at him. 'They told me this was big-time.'

'This? No' really. It's all right, but the bigger shows are on cable telly.'

I turned back to the host. 'So what about it, Bong? Your producer told me you've got the biggest viewing audience in South East Asia. My friend in Britain, Mr Parkinson, won't be very impressed when I tell him you've been pulling my chain.'

'We have huge audience.' The little man chuckled, his lips tightening. 'Huge.'

'Maybe yes,' I conceded, 'maybe no, but you do have an intelligent audience, because they've chosen to come and listen to me and Eric the Red. Tell you what,' I said to them, 'between now and the commercial break, why don't we all just have a chat among ourselves?' The host opened his mouth, but I cut him off, still being careful to smile. 'Relax-lah, Bong: you know it makes good telly, and good publicity. You'll be on the news pages tomorrow.' I held up my hands and made quote marks. 'Can you see the headlines in the *Straits Times?* "Rowdy Scottish actor tells Mai Bong to piss off on his own show." That won't do the ratings any harm at all.'

I scanned the crowd. 'Okay-lah,' I said. 'Hands up all the people with the planted awkward questions designed to embarrass the guest and make the host look good. Come on,' I laughed, 'enter into the spirit of the occasion. Like Delia Smith said, let's be having you.'

In the second row, an arm rose, tentatively; it was followed by two more, one in front, one at the back. 'Okay, you three,' I told them, 'you're clearly production assistants; you can piss off too.' The rest of the audience were well into it now: they hooted with laughter. 'Go on,' I insisted, 'I'm serious. You're not real punters; you don't belong there.' Off-camera to the right, I saw a floor manager signalling to them to leave. I waited as they rose from their seats. 'Don't think about coming back during the commercials,' I yelled after them. 'Mr Cantona's watching at the back, he'll know who you are.'

I smiled at Marie in the front row, giving a nod of approval to her legs, which I'm sure she understood and appreciated. 'What do you think of the show so far?' I asked her.

'Excellent, Oz,' she replied; her voice had a lovely laughing lilt to it. 'A big improvement on the usual format.'

'Thanks, you've got the floor. Ask me a question if you like; a real one that the people of Singapore want to hear.'

'I think we'd like to know what sort of a trip this is. Is it pleasure, is it business, or is it research? Are you planning to come back to make a movie here?'

'Nice one. The honest answer is that I have no current plans to make a film here, although I'd like to, and I'd like to cast you in it.' I looked into the live camera. 'This is Miss Marie Lin, ladies and gentlemen, a very fine young Singaporean actress. Remember the name and the face.' I looked back at her and saw another camera focus on her and go live. I let it linger for a while then carried on. 'It's a pleasure being here,' I said, 'but it's business that brought me, something I have to do for a family member. I was trying to trace someone I thought might be here, but she may well be off the island by now.' What I'd said had been entirely spontaneous, and I didn't know how it came out, or why. Looking back, I think I was trying to put up some smoke for the bad guys on the off-chance that they had been watching Maddy and knew of our connection.

Then something else escaped from my mouth when I wasn't looking. 'Can I ask you a question now, Marie?'

'Of course?'

'Meet me for a drink in my hotel later on? About ten thirty? I've got a special pass to the New Asia.'

She smiled back at me. 'Okay, but I prefer the City Space bar; it's quieter.'

Fuck me! I'd made a date with a woman, on live television! Susie was going to kill me, twice.

I picked out another audience member: a bright-looking man in his twenties. He asked me what I thought about the possibility of a casino coming to Singapore.

'Far be it from me,' I replied carefully, 'to become involved in local politics on a flying visit, but looking around at the prosperity here, I have to question whether you need it. If it's allowed, will it stop at one? I doubt it.' I tapped my T-shirt. 'Much as I love Las Vegas, I reckon it belongs in the middle of a desert in the USA and nowhere else.'

That led to a lively informed discussion on the pros and cons, which went on until I saw the floor manager hold up a sign that read, 'One minute to break.' Mai Bong tried to cut back in, but I wasn't having it. I've been stitched up by experts in my time; he was a rank amateur. The minute must have passed slowly for him, but eventually I did a wind-up, thanked the audience and shoved myself out of the silly seat. I extended my hand to Mai so that he couldn't avoid shaking it, waved to the benches and walked off set, just as the floor manager signalled, 'Cut to commercial break.'

As I headed for the exit and the limo, I stuck my head back into the green room. 'Tell them you're not going on,' I advised Cantona, who's put on a bit of weight since he quit playing, 'unless they give you a proper chair. There's no chance of you fitting into that one out there.'

24

I don't know why the hell I did all that, but it felt good. I suppose it was my way of getting my own back for the nonsense that had been happening to me since I arrived in Singapore. Or maybe I did it to take my mind off the prospect of shelling out fifty thousand bucks to a blackmailing bitch when I could simply have waited for a couple of days in the likelihood that the bad people would take her out of Harvey's hair, and out of everything else.

I was about to step into the stretch Honda when I heard a shout. 'Hey, Oz.'

I turned and there was Sammy heading towards me. 'Didn't you fancy the Frenchman?' I asked.

'They didnae fancy me any more,' he replied, with a satisfied smile. 'The boy on the floor asked me tae leave. He said Ah'd upset Mr Mai. Ah'm barred for life, as well.'

'You'll be pleased with yourself, in that case. Being barred from places is a badge of honour for you Weegies. Won't that get you into bother at work, though?'

He laughed. 'Oz, pal, the money Ah make for that bank, nothing short of bein' arrested for murder is going to get me intae bother.' He tapped the roof of the limo; the driver frowned but said nothing. 'Any chance of a lift?'

'Sure, where do you want to go?'

'Back tae your hotel will do fine. I can get a taxi from there. I'm going down to Harry's bar.'

'In the Esplanade complex?' I'd noticed a pub sign that morning.

163

'Naw, the one on Boat Quay. There's a few Harrys now; one at the airport, even.' I held the limo door open for him, then followed him inside. 'Hey,' he exclaimed, when he saw the booze compartment, 'is that self-service?'

'It is now,' I told him, taking a 7-Up, as he chose a Grolsch.

He nudged my elbow as we pulled out into the traffic. 'Ah see you've got yourself fixed up for later on,' he murmured, or came as close to murmuring as a Glaswegian can.

'Don't read anything into that,' I warned him. 'I met her this morning down at the theatre. She works there.'

'Ah'm saying nothing, Oz.'

'Keep it that way.'

'Trust me. Wish it was me, though. A right tasty lass, she looked.' He winked at me, then forgot his promise to say nothing. 'You're sure of yourself, trying there. If you crack her I'll bet you're the first. If that's what bein' a movie star gets you I wish Ah was one.'

He really was a cheeky bastard. 'Actually, Sammy,' I said, 'I'm going exploring first. Ever heard of a pub called the Next Page?'

'Oh, aye. There's two of them, down near Robertson Quay, the Front Page and then the Next Page, side by side. The Next Page used to be a couple of doors up, but it moved and got smartened up. That was a while back.'

'How long have you been here, Sammy?' I asked. 'In Sing, I mean.'

'Eight years. Ah came out when Ah was twenty-one. There was nothing for me in Glasgow, except unemployment and maybe the jail.'

'Do you still have folks there?'

'My mother, my sister and two nephews.'

'Do you ever see them?'

He took a pull of his beer. 'Ah go home every couple of years. Ah could get a job there now, or in Edinburgh, but Ah like the life out here. Ah'm a resident now.'

I found myself wondering if there was a woman in his life, but I held myself back from asking. I didn't want to get too involved in the background of a guy I'd probably never see again.

The limo pulled up outside the Stamford. I wished him luck as we parted, and watched him head for the side door that takes you direct from the foyer into the Raffles City Mall, and on to the MRT.

Dylan was waiting for me up in the New Asia bar. We ordered a dozen mixed satays each, not knowing whether we'd have time to eat later. 'That was a performance,' he said, as we waited for them to arrive.

'How do you know? You had a job to do, remember?'

'And it's done, don't worry, but I still had time to catch your local TV début.'

'What did you think?'

'I thought you were arrogant, aggressive, and a touch conceited, but very funny. What's it worth for me not to tell Susie about the girl?'

'There'll be nothing to tell, but it'll cost you plenty if you do. *Blue Star Falling* will never get made.'

'Bastard. Has she got a mate?'

'Ask her yourself. You can come with us to the City Space if you like.'

'We'll see when the time comes. We've got somewhere else to go first.'

'We? I'm going on my own.'

He shook his head firmly. 'No, you're not. This might be the safest city in the world, and you might be more than capable of handling yourself in a bundle, but you're carrying fifty large to a meeting with a dodgy woman who's on the run from one of the deadliest criminal organisations in the world. You can make the trade yourself, but on the way there you're having a minder, and that's that.'

I blinked: it had been a while since anyone other than my wife had laid down the law to me. 'Okay,' I said. 'If it makes

165

you happy you can chum me, but when we get there you wait outside.'

'That's not going to happen either. How well do you know this woman? Not at all: she gave you a rabbit-in-the-headlights act and you took it at face value. I know this part of the world, Oz: I spent a few dark years up in Thailand after the Amsterdam thing. Singapore might be more ordered and civilised, but it's still Asia and all sorts of things can happen here. If you want proof of that, this friendly place executes more people per million population than any other country in the world, although they're careful never to publish the statistics. What if you're the target here, not her? The Triads get up to many things, and kidnap for ransom is one of them. You're rich and you're high-profile.'

'That's probably why I'm safe,' I pointed out. 'If these people are as secretive as it seems, they won't want the publicity that would come from snatching me. But if you want to make sure, you can come in with me. You really did dump that thing in the river, didn't you?'

Eventually he convinced me that he had; by then we had finished the satays, and it was time to head for my meeting with Maddy. I picked up the money from the safe; it was in a mix of twenties and fifties, too bulky for an envelope so I packed it into a small tote bag that I had bought for the purpose in the Raffles City Mall.

The Stamford doorman found us a taxi, and as usual got himself a ten-dollar tip in the process. The cab had barely pulled away before I found myself focusing on what I was about to do. I was going to buy Harvey's peace of mind, then abandon a woman to her fate, which could well turn out to be a very grisly death.

'Should I be doing more here, Mike?' I said quietly. The radio was on loud, so I wasn't worried about the driver overhearing; he was a big sullen Indian bloke who hadn't smiled, who had been singularly unhelpful until the doorman had given him a hard word, and who was getting fuck-all tip from me at the end of the trip, which I realised very early was going to be longer than it need have been. 'Should I be doing more to help her?'

'Why? She's a blackmailer.'

'Yes, I know, but she's a . . . she's a woman!'

'Let's get specific here: she's a white woman, and some nasty Asian gangsters want to kill her. If she was a Filipina housemaid you probably wouldn't give a toss.'

'Hey, that's not true!' I protested.

'Maybe not entirely,' he conceded, 'but you wouldn't feel as strongly; you'd probably think it was a shame but too bad, she's caught up in something within her own culture. This Madeleine woman, she's done something stupid . . . she's upset people in a culture she doesn't understand.'

'So I let them kill her?'

'How are you going to stop them? You being famous doesn't count for anything in this situation.'

'I know, but there must be something I can do.'

Dylan sighed and tapped his chest. 'You know, mate, some-where deep in here I'm still a police officer. Corrupt, yes, beyond redemption, yes, but I'm still a copper. The only thing you can do is the same as Maddy should have done in the first place. She should have gone to the police: someone who can identify a top Triad member would be very valuable to them. She'd be under their protection, and she'd probably be helped out by Interpol and the DEA as well, just as I was. She'd probably turn up in Greenwich Village as Mrs Benny Luker,' he added, mournfully

Even in the circumstances, I had to laugh at that. 'The couple from hell,' I said. 'I'd hate to live next door.'

'I don't have a next door. I live in a loft: I have an up and a down.'

'In truth, Mike, I'd hate to live in the same city as you and her. But are you sure, dead sure, that the local police wouldn't just arrest her for attempted extortion?'

'Not if she has something to give them. Did Tony Lee take her film from her?'

'I guess so, but I don't know for sure.'

'Then find out; if she still has it, or even a print, that would do, try to persuade her to go to the police with you. You're even more famous here now: you've just made a charlie out of a local TV star so you're a man of influence. If she won't do that, give her the money and let her run as far as she can.'

'What about the British High Commission? Maybe she'd agree to go there.'

'They couldn't protect her: they'd have to involve the police. Besides, they employ a local workforce. There's a fair chance that the Triads will have a source there. No, it's the bizzies or run.' He paused. 'Of course, it'll suit you better if you don't have to take her to them.'

'Why's that?'

'It won't ruin your chances of getting your leg over that girl from the TV show.'

'Forget about that. I told you, she's . . .'

'I know, I know: she's a nice girl and you're a happily married man. Let me tell you something: if all the happily married men who shagged nice girls on away trips were laid end to end, they'd encircle the globe several times over.'

'Cynical bastard.' I laughed. 'Is there no purity in your life?'

'Not since the former Mrs Dylan caught me with a nice girl on an away trip, no.'

As he spoke the taxi pulled into a space just along from our destination. 'Mohamed Sultan,' the driver growled. It was a couple of minutes short of nine; I asked the guy to wait for a while. 'You're here,' he barked. 'Where you want go. Okay?'

Mike leaned forward and gave him some quiet advice; whatever it was, it worked. We sat there until two minutes past nine, when I decided it was time to go. I paid off the driver . . . no tip . . . and we stepped out into the humid night.

The front of the Next Page was not what I would have called welcoming: its blue-painted doorway and small obscured windows made it look like a stretch Tardis. Doctor Who's assistant was seated on a stool at a tall desk by the entrance; she had taken the form of a fat Malaysian girl. 'Twenty dorrah,' she said, as we made to enter.

'This is a pub, dear,' Dylan pointed out.

'Sure, but twenty dorrah. You get a drink and there's a free draw.'

'Are we sure to win the free draw?'

'No.'

'Then it's hardly a bargain, is it, dear?'

We weren't there to haggle: I thrust a couple of notes at her, took the two tickets she offered me and led the way through the door. Inside, a man in a suit wanted to search my bag. I told him to fuck off. We had a small stand-off until Dylan whispered in his ear; he stepped aside and let us past.

'What did you say to him?' I asked, above the thumping sound of the inevitable music, as we made our way towards the bar; the Bose speakers were proving their excellence once again. The place wasn't as busy as Maddy had led me to believe; maybe the cover charge wasn't such a good idea after all, I thought, but in the circumstances I wasn't bothered about that.

He leaned close to reply. 'I told him we were the special police, and that if he didn't get out of the way we'd take him out back and kick the shit out of him. Works every time; I told the taxi driver much the same.'

I looked around the bar: I'd been expecting old Singapore, and the Next Page was trying to be that. It was a designer boozer, all themed up with hanging lanterns and Oriental carvings, the sort of classy hang-out you'll find in every modern city. It was one long room; at the far end, beyond a central light well, I could see a blue-covered pool table, and just before it, a series of booths.

I gave Mike the tickets to exchange for drinks, and was about to head for the back area when I heard a voice that had become familiar. 'Hey, boys.'

I stopped. 'What the hell are you doing here?'

169

'Ach, Harry's was like a tomb and the band was shite, so I thought Ah'd come here and catch up wi' you guys.'

At that point in time, I did not need him around; in fact, he came very close to having his head bitten clean off, until Dylan's hand fell on his shoulder and hauled him towards the bar. 'Sammy, wee man,' he drawled, 'let us get you a drink. What's best in this fucking palace of sin?'

I didn't hear the reply: by that time I was heading in the direction of the pool table with the blue cloth; I was happy to see that no one was playing that night. (If I was God I would remove all pool tables from pubs with a single flick of My Finger, but that's just another quirk of Mine.)

As I approached I saw four booths on my right, very dimly lit, each with a table and a bench on either side: I checked them one by one. The first three were unoccupied, but a man sat in the fourth on the bench that faced me. Even with the lack of wattage, it took me half a second to recognise him: I'd seen him before, larger than life, in a poster on the door of the Heritage Theatre Company office at Riverside Point.

He didn't react as I slid on to the seat opposite him. 'I don't like this, Mr Lee,' I murmured. 'My meeting was with Madeleine. You may have decided to come along in her place, but that isn't all right with me.' I touched the bag on my shoulder. 'You get nothing until I see that she's all right.'

Tony Lee said nothing. He simply stared at me across the table. I'd heard of inscrutable Orientals but this bloke was an extreme case.

I wasn't having it: I reached across and poked him with my right forefinger, hard, in the chest. 'Do you hear me?' I snapped.

He didn't. The force of my prod sent him back into the wooden divider. He recoiled from it and pitched forward, slowly, across the table. As he did, a fountain of blood exploded from his mouth, and much of it splashed over me. Siegfried and Roy's white tiger would never be the same again.

Startled is not the word to describe my reaction. You know,

170

because I've told you, that I've encountered a couple of stiffs in my time, but this one took me completely by surprise. 'Fucking hell!' I yelled, and dived inelegantly from the booth, tripping in the process and falling on to the floor.

The music drowned my shout for most of the crowd, but Dylan had been looking in my direction. By the time I'd picked myself off the floor, he was by my side, and Sammy Grant was by his. His Glaswegian eyes widened as he saw Lee's glazed eyes, and my ruined shirt.

'Oh, my Christ,' he squealed, as Dylan reached across the body, going through the vain formality of trying to find a pulse in the neck.

By this time we had attracted an audience: people were watching us from the busier end of the place, and one or two, including a couple of girls, started to wander in our direction to see what was up.

Dylan stepped towards them to head them off. As I watched him, still slightly numbed by the shock, Sammy grabbed my elbow. 'Oz, you've got to get the fuck out of here before the polis arrive.' His voice was insistent, and sounded more than a little scared. 'You don't want tae get involved wi' those boys. They're no' nice.'

'No, pal,' I told him. 'I do want to get involved with them; that's exactly what I intend.' I glanced at Lee. 'Now, what's happened to him, that really is not nice. You get the fuck out of here, Sammy, if you'd rather; I'll keep you out of it. In fact, there's something you can do for me. Go back to the Stamford and wait for Marie Lin; tell her I'm sorry I've been delayed and that I'll call her whenever I have a chance. Go on, scoot; get your arse out of here.'

He looked at me gratefully and scooted. His arse was through the nearest emergency exit in under ten seconds.

By then, Dylan seemed to have the situation in hand. The manager had appeared, down a spiral staircase that led from the office area, the doormen had been ordered to keep any potential

171

gawpers back from the booth, and the police were being called by the barman. The music had been switched off.

'What's happened?' a wide-eyed American girl asked, her question aimed at nobody in particular.

'A man's died,' I told her.

She stared at me and then at the bloody tiger on my chest. 'How?' she mouthed.

'I'm no doctor,' I replied, 'but I have done advanced first aid. A perforated ulcer looks like a possibility.' That was true, but as far as I was concerned it was an outside chance: I reckoned that the cause of death had a lot to do with a small tear I had spotted in the side of Lee's powder blue jacket as he lay across the table.

Dylan grabbed me and pulled me away from the small throng. There was an air of authority about him that I hadn't seen for a long time. When he told the barman to go to the door and let nobody in but the police, the guy obeyed without hesitation. 'What happened?' he asked me quietly.

'Nothing. I sat down beside him and spoke to him, till I realised something was up. Then he fell forward and gobbed blood all over me.'

'Don't go and look or anything, but there's a long-bladed knife on the floor under the table. You didn't touch it when you fell off the bench, did you?'

'No. At least I don't remember touching it. I was too busy hauling ass out of that booth, just like Jackie out of the car in Dallas.'

'I'll leave it there in that case. If your prints do show up on it we can explain them away by saying you grabbed it by accident when you hit the floor. If they don't, someone else's might; although I doubt it. This is a real pro job. Someone just slid into the booth beside him, spiked him, dropped the blade and slid out again without anyone noticing.' He glanced at the crowd. 'He could still be here. She for that matter, this didn't need strength, just skill and the ability to get a blade past the doormen . . . and as we've seen it isn't too difficult to get something past them.'

172

He stopped, as a commotion at the door indicated the arrival of the police. 'Go along with what I say here, Oz,' he hissed, 'no messing.'

There were three of them, a sergeant and two corporals, one a woman. The manager stepped forward, but Dylan beat him to it. 'Are you guys Criminal Investigation Branch?' he asked.

'No,' the three-striper replied. 'We're Patrol: we were told this was a sudden death.'

'It's that all right, but it's murder; a Triad hit, I would say.' He didn't pause, didn't give the man time to think about anything. 'Call your CI people at once, and keep that area of the bar sterile.' The sergeant nodded, then opened his mouth as if to ask who was giving the fucking orders. But Dylan cut him off again. 'One more thing, and this is very important. Have someone contact Superintendent Tan, wherever he is, and tell him that Martin Dyer is here. That's Martin Dyer,' he spelled it out, 'and tell him that he's here, looking after Mr Oz Blackstone.'

The copper looked at me for the first time, and his eyes widened; the female corporal had already clocked me, knew who I was. 'Sah!' he barked, and reached for his radio.

I pulled Dylan to one side. 'Who is Superintendent Tan?' I hissed at him. 'And who, the fuck, is Martin Dyer?'

173

25

He was, of course. It was the name, the new identity, they had given him after the Amsterdam débâcle, when he had come back from the dead and had been more or less conscripted as an Interpol agent. He reckoned that calling him Dyer had been someone's idea of a joke.

Superintendent Tan Keng Seng (known universally as Jimmy) was, he told me, the head of the state-security section of the Singapore Police, the sort that every force has but doesn't like to talk about. He worked in association with his opposite numbers in the neighbouring countries and with various international agencies. He reeled off a list that made my eyes water: Interpol, the American DEA, the CIA, occasionally the FBI, (apparently the Americans didn't share information with each other unless ordered to), our own Secret Intelligence Service and the Russian SVR.

Wherever the superintendent had been, getting word to him must have been given top priority for he arrived before the detectives. He walked in like God; he had a presence that parted crowds like the bow of a ship cuts through water. He was aged somewhere in his fifties, with baggy eyes and a yellow complexion. His grey-flecked brown hair was parted roughly on one side, and he was dressed all in black, a collarless silk shirt with slacks and slip-on shoes.

He stared at Dylan for a long time, then ushered both of us ahead of him into the area that had been sealed off. 'Jesus, Martin,' he said, when we were out of earshot, 'they told me you were dead for real, that you'd been wasted in that big drug operation in Bangkok. What for the hell you show yourself here? It's crazy, man. If these Triad boys find out you're alive, they'll work out who set them up. They chop you to pieces. What you do now, private security for Mr Blackstone here?'

'I'm a friend of Mr Blackstone, Jimmy. My name is Benedict Luker now, and I'm an author. I'm here because Oz has private business, and he's asked me to come along to help him.'

'Tell me rest later.' He looked towards the booth. 'What is this? Mr Blackstone's shirt tells me that you know.'

'His name is Lee Kan Tong,' Dylan replied, 'known as Tony Lee, when he was in London. He's the head of a theatre company called the Heritage, but our information is that he's a member of a Triad society, in Singapore.'

'Ah,' said Tan. 'I get it. He saw you and recognised you, so you killed him. Don't worry, son. The autopsy will say it's a heart-attack.'

'No, Jimmy, that's not what happened. Oz, tell him the story.'

And so I explained to the most powerful secret policeman in South East Asia, that I, one of the most recognisable faces in the Western world, had come to his country on a fool's mission to get my brother-in-law out of a situation which now, in the light of all that had happened, looked very trivial indeed. I told him I had come to meet Lee's girlfriend, not him, and I showed him the fifty grand in the knapsack. 'But he turned up instead. He's probably killed her already, and thought he'd collect fifty grand from me for Harvey's photographs. The big problem for him is that the Triads had him under observation instead. My guess is that they thought he'd come to sell me Maddy's pictures of their top guy, and they got to him first, maybe in a way they hoped would incriminate me.'

'And they fucking would do that,' Jimmy Tan exclaimed. 'We know just about everything about Triad in Singapore, but for one thing. We don't know who top man is, not his name, not what he

176

looks like, not nothing. These boys don't ride in Popemobile waving to crowds, although they have same influence in Chinese communities; they ride in cars with windows blacked out. This one, this Lee Kan Tong, I don't know, but if he's new back from London, that would explain why. Let's see what he's got on him.'

Two more police had arrived; I guessed they were the detectives. Tan shouted to them, 'Clear the place. Get everybody outside, take names and addresses, and see ID, then let them go. Quick now.' He watched as his orders were obeyed.

As soon as the bar was cleared, he turned. 'Let's see what we've got,' he exclaimed, then walked over to the booth, reached in and grabbed the body under the armpits. 'Wait,' he muttered, as if he was talking to it, then looked over his shoulder at me. 'Mr Blackstone, you a big guy and you got blood on you already. Can you do this?'

'You mean haul him out?' What about scene-of-crime technicians and such? I used to be a copper too, I should tell you.'

'But now you a movie star you don't want to get your hands dirty?'

Mockery has always got to me. 'Shift,' I told him, then leaned over and pulled Tony Lee's body out from the bench seat, awkwardly, because I really didn't want to get any more of the gore on me. The trouble with blood is that you never know where it's been, or what's in it. He hadn't been a big man; even dead and flopping he didn't weigh all that much, so I didn't have any trouble holding him up. 'What do you want me to do with him?' I asked.

'Put him on the pool table.'

I hefted him across to the blue baize; it wasn't full size but it looked to be just about big enough. It was racked for a game and Mike had to sweep the balls into the pockets before I could lay him out. As soon as I had, Jimmy Tan stepped past me and began to search him. He found keys, to a BMW, and I guessed to his home, in the right trouser pocket, and some change in the left.

The inside pockets of the jacket held a wallet, stuffed with Sing dollars and Malaysian ringit, and a Singaporean passport. A compact Beretta Cheetah automatic sat in a holster strapped to his right ankle. But nowhere did the superintendent find any film or prints.

'Whoever killed him came for pictures and he got them. He's in for big surprise when he looks at them.' Tan laughed. 'He expect top man in Triad, he get Scotsman's bollocks. You no worry now,' he said to me. 'Your brother-in-law is okay. They won't understand those, they'll throw them away.'

But I was worried, and I'd continue to be worried until I knew for certain what had happened to Maddy January. It worked on two levels: I didn't trust that lady as long as there was breath in her body, and yet, having met her, I found that I wanted to reassure myself that there still was.

'I need more assurance than that,' I replied. 'I still need to know what happened to the woman.'

Tan shrugged. 'What matter? Fuck her, she's in the sea.'

'The Triads will want to make sure as well,' I pointed out. 'If she's still alive, and maybe still has the pictures, she's a threat.'

'Then let them have her, and for sure she won't be a problem any more.'

'And you still won't have identified the top banana.'

'True,' he conceded. 'What you wanna do? Got any ideas?'

'I want to see where this guy lived. If we find her there, dead, okay; if not, maybe there'll be something that'll give us a pointer to where she might have gone.'

Jimmy Tan picked up the keys from the pool table . . . that cover was never going to be the same again . . . and tossed them in the air. 'Okay,' he said. 'I can find out his address no problem . . . and we have no problem getting in either.'

He grinned at me. 'Now I take you back to your hotel, but first we better fit you into one of those T-shirts on show behind bar. You can't turn up for your girl in that one.'

I stared at him: secret fucking policemen. 'How did you know about that?' I demanded.

He laughed out loud. 'Mr Blackstone, you forget: you made your date on television.'

26

Fuck! Live television! That stuff gets everywhere these days; no bookie in the world was going to give me odds against Susie switching on Chris Tarrant one night, and looking at footage of me trashing Mai Bong and his show, and picking up the beauty in the front row into the bargain.

Confession may or may not be good for the soul, but it can be a wise precaution. I decided that as soon as I got back I'd phone Susie and fill her in on every detail of my exciting evening, including my fixing up a meet with Marie Lin to talk a deal about a part in the movie of *Blue Star Falling.*

That's what I'd planned, honest; Susie would believe me . . . of course she would.

It was eleven thirty by the time Mike and I got back to the Stamford. It hadn't occurred to me for a moment that Marie would still be there, but she was, at a table in the foyer bar, close to the waitress station. I nodded good night to Dylan and headed towards her.

'Hey,' I said, as I approached, 'what are you doing? A woman on her own at this time of night? There's flight crew coming in and out of this place all the time. You don't want anyone to get the wrong idea.'

She laughed quietly, as if she was amused by my concern. 'They only get the wrong idea if I give it to them, and I won't do that. I waited because your friend said there had been trouble at the Next Page.' She looked me up and down, as if she was checking that I had no bits missing. 'Are you all right?'

'I'm fine, honest.'

'What happened?'

I had hoped not to get into that with her. 'A man died there. We had to wait for the police to come.'

She frowned. It was the first time I had seen her without a smile on her face; it didn't make her any less beautiful. 'What happened to him?'

'The policeman who came said it looked like a heart-attack.' I hoped that Sammy Grant hadn't told her anything different.

'Oh dear,' she murmured. 'What a pity. Who was he? Do you know?'

'It was the man I was looking for this morning at Riverside, Lee Kan Tong.'

'Ah, did you go there to meet him?'

'No. I was surprised to see him there.' I gazed around, the place was virtually deserted. 'I guess the City Space will be closing soon,' I said.

'I think midnight,' Marie replied.

'I have my own bar, and it's almost as high. Would you like to come up?' I had to go up anyway: I was still carrying fifty grand US in a knapsack.

'That depends,' she murmured, 'on what I'm coming up for.'

I dug out my wallet from my pocket and showed her the photo of Susie and the children. 'Does that answer your question?'

The smile was back. 'Not really, but I'll come.'

The suite wasn't as gaudy as some I've had, but it was pretty comfortable. The evening chambermaid had been in, the lighting was dimmed, the folding doors that led to the sleeping area were open, and the cover on the Olympic-size bed had been turned down. Marie took a seat on the sofa in the sitting room, while I put the cash back into the safe, poured two glasses of dry white wine and pulled back the thin gauze curtain to give us an uninterrupted view of the city.

'Where do you live?' she asked, as I sat beside her.

'I live in a few places; at the moment my family are in our house in Monaco.'

'Monaco?'

'Monte Carlo.'

'Ah, yes, I have heard of it: the fairy-tale kingdom, the place where Grace Kelly went.'

'The place where Grace Kelly died. I saw their graves a few days ago, hers and Prince Rainier's. They're in the cathedral, near the Grimaldi palace.'

'My mother loved Hollywood movies,' she said. 'I think that's why I'm an actress. She told me the story of the beautiful American actress who became a princess. I thought it was wonderful . . . that they lived happily ever after.'

'But they didn't,' I had to point out. 'Nobody lives happily ever after. She died in a car accident and he spent the rest of his rich and powerful fairy-tale life grieving for her. Now their bones are under two slabs behind the altar. Where their spirits are . . . well, that's the part we hope for, that's what faith and religion and all that stuff is about. Forget about ever after, Marie, just live happily when you can.'

'You sound cynical.'

'I'm not a cynic, I'm a realist. Up until six years ago, I was a dreamer; I accepted all that romantic stuff too. Now I know the truth: in life there are more horror stories than fairy-tales.'

She slid her hand into mine; I don't remember ever feeling the touch of softer skin. 'What happened to make you believe that?' she murmured.

'I can't talk about that, not any more. I've had a second chance, though, and I'm going to protect it. Anyone who tries to threaten my family will have to deal with me and, when I'm away, with a man called Conrad. They shouldn't, though; either one of us would kill them if we had to.'

'It must be very scary to be loved by you.'

'What?'

'You're so intense. You aren't a bit like they make you seem in the movies.'

'But scary?'

'What you feel is so strong. For a moment, I had a flash of what it would be like to be your enemy; it wasn't nice.'

I gave her hand a gentle squeeze. 'I'm sorry,' I told her. 'I shouldn't let you think of me that way. I saw someone die tonight, just three hours ago; I guess it's affected me.'

'Then stop thinking about it.' She touched my face gently, turned it towards her and kissed me. It was very gentle, and very tender, and it went on for quite a long time. When she broke off, I felt soothed, softened, my hard, jagged edges rubbed away, and the night didn't feel quite so dark.

She laid her head on my shoulder and we looked at the lights of Singapore; there were still monsters out there, I knew. One of them had shoved a blade through Tony Lee's heart, and would get away with it, because that's the way things are sometimes. But with Marie, in that room, I felt as if I was in a beast-free zone. There was something about her that seemed to build around me the same kind of invisible security forcefield that being with Susie and the kids gives me. They're my island of tranquillity and at that moment I needed them badly: they were far away, but Marie was there, and her goodness was hauling me back from the places I'd been since I'd met Maddy January in Fort Siloso.

Without her being aware of it, she was reminding me of something I knew, that monsters threaten us on two levels: first, because they are what they are, but also, because when we get down there where they live and tackle them on their own terms, as sometimes we must, then all too easily, without realising it, we can become like them.

27

She stayed with me until after two. I think I dozed off for part of the time, and maybe she did too; eventually I asked her if she wanted to go home. Maybe I was really asking her if she wanted to sleep with me, although honestly, I don't think I was. In any event, she said that she should, so I saw her to the elevator and down into the lobby.

There were no taxis at the rank outside, not unreasonably since it was the middle of the night, so we walked round to North Bridge Road, where I could flag one down. 'Are you working tomorrow?' I asked, as we waited. 'Will I find you at the theatre if I'm free for lunch?'

'No,' she replied. 'I'm never there on Mondays. Tomorrow I have to see about auditions: there are some productions coming up and I hope to get work.'

'I'll have a part for you,' I said, 'once I get back to work. I've bought the rights to a book; I don't know for sure when we'll make the movie, not this year, but probably next. Meantime, if you really want to leave Singapore and can sort out a US visa, I can find you some other work.'

'But you've never seen me act, Oz.'

'Miles Grayson had never seen me act either, before he cast me in my first movie. He took a chance and it paid off. I'll do the same with you.'

She looked me dead in the eye. 'Why?'

'Because I like you.'

'You don't just want to get into my pants?'

'No, but could I, if I did?'

She smiled. 'Could I get into yours, if I did?'

I grinned back at her. 'Maybe you just had a chance. We'll never know.'

'Let's just say now is too soon,' she said quietly. 'I don't know you well enough.'

'Only one person ever really knew me.' There was something about the girl that had me saying things without even thinking about them.

'Your wife?'

'My sister: half-sister.' I said it naturally: I'd never think of Jan as a wife again. Our marriage was never legal, in the eyes of the law, at any rate. No, what we had was much more complex, much deeper than a marriage, even if I hadn't known it at the time.

'Where is she now?'

'Her bones are in a cemetery in Scotland. Her spirit's never far away.'

'That's what you didn't want to talk about earlier?' I nodded. 'What happened?'

'She was murdered.'

'Aah.' She sighed. 'That's why you can seem scary inside. And the man who did it?'

'People. The man who did it was under orders. They're dead; all dead.'

'Did you . . .?'

'Ssh!' I whispered. 'Let's not go there. It's better that you don't know about the feelings you have in your heart when something like that happens.'

'Maybe not.' She looked up at me again, as if she had closed one chapter and moved on to the next. 'Do you leave Singapore, now that this Lee Kan Tong man is dead?'

'Not yet. I didn't come to find him, but the woman who's with him. She has something that I need.'

'Do you know where she is?'

'No. But if I find out, I'll go after her. I'll know better

186

tomorrow morning . . . this morning.' In a corner of my eye, I saw the traffic-lights change. A taxi with an illuminated sign came towards us: I flagged it down.

'He'll think I'm a prostitute,' Marie said, laughingly, as it drew to a halt.

'You're too good-looking to be a hooker.'

'You don't know Singapore; I'm not good-looking enough.'

I raised an eyebrow as she slid into the cab. 'Maybe I'd better check those guide-book ads again.' Impulsively, I bent and kissed her. 'I'll call you later,' I promised, 'even if it's only to tell you I'm leaving.'

28

I slept late next morning, late for me, that is. It was nine o'clock when I was wakened from a troubled sleep by a knock on the door of the suite, followed by the sound of it opening and a shrill cry of 'Housekeeping!'

'Later!' I yelled. I'd hung out the privacy sign when I'd got back from seeing off Marie, but often that means nothing. Rita Rudner, the comedienne, who's big in Vegas and spends a lot of her life in hotel rooms, once claimed that she was driven to creating her own 'Do not disturb' sign to get the message across. It showed a maid with her neck in a noose.

I'd probably have been more polite if it hadn't been for the dreams. Several times that night I'd seen Tony Lee sitting across from me in the Next Page booth, then toppling forwards. On each occasion even more blood came my way, until finally I was drenched in the stuff. But that wasn't the only vision I'd had in my sleep. I saw Maddy January's darting, frightened eyes. I saw Jan, lying dead on our kitchen floor from a massive electric shock; I wasn't there when it happened, but that doesn't shield me from its full horror. I saw Susie and Prim, in the pool in Monaco, both of them naked and swimming towards me. I saw Jack Gantry's maniacal, evil face lose all its colour as he realised he was going to die. And I saw Marie Lin, black hair spread on the pillow, long legs apart and stretched out as she lay beside me in another bed, in another room, in a place I couldn't recognise. That was where I was when the maid opened the door and shouted. If she'd looked round the corner into the sleeping area she'd have seen the duvet on the floor and me with an erection that would have made Shergar feel inadequate.

I swung out of bed, feeling incredibly guilty, and snarled my way to the bathroom, where I took a long, cold shower, until I was back to something approaching my normal temper and size. I was shaved and dressed when I heard another knock at the door. I opened it, ready to apologise to the chambermaid for the delay, only to see Dylan standing there.

'Who bit your arse?' he asked, cheerfully. Clearly my temper still didn't look as normal as I'd thought. 'She's not still here, is she?'

'Don't be a fuckwit,' I growled. 'It's not like that, I told you. What do you want anyway? We haven't missed breakfast, have we?'

'Relax, we've still got half an hour before it closes. I've had Jimmy Tan on the phone; he's found out where the late Mr Lee lived, and he's willing to let us join him to look it over.'

I took a fresh look at him as he stepped into the room. Sometimes you don't see people at all, no matter how well you think you know them. In Glasgow, my boiled-down opinion of Mike was that he was an amiable clown. (Come to think of it, that's how I wanted people to regard me.)

'You're in deep with him, aren't you?' I asked.

He nodded. 'When I was under cover, only four people out here knew who I was. Jimmy was one of them, but even he didn't find out until the last operation, the big one in Thailand, was ready to go down. The DEA and Interpol set me up with an escape route through Singapore, so he had to know then. But that was a phoney: they pulled the Amsterdam thing again, and when the police and troops moved in to take down the drug runners they shot me too, only they didn't use real bullets on me the second time. There were only two survivors from the gang; they both thought they saw me die. We know this because they spoke about it in jail, and they never did twig that I was an agent. When it was all done, Interpol told everybody that Martin Dyer was dead, including Jimmy. They flew me out to India on a freight plane and on to Europe from there, on a new passport.'

'Was the Singapore Triad part of the network you brought down?'

'They had people involved; not the top guy, though, he stayed out of the picture. I got the impression that everybody deferred to him, except maybe the Burmese warriors who control the poppy production.'

'Tan's right, Mike. You should not be around here. Why the hell did you agree to come with me?'

He grinned. 'I never did make it to Singapore. I wanted to see the place.'

'Is that right? It never occurred to you that I might get caught in the cross-fire?'

'That's what friends are for. Come on, let's see if there's any breakfast left, then go and meet Jimmy. He's expecting us at ten thirty.'

As it turned out, the buffet had been devoured by an invasion of gluttonous Americans, who compounded the felony by commandeering the centre of the room and discussing, twice as loudly as was appropriate, their tactics for maximising the grant payable by the Singapore government towards whatever project had brought them there.

After the phrases 'bottom line', 'hidden inducements' and 'participating bonus' had been mentioned for the fourth or fifth time, Dylan leaned over the apparent ring-leader as we left the room and said, in what appeared to be a perfectly honed New York accent, 'What makes America great, guys, is that the fucking IRS is everywhere.'

Having planted that seed of terror, we were grateful when a lift opened at the first touch of a button and took us down to the foyer. We pulled a taxi; as we got in Mike leaned towards the driver and said, 'Makena Condo, Meyer Road, Katong.'

'You know number Meyer Road?' the driver enquired.

'Afraid not.'

'No worries, I find it. Meyer Road pretty straight.' By this time I had discerned that there are two kinds of taxi drivers in Singapore, the Chinese (helpful and talkative) and the rest (neither). Ours headed west, out of the crowded heart of the city, past the enormous Suntec complex, then turned on to East Coast Parkway.

He didn't fanny about: he took the first available turn-off for Katong, which wasn't very far, then found Meyer Road. As he'd said, it was straight, but straight for a long way. He cruised along it, slowly, until finally he spotted a group of high-rise buildings, set within a secure boundary fence. 'Ah, yes, I remember now,' he chirped. 'That the Makena.'

He swung through a gate, nodded his way past the security guys in a booth to the left, and dropped us in front of the first building. He got a respectable tip. He glanced at it and said, 'Thanks. I hope I get you guys again.'

I waved him goodbye, then glanced upwards. The Makena towers weren't in the same league as the Stamford when it came to height, but they were taller than anything I'd seen in my home country, even in Glasgow, where for a while the city fathers seemed to be conducting an experiment to determine how many unhappy people they could cram into a single structure. There seemed to be nothing unhappy about this place, though, as Mike, who seemed to know where he was going, led us along the entrance driveway and round a corner.

Jimmy Tan was waiting for us, standing in the shade of the building. The black gear from the night before had been replaced by a white linen suit. The jacket was loose-fitting, the sign, once you learn to read it, of the plain-clothes policeman everywhere. Behind him, unconcerned by the fact that they were in the morning sunlight, stood half a dozen dark-uniformed troopers, wearing flak jackets, Kevlar hard hats and carrying automatic weapons. I looked beyond them to a central courtyard area surrounded by five apartment blocks. Most of it seemed to be taken up by the biggest swimming-pool I had ever seen, but since the community probably contained, at first glance, more individual residences than my home town of Anstruther, maybe that wasn't surprising. For all that it was vast, it was almost deserted: this wasn't a tourist hang-out but a working community, so the parents were at work and the kids were at school. I could see maybe half a dozen people in and around the pool, but only a couple of them were aware of what was going on.

'What the fuck is this, Jimmy?' Mike barked, as we approached. 'Why the SWAT team?'

'This is a Triad house we go into,' Tan replied. 'Best these boys in first.' I had no objection to that.

'What about Lee?' I asked.

'What about him?'

'He was murdered, remember?'

Tan shook his head. 'He had heart-attack, like I said last night.' The look on my face must have merited some further explanation, for he continued: 'Listen, Lee was Triad member, that wasn't just a story. My sources confirm it. He was senior guy, quite near the top, involved with drug distribution and prostitution, as he was in London. He the sort of guy we never catch with anything on them; the boys and girls on Death Row are all mules, well down the chain. I'm not going waste time investigating; we never catch who did it anyway. Fuck him.'

I nodded: it made sense, in a cynical sort of way, and he was the guy with the local knowledge.

We rode the lift together to the seventh floor. When we got out, Tan told us to stay where we were until he called to us, then led his batter squad round a corner to the left. A few minutes later we heard some shouts; whatever the Chinese is for 'Armed police!' I guess that's what it probably was.

It didn't take long, only a couple of minutes, before one of the squad, a corporal, returned and signalled to us to follow. Tony Lee's apartment was quite something: the floors were marble, and the main living space was split level, with dining furniture topside, and a couple of steps down to a sitting area with two leather chairs facing a big plasma television, and a unit which housed the best music system that Mr Bang and Mr Olufsen produce. The main attraction of the upper level was an aquarium, which seemed to cover most of the wall opposite the door. Jimmy Tan stood in front of it, with his hand on the shoulder of a very frightened woman in a black tunic.

'Maid,' he said. 'Filipina; she says she doesn't speak English, but I don't buy that. We find out for sure later.' The woman flinched, proof enough that she understood him.

'Maddy January?' I asked.

'Not here, alive or dead.'

'Can we look around?'

'Be my guest, but what you looking for? We won't find drugs here, or anything else that ties to Triads.'

'I don't know what I'm looking for. Anything that gives us a clue to where Maddy might have gone, I suppose.'

'Okay. She's nothing to me; you want to look for her, Mr Blackstone, that's fine.'

He dismissed the troopers as Dylan and I moved off to search the place. We started in the kitchen: it was as well equipped as the living areas had been. All the appliances were state-of-the-art. We opened cupboard after cupboard and found nothing but food, drink and cleaning products; the place was well stocked, though. 'Look at this,' said Dylan, waving a piece of paper he had picked up from the counter. 'It's a supermarket till receipt. Somebody did a big food shop on Thursday. The shit must have hit the fan after that.' Calamity had fallen on Maddy and Tony suddenly.

Beyond the kitchen we found a small back room, with a bed, a small hanging wardrobe, and a dressing-table with a couple of drawers. 'Maid's room,' I said. 'Look at that.' There was a magazine on the bed: English language.

Dylan wasn't listening: he had opened a door that seemed to lead out on to a small, shaded balcony. (Shade is difficult to find in Singapore, because it's almost on the equator, so the midday sun's directly overhead but the architect who planned the Makena

194

had built it in wherever possible.) It housed a big condenser unit for the air-conditioning system, and more than that: a wetsuit, black and blue in colour, mask and flippers, lay there. There was other scuba equipment too, a tank and a regulator. I've done some diving, so I was able to recognise them all as top quality, and I realised something else: the suit belonged to Maddy. Tony Lee hadn't been a giant, but he'd been too wide to fit into it.

I logged the fact away as we moved through to the rest of the apartment. There were three bedrooms; we looked in the master with its en-suite, then moved into another that was furnished but appeared to have been used only as a store. We checked what had been Maddy's wardrobes, her drawers, her cosmetics table; they were all well stocked, but we had no way of telling if anything was missing. There was a Tampax box in the bathroom. It was almost full, but I read nothing into the fact that it was still there: Susie carries a couple of the things in her handbag like she carries lipstick. If the woman had done a runner, she'd have taken what she needed and no more.

Next we checked Tony's space. There were two empty hangers that might have held suits; the one he'd been wearing when he'd been killed, and maybe he'd packed another. He'd been ready for flight, I reckoned that was for sure. Somewhere in the city there was a BMW that would be attracting parking tickets, unless Jimmy had found it and had it towed.

'Look,' said Dylan, pulling the hanging clothes apart. Behind them, set into the wall, there was a safe, open, and empty, 'I'd guess Maddy's got some cash. He had some in his wallet last night, but less than you'd bother to keep in the safe. My bet is that he sent her on ahead with most of their stash, then went to do the trade with you and follow her.'

'Or rob me. He had a gun, and he was a criminal.'

'Maybe, but I doubt it. You're high-profile: robbing you could have drawn attention to him and that was the last thing he wanted.'

The third bedroom had been converted to an office, with a

desk, a filing cabinet and a message board on the wall. It was covered in yellow message stickers. I read a few. 'Tony: lunch 1.30 Rubino's.' 'Hairdresser: 11 a.m.' 'FW, Riverside, 7 Friday.' Nothing signified: there was nothing, for example, about meeting me on Siloso the day before. However, there was a photograph, pinned to the board. It showed Maddy and Tony, smiling in the midst of a group of people in a bar; a sign in the background read 'Café Narcosis'. That told me at once that it was a hang-out for divers. Who else would use a bar called after the clinical name for the bends?

There was an HP computer in a separate housing unit, with an all-in-one printer–fax-scanner attached, and also a docking device for a palmtop. The screen was blank, but the soft hum of the tower unit, and the warmth of the room, told me it was running; whoever had used it last had neglected to switch it off. I moved the mouse and waited as the screen came to life. I spotted an AOL start-up icon on the task bar and hit it. I grinned as it started up: automatic log-on is very convenient, but in certain circumstances it can be very silly. It took me straight in there without my having to know a password or anything else. I stopped smiling pretty soon, though: the mailbox contained two spam stock tips and one Viagra ad. The 'old' and 'sent' e-mail files were empty, wiped. There was a Messenger icon as well, I hit that and, again, was signed in automatically, but there was nothing there either, not even an address book.

I closed the applications and turned to the hard disk. For a moment I got a buzz when I saw three folders: 'Tony', 'Maddy', and 'Maddy's pix'. But that evaporated pretty quickly too. They had been emptied, then flushed away by clearing the waste basket. I checked the Adobe Photoshop software I found among the programs, but that had been cleaned out as well. Chucking the thing into a car-crusher would have been less efficient than the wiping job that had been done.

We looked in the desk drawers: we found stationery, and two cameras, a very expensive Nikon 35mm SLR job, and a pocket-sized Pentax digital. They worried me: would a keen, professional-class photographer have left them behind? Maybe, I told myself, if she wanted people like us to think she was dead.

We went back through to the living area. Jimmy Tan was still there with the maid, who had remembered her English. 'She says she know nothing. The woman left on Friday, is all she tell me.'

'Who was her hairdresser?' Dylan asked her. 'You want to find what a woman's been up to,' he murmured to me, 'ask her hairdresser.'

'She go to a place in Ngee Ann City, up Orchard Road; Kingsley, I think it called.'

'What's FW?' I tried, remembering the name on the message slip.

'Don' know.'

'Who did she dive with?'

'Don' know either. She never tell me; Miz Maddy never tell me much, only 'bout Mr Tony.'

'What did she tell you about him?' Tan snapped at her, as if he was annoyed that he hadn't extracted that piece of information.

'Not so much tell, more ask. She ask me if I ever answer phone to women looking for Mr Tony.'

'What did you say?'

'I say once or twice woman call for him, young woman, Singaporean.'

'Did she give a name?' I asked.

'No.'

'Leave any messages?'

'No.'

'What did you tell Ms Maddy?'

'That what I tell her, same as I tell you.'

'When did she ask you this?'

Somehow, the maid managed to shrug her face. 'I don' know,' she mumbled. 'A few times, maybe over last month, six weeks or so.'

'And that's why she tailed him with her camera,' I said to Jimmy Tan, 'and got herself into this fucking mess.'

'Looks like,' he agreed. 'What you find back there? Anything to help you?'

'Nothing. Tony's cleaned the house pretty efficiently; don't know why he needed a maid.'

'You look at garbage?'

'No.'

He chuckled. 'That why you actor not cop, Mr Blackstone. We always look in garbage.'

'What did you find?'

'Go back and see, in kitchen.'

We did as he said; what we'd overlooked was a green bin-bag. We unfastened the wire that closed it and peered inside. What we saw was a mess of wet ash and melted plastic. We resealed it and went back to Tan. 'Lee had a fire,' he told us. 'She says that yesterday in the evening, before he went to meet you, he burned all his papers and Ms Maddy's photographs in the shower in the second bathroom. She cleaned it this morning and was going to dump the bag down garbage chute when we come in.'

'So what do you think, Jimmy?' Dylan asked him.

'I think she not a threat to Mr Blackstone's brother-in-law any more. I think she maybe dead, and that Lee tried to get money from Mr Blackstone to help him go on run himself from Triads. Or maybe they run together. I don't care: the photograph of the Triad top man doesn't exist any more, so there nothing in this for me. The Triads can have them both, if they catch them . . . and they usually do.'

29

Jimmy gave us a lift back into the city. He was going to take us to the hotel, but Dylan asked him to drop us in Orchard Road instead. The wise old guy knew where we were headed: he took us straight to the vehicle entrance at the back of Ngee Ann City.

It's quite a place, a bloody great edifice of red granite and marble, which has managed to attract some of the world's leading names in consumer and luxury products. They look after the ladies too. We found the Philip Kingsley Trichological Centre on level five. It's world famous and its published client list includes Barbra Streisand, Cher and Mick Jagger; Maddy had been mixing in exalted company and, into the bargain, enjoying a lifestyle beyond the means of your average theatre-company director.

It was a dead end, though . . . or maybe that should be a split end. Philip Kingsley is not your average barber shop: it's a highly specialised place, which focuses on the health of its customers' hair rather than on cutting it into attractive shapes. It's not a business where the ladies go for an hour's chat under the dryer, and if they do, anything they say is treated with the confidentiality of the confessional. That's more or less what they told us; the head trichologist didn't even confirm that Maddy had been one of their clients. I wound up buying a stack of remoisturising products and telling them they could add my name to their celebrity client list, if they chose.

We didn't have time to shop, or I could have done some damage to my credit card. Instead, we found the taxi rank; we had interviewed and rejected four drivers before we found one who convinced us that he knew for sure where Café Narcosis was. (Note for Singaporean cabbies: knowing the address of the place to which you're taking your passengers helps to reassure them.) He took us downtown past Clarke Quay and across the river, stopping almost at once in front of a building called Riverside Walk. 'In there,' he said. 'Next to Friendly Waters.'

'Who?'

'Friendly Waters; they organise diving trips. Okay-lah? That seven dollar fifty.'

I gave him ten and we stepped out into the rising heat. The early-morning cloud had gone: it was going to be seriously warm. I led the way up a few steps to the second level of the building; at the top, a sign faced us, 'Friendly Waters Seasports Services' with an arrow, pointing to a shop-front. 'FW,' I whispered.

The place had a glass door, and this time I could see inside. It was small and crammed with dive gear. I tried the handle and stepped inside; when I say 'small' I mean that there wasn't room for both Dylan and me. There was an equally cramped office to the right, with a Singaporean guy, in his thirties, sitting at a cluttered desk tapping away at a laptop keyboard.

He looked up; dark hair, brown skin. 'Can I help you?'

'You run this place?'

'Yeah. My name's Dave. How can I help? You want to book a trip?'

'That depends. I'm looking for a friend, her name's Maddy January, I can't find her. I know she dives with you, so I'm starting here.'

He nodded. 'She does. Reason you can't find her is she isn't in Singapore. She's on Aur.'

'Where?'

'Pulau Aur, off Mersing. It's where we have our divers' lodge. Maddy headed up there on her own last night; she came in around five and booked in for a week, said she'd drive straight up there and catch the supply boat on its way back from dropping off the weekend dive party. She was lucky: normally I'd have been with them and this place closed, but my buddy took this group up for me. She told me a man would be joining her, paid for him too, but I thought he was going up last night. You him?'

When I nodded, his eyes narrowed a little, his face became a little less friendly. 'Then you've got competition. Another guy ask after her this morning. What's going on?'

That was not the news I'd expected or wanted to hear. I fixed him with a stare. 'Believe me, I'm the person she wants to see.'

He looked a little harder, then the light came on. 'Hey, you're the guy in the movies; you tore up that creep Mai Bong last night. You're in *Straits Times* this morning.'

'How do I get to Mersing quickly?' I asked.

'You need to drive, I reckon.'

'How far?'

'Little over hundred and fifty kilometres.'

'And to Aur?'

'You need to wait for a boat going out there, unless you charter. The islands are around sixty kilometre offshore.'

'You got a map?'

'Sure.' He picked one up from the morass on the desk and handed it to me. 'You going to dive?'

'Only if I have to. Don't worry, I've got my PADI advanced open water, and rescue.'

'Okay then; we got stuff in the lodge you can hire if you need it.' He reached out a hand; we shook. 'On you go, enjoy and say hello to Maddy for me. You find the other guy, tell him not to take the piss from Davey again.'

30

We went back to the hotel and asked the concierge to rent us a car, as quickly as possible. For once Hertz tried harder than Avis and a Mondeo was delivered to the front door at one thirty. Mike insisted on driving; he said he'd done a police advanced driving course early in his service. That did nothing for my confidence, for I've seen some of those maniacs behind the wheel, but I didn't argue the point because I preferred to navigate.

We took the Seletar Expressway heading north. I had the knapsack with the money; I didn't know what the police would say about that if they searched us at the border crossing, but if push came to shove I was prepared to use Jimmy Tan's name to get us through.

As it happened, my British passport and Benny Luker's US version got their respect, and opened the gateway for us, no problem. We crossed the causeway into Johor Baharu, then went east on Highway Three, heading for a place called Kota Tingii. It's a fine old road, built by the British in the 1930s. Unfortunately they were so self-assured, or naïve, in those days that they forgot to take the elementary precaution of mining the bridges, and the Japanese were able to use it to great effect in 1942.

The drive was straightforward; the only exciting moments were provided by local nutters who seemed to think that a Proton is a racing car. We let them get on with it and arrived at Mersing jetty just before three thirty. We found a secure park for the Mondeo, then went in search of a vessel to take us to the islands. There were all sorts there, but none had a scheduled sailing.

Finally we found a quayside office with a sign in English saying 'Charter'. The boat on offer looked sleek and fast; it was a thirty-foot cruiser, extravagantly named *Malay Goddess* and modern, unlike most of those moored next to it, which resembled the river taxis in Singapore. I did a deal with the guy behind the counter, and paid him with Visa for twenty-four hours' hire.

'When will you be ready to leave? I asked him.

'You leave any time you like, boss. It's self-drive.'

'Jesus!' Dylan shouted. 'What the fuck have you got us into?'

The prospect didn't faze me too much; I'm no sailor but, as I told you, I've cruised with Miles on his yacht, and taken my turn at the wheel. The owner gave me a run-down of the controls, and told me that reaching Aur was pretty easy, in daylight at least. All I had to do was cruise past Pulau Tioman, and it would be in sight, a large island with some smaller ones dotted around. Finding Tioman, he assured me, would be no problem.

He was right: we could see it in the distance as soon as we cleared the harbour. It was bigger than I'd realised, though, and further away. The sea was choppy but not too bad; still, I made Mike lie down in the cabin to ward off any seasickness. Eventually he called up to me, 'Ever seen *South Pacific*?'

'Of course. It was my mum's favourite.'

'She'd have liked this, then. According to the magazine I'm reading, Tioman Island is what they used for Bali fucking Hai.'

Fortified by that useless piece of information I cruised on, at three-quarter speed to conserve fuel. The guy had assured me that there would be enough to get us there and back, but I wasn't taking any chances.

It took us three hours, but finally I found myself piloting the *Goddess* into a strait, towards the landing-stage on Pulau Aur where three boats were moored already. As our guide had said, there was another island, much smaller, on our left . . . Sorry, on the port side. It had a jetty too, but it was deserted.

I slung two fenders over the side and eased alongside, while a grateful Dylan tossed a rope to a lad on the quay. He tied us off, fore and after, I cut the engine and we scrambled ashore.

'We're looking for the Friendly Waters Lodge,' I told the youngster. He was fresh-faced and looked about sixteen.

'That's me,' he replied. 'Or, at least, I work there. None of other guys around, though, and no divers. You only ones here.' He peered into the boat. 'Where your gear? You need hire?'

'What about the lady? Ms January? She's supposed to be here, or so Davey told us.'

'No, she on Dayang, over there.' He pointed to the smaller island. I looked across and saw, behind the landing, a silver-white beach, lined by tall coconut palms, and beyond a small wooden building, not much more than a hut. 'I tell her she crazy; we don't use it no more. There no water supply over there other than the rain, and toilets don't work well, but she insist. So she take some food and water and I take her over in boat.' He frowned across the water, then back at me. 'Other man come looking for her earlier, in hire boat like you. I send him across, but he must have gone. Boat not there no more. Never saw him go.'

Dylan and I exchanged glances. 'Come on,' I said. 'Untie us,' I told the boy. 'We're going across.'

I fended the boat off then started the engine. The current was strong in the strait, flowing across us, but I leaned the cruiser into it, keeping the speed as steady as I could. When we reached the Dayang jetty, Dylan jumped ashore with the rope this time. 'You know what we're going to find here, don't you?' he murmured, as I joined him on the wooden walkway.

'I fear that I do.'

'Ever seen a headless woman?'

'A couple of post-modernist sculptures, but never in the flesh, so to speak.'

'It's just as well oral sex is illegal in this part of the world.'

'Wash your mouth out,' I replied tersely.

We walked up the jetty. There was a barbecue area in front of the old lodge, with a few tables and benches that hadn't been oiled or varnished for a while. On one of the tables, there was a large blue plastic cool-box, big enough to hold a day's supply of beer for two . . . or something else. While Mike kept an eye on the lodge, I opened it, wincing as I raised the lid, but it contained only a few frozen blue blocks; I found that I was able to breathe again.

Dylan slid a hand into his trouser pocket and produced the gun I'd taken from Madeleine. 'What the . . .' I began.

'So I lied,' he said.

The door of the lodge was barely open, no more than an inch. I don't know what made me call out, 'Maddy!' but I did. Dylan gave me a sneering look, and pushed his way into the building, the tiny pistol held ready.

There was a body on the floor, all right, but it still had its head on its shoulders. As far as I could see, it still had most of its bits: hands (one held a long, sword-like knife), feet, dull blue eye staring into the wooden floor, and its penis, for there was a pool of urine beneath it. The hair was scorched just behind its left ear, by muzzle-flash, I guessed, and a single line of dried blood ran down its neck into a very small puddle. I keep saying 'it', and I suppose that technically I'm correct, but it had been a 'he'.

It had been Sammy Grant.

31

'What do we do now?'

'Panic would seem like a logical first step,' said Dylan.

'Let's do that on board. But first, let's get the fuck out of here.' There was a gun on the floor beside Sammy's body, another Beretta, the twin of the one Tony Lee had been carrying in the Next Page. I picked it up. It must have been loaded with soft-nosed ammo, for the opposite wall was a mess. I thought I saw another eye stuck there among the gore, but I didn't investigate.

We didn't high-tail it. Dylan untied, I eased the *Goddess* away from the landing and steered her smoothly out of the strait and past the third tiny island, which seemed to be guarding the entrance.

Then we high-nosed it: I opened the throttle, driving the twin propellers deep as they cut through the water and thrust us back towards Mersing.

I had my fingers crossed all the way against two possibilities: the first and less serious that we would run out of fuel, the second and more likely that the kid on Aur would decide to go across to Dayang to investigate, and that we'd find the police waiting when we got back to port.

Fortunately, the owner had been right about the tank capacity. Even more fortunately, the kid had not been inclined to do anything that wasn't in his job description. We made it back to Mersing by eleven and moored the *Goddess* in her own empty berth. The charter office was closed, so we posted the keys through the letterbox and checked the Mondeo out of the car park.

I overtook every fucking racing Proton we encountered on the road to Johor Baharu, and we made it back to the hotel just before one. The gun? That, and the tiny one Mike had been carrying, were at the bottom of the China Sea, or on their way there, depending on how deep it was at the point at which I'd watched Dylan throw them over the side.

In the relative safety of my suite we started to think for the first time in several hours. The first thing we contemplated was self-preservation. Jimmy Tan had given Dylan a number. 'Day or night,' he had said, so we took him at his word. Mike called him; I switched the phone to speaker mode as he answered.

'Martin.' His amplified voice sounded fresh, as if he had been awake. 'What the fuck you call this time for?'

'We've had a little trouble up in Malaysia. We got a lead to the woman and went looking for her, on an island called Aur, out past Bali fucking Hai, whatever its real name is. Someone got there before us, though.'

'She dead this time, then?'

'No, he is. She's not dumb: she placed herself on a small island, in an old dive lodge, where she would see anyone approaching. When someone did show up, as soon as he stepped through the door she put one behind his ear, then took his boat and got out of there.'

There was a long silence . . . or almost a silence: music was playing somewhere in the background. 'The dead guy,' Tan finally said, 'what about him?'

'He was European, Scottish. He was a guy who latched himself on to Oz and me the night we arrived, and he's been sort of following us around ever since. His name's Sammy Grant; at least, that's what he said it was. He was in the Next Page when we got there, when Tony Lee was killed. He seemed nervous about being there when your lot showed up; we actually told him to get out. He stabbed the guy, and we got him out of there. Sorry, Jimmy.'

'No matter, he dead now; save me the trouble of hanging him.'

208

'Fine, but the problem is that sooner rather than later someone's going to find him. A couple of days and the fucking smell will drift over to the big island, suppose nobody goes over before then.'

'We hear rumours,' the superintendent said slowly, 'about a Westerner that the Triads sometimes use for business like this, when a Chinese might stand out. Never find him, though. Sammy Grant, you say?'

'Age late twenties, medium height, fair hair; he told us he worked as a dealer in the DRZ Bank.'

'Then they got a vacancy. No worries, Martin: I have colleague in Kuala Lumpur. I explain to him and this boy be fish food.'

'You won't tell him about me, though,' said Dylan, quickly, 'that I'm still alive.'

'Don't worry, boy, that secret safe with me.'

'Where would she go, Jimmy, from Mersing?'

'You still want to find her? Sound as if this woman don't need help.'

'I still want to find her,' I said.

'That you, Oz? You still worried about brother-in-law?'

'I made him a promise. A judge's ex being murdered by Triads won't make nice headlines in Scotland either.'

'Maybe not. Well, she won't come back to Singapore, that dead fucking sure. So I reckon she have to go to KL. From Mersing she get there by bus or by KTN, the national railway. Hell, she could hire car, or take taxi. Once she in KL, you lost her: there are many ways out of there. And she could be in KL by now.'

He chuckled. 'Go home, boys, you done here. Martin, go back be dead. Oz, go back pretend in movies. 'Bye.' There was a click as he hung up, then a buzz.

'Sounded like good advice to me, Oz,' Dylan murmured. 'We've got a better chance of finding Nemo than of tracking her down. We've lost her.'

I couldn't argue with that. The thought of getting back into the

Mondeo and driving to KL did flash across my mind, but I let it pass through and out the other side. Still . . .

'What about the boy Sammy?' I said. 'Weird, him just latching on to us like that.'

'Maybe, but weirdness happens sometimes. Fuck, look at you. Look at me. We're weird, but we're real.'

'I need to know about him, though.'

'Don't look at me. I can't help you there, not any more.'

'No, but there's someone who might: your old boss.' I dug out my mobile and called an Edinburgh number I had stored there.

'Ross,' a voice answered smoothly.

'Ricky, how goes? It's Oz here.'

'It goes fine, and so does your estate.' Ricky's security firm looks after Loch Lomond for us while we're away.

'Good, because my dad will be through there soon, to recuperate.'

'Aye, I heard he'd been ill. He's on the mend?'

'He's going to be fine. Listen, I'd like you to do me a favour. I've run across a Scots guy who says his name is Sammy Grant; claims to have left Maryhill eight years ago, when he'd have been early twenties. Can you check him out?'

'A picture would help.'

As it happened, I could do that: when we'd all had a few in the Crazy Elephant, I'd taken a couple of snaps with the camera on my mobile. Sammy had been in one of them. 'I'll send you what I've got through the phone. The quality won't be great but you'll be able to do something with it.'

'Okay. Where are you?'

'Singapore.'

'Movie business?'

'No, just a stag trip, scuba-diving with a pal.'

'I didn't think you had pals like that any more, not since Dylan copped it.'

I laughed. 'There was only one Mike Dylan, right enough. Call me on my mobile if you get anything before Wednesday. We'll be heading back to Monaco tomorrow night.'

I killed the call: Benny Luker was gazing at me, with a sad look in his eyes. 'It guts me sometimes,' he said. 'I liked Ricky Ross, but I can never see him again, because he's in Scotland and I can never go back there. Too many people know me. My mum's still alive, too, and I can't even send her a fucking birthday card. I can't send her an anonymous bouquet of roses, for she'd wonder, and tell her friends, and they'd wonder, and soon every fucker in Edinburgh would be wondering. I'd love to go back home, Oz. I'd love to walk into my mum's kitchen and make myself a coffee and just sit down and wait for her getting back from the shops.'

'And watch her have a heart-attack when she saw you sitting there? Michael's dead to her: that was part of the deal you made.'

There were tears in his eyes now. 'I know. But it's hard, man, it's really fucking hard.'

'But you came back to us, to Susie and me.'

'Because you're not in Scotland, and because you're the only two people in the world I can trust, other than my mum . . . and if she knew, she couldn't keep it to herself.'

'But there are others. You're trusting Prim, and now you're trusting Miles and Dawn. I haven't had a chance to tell you: they're okay with the deal. You can trust me on something too. Your mum gets a birthday card every year, and a Christmas card, and roses. She gets them from me, and every time I'm in Edinburgh, I go to see her; the last time was ten days ago.'

The tears had escaped, two big, slow rollers. 'How is she?'

'She's fine, man, fit as a fiddle. You know what? Once we announce this deal, once we make the movie, once your book sales shoot up as a result, and you get a chunky advance on the next one, you'll be able to pluck her out of Edinburgh, if you wish, and have her live with you in the US.'

'How?'

'I'll invite her to our place in Los Angeles. You can take it from there.'

211

He frowned at me. 'For a slightly psychopathic egomaniac who's risen way above his station and is reaping good fortune far beyond what his talent or behaviour merit, you're not a bad guy.'

32

As summings-up go, that one was pretty near the mark. 'Doesn't make you a bad person,' Rod Steiger once said, in one of the greatest ad-libs ever filmed. That's how I try to look at my less user-friendly side.

I got some sleep; not a lot, but enough, I woke at seven thirty and went straight down to the gym, where I ran the treadmill, rowed till it hurt, then slammed a hell of a lot of weight up in the air. I was punishing myself. Why? Because I had a sense of failure, that's why. I had seen myself going back to Scotland and handing Harvey a slim, if expensive, envelope, then watching while he reduced it to crispy black ashes. Instead I was going back with the news that his former wife . . . since he'd married the woman, he must have loved her at some point . . . was a killer, out there somewhere, on the run. Or maybe not: maybe she wasn't running any more, maybe she'd been caught in KL and her pickled head was in some Triad chieftain's trophy cabinet. If it was at least her hair would look good: the Philip Kingsley Trichological Centre had made sure of that. (*You're a bastard, Blackstone, you really are.* No, I'm not; not that bad at any rate. We all have our own ways of dealing with horror when we meet it, that's all.)

I was punishing myself for giving up, too. I had met the woman; I had reached an agreement with her. There was a bond between us, a shared obligation. Just because she wasn't in a position to honour her side, did that absolve me of mine? There was even more to it than that. Maddy January was a chromium-plated bitch, no doubt about that, but when we had met in that steaming hot place, I had seen something in her, buried pretty deep, I'll grant you, but something I liked. Maybe she showed that to all the guys, but I didn't care. I didn't like the idea of someone cutting it off at source . . . or at the shoulders.

I felt better when I'd finished: I went upstairs and rang Lufthansa to get us on to their evening flight, then called Reception and arranged a late check-out. Once I'd done all that and showered, it was nine thirty and I was ready for the day. I called Mike, but he wasn't, so we agreed to go our separate ways and met up at five thirty, to check out, dump the bags and have a drink in Raffles before we headed for the airport.

He mumbled something about sightseeing, but there was only one sight in the city that I wanted to see before I left, so I called her. 'Hiya,' I said, as she answered her mobile. 'Are you working today?'

'Reading scripts,' Marie replied, 'but I don't have to. You call to tell me you leaving?'

'I'm afraid so. I only have a few hours left in Singapore, and I was hoping I could spend some of them with you.'

'You want to get in my pants now?' Her voice had a lovely laugh to it.

In other circumstances I'd have said, 'Yes,' no hesitation. As it was I just went along for the ride, so to speak. 'And if I did?' I asked.

'Maybe still too soon.'

'Let's just meet up, then.'

'Okay, let's go to the zoo. You like animals?'

Fact is, the animals I like most are those I eat, but I wasn't going to tell her that. 'Sure,' I said. 'I have a hire car, can I pick you up?'

'No, I meet you there. I take a taxi, it's quicker. I see you ten thirty.'

I can take or leave zoos, leave them mostly, although I have taken the kids down to San Diego. It's bigger than Singapore, but probably no better. Marie seemed to know it like the back of her hand. The girl in the ticket booth seemed to know her too, for she smiled at her as I bought the tickets and said something quietly in Chinese.

'What did she say?' I asked, as we moved off.

'She asked if you are my lover.'

'What did you tell her?'

'I said you were my friend . . . for now.'

'Time we saw the zoo,' I said, and let her lead me to the tram ride.

We spent three hours there, getting to know every part of the place. There was a sound commentary on the tram, but Marie overrode it, acting as my personal guide. As you'd expect, the orang-utan, a near native, is the star of the show, but there was just about every other species of mammal on display, or so it seemed. The only part I didn't like was the polar-bear enclosure; as I watched the poor bastard parading back and forward, forward and back, oblivious to the gawpers on the other side of the glass screen, I knew, instinctively and beyond doubt, that it had been driven quite insane.

When we were done there, I took her for lunch. I expected her to choose a fish restaurant, but she took us to an Italian place called Al Dente, on Boat Quay, where she said they did a killer lasagne. It looked pretty good, but I passed and chose a shark steak, and a nice bottle of well-chilled Frascati to go with it.

Our table was by the river, shaded by an umbrella but still hot. That was okay by me: too much air-con is bad for you, and probably explains why half the people in Singapore seem to suffer from fairly noisy sinus conditions.

'Are you serious about the film part, Oz?' she asked, after we had eaten and were staring into a couple of cappuccinos.

'Of course. Why would I not be?'

Her answer was a smile and a raised eyebrow.

I replied in kind. 'And when will you have known me long enough?' I asked.

She looked at me with honest open eyes. 'I don't know; maybe never. Or maybe this afternoon. I'm a very careful girl. I don't know how to be impulsive, but maybe I can try.'

I took her hand, drew her across the small table and kissed her. 'Marie,' I told her, 'you go on being careful. Impulsiveness is for guys like me, not girls like you, and now even I avoid it like the plague. It can get you into a hell of a lot of trouble.'

I said that, yet I confess that my impulse was to take her back to the hotel and make love to her until it was time to go to the airport. The harder I resisted it, the more I found myself wondering what it would be like. Resist I did, though.

'The movie part is yours,' I promised, 'without conditions before or after the event. You give me an address where I can write to you.'

'I have a post-office box,' she replied. 'It's best here.' She wrote the number on the back of a restaurant card and gave it to me. 'Thanks, Oz. It's been wonderful to meet you. I will think about everything, I promise.'

I parted from her there; she said she wanted to catch the MRT, so I walked her to the Clarke Quay station. We kissed goodbye . . . it was meant to be just a friendly peck, but it wound up going on for a little longer than one of those. The last I saw of her, she was waving, as the escalator took her down and out of my sight.

33

I was still thinking about Marie when Dylan and I met in the foyer at five thirty, as arranged. I went through the check-out procedures and paid the bill. Then we dumped our cases with the valet, who would look after them till 'Go to Changi Airport' time. I'd arranged for Hertz to collect the car.

We were waiting to cross Bras Basah Road, heading for Raffles, when my mobile sounded. It was Ricky Ross.

'Can you speak?' he asked, as the green man showed.

'Yes, but it'll be cooler once I get into the shade.'

'What time is it with you?'

'Tea time.' I stepped into the shadow of Raffles and leaned against the wall. 'Do you have something?'

'Too right. This guy you met, his real name's Sammy Goss and he is well and truly on the run. He did indeed leave Scotland eight years ago, but not from Maryhill. He escaped from custody on his way to a committal hearing; he was due to stand trial on two counts of murder in Glasgow, and after that he was going to London for a third. All three of them were gang-related.'

'Any Chinese connections?'

'Why do you ask that? As it happens, two of the victims were Chinese. The London case was a guy who'd upset some people in Chinatown. When Goss was picked up in Glasgow, the gun he'd used in one of the killings there was matched to that one.'

'What did he use in the third?'

'A knife. He was linked to several other hits, but those were the only ones they could proceed on. Are you telling me he's in Singapore?'

'Not any more.'

'Oz, I've pulled some strings for this information. The people I've talked to want to know why I'm asking.'

'Tell them to cross him off their list. He's dead.'

'How do you know?'

'I have the word of a reliable witness,' I told him. 'It seems Sammy underestimated somebody and took one in the back of the head.'

'Will the Singapore police confirm this?'

'It happened in Malaysia, not Singapore, but nobody's going to confirm it, because there isn't going to be a body.'

'Fucking hell, Oz,' Ricky gasped, 'what have you got yourself into?'

'Nothing at all. I'm catching a plane in a few hours and I'm heading back home, clean as a whistle. Did Goss have any family? He told me he had a mother, a sister and two nephews and that he went home every couple of years or so.'

'He was kidding: his father died in a pub fight twenty years ago and his mother boozed herself to death. No sister, only a granny; the police check her out every so often, but he's never shown up there. Do you know who killed him?'

'You didn't ask me that; just tell your former colleagues on the quiet that they can stop staking out his granny's. If they ever see anything of him again, it'll be in a can of fucking tuna.'

'You wouldn't like to tell me what brand, would you?'

'That's a hard one. If you like the stuff, I'd build up a big stock now, if I were you, before Sammy's had time to get into the human food chain.'

'Jesus, Oz. You definitely hung around with Dylan for too long, d'you know that?'

34

With the time difference, I made it home to Monaco for a late breakfast on Wednesday. Dylan and I had parted in Frankfurt, since I had done a complicated ticket transfer to see him back home to New York, through Paris.

If I said that the kids were pleased to see me again, I would be guilty of the sort of understatement that I abhor. They were ecstatic, at least the two older ones were, and wouldn't let go of me not even after I'd given them the toys I'd bought for them in the Raffles shop and in a place in the Citylink Mall that had just about everything for kids.

Even with the melatonin I was running on empty, but we spent a couple of hours on the pool, and then I took them to the Cousteau Institute aquarium . . . again . . . and to the motor museum, of course. I had to tell them about Singapore too; as much as I could, at any rate. By the time I'd finished I'd promised to take them there as soon as their mum said they were old enough to go, although to be honest, after what I'd seen, I was glad that would be a right few years away.

Susie was pleased to see me too, you understand, although she kept her ecstasy under control better than they did. The fact that I was twenty-four hours late might have helped her in that. In fact, she kept it to herself until they had gone off with Ethel to start the getting-ready-for-bed process.

Afterwards, as we lay side by side looking out at the blue sea and at the red ball of the sun as it began to dip towards the horizon, she nudged my shoulder with her head. 'That was pretty good, considering the trip you've had, and the time it took you to get back, and the fact that you haven't been in touch since Sunday. Are you going to tell me now? Did you get Harvey's pictures? Did you pay the woman off?'

'No.'

'What did you get?'

'I got my Siegfried and Roy T-shirt ruined and I nearly got arrested twice.'

She propped herself on an elbow, eyes wide, 'What for?'

'Murder.'

'Murder!'

'Don't shout, for Christ's sake, the kids will hear you. I didn't do it, either of them, honest.'

'Who did?'

'A wee Scots guy called Sammy did the first one: he knifed Maddy's boyfriend just before I was due to meet him in that bar on Sunday night. Then Maddy killed him. That was self-defence, though: he was going to cut her head off and take it to the Triad chieftain because she'd upset him.'

She put a hand on my forehead. 'Oz, are you feeling all right? You haven't got malaria, have you?'

'It doesn't take effect that quickly.'

'Has Mike Dylan been trying out his next book on you?'

'No, he hasn't, and you must be very careful never to call him that again, not where anyone can hear you. There are people out there who would kill him with a blowlamp if they thought he was alive.'

'Are you trying to tell me you're serious?'

I pointed across the bedroom. 'See that knapsack on your dressing-table stool?' She nodded. 'Go and get it, there's a girl.'

'Why don't you get it yourself?'

'Because I like watching you in the buff.'

'Oh. That's fair enough, then.' She got up from the bed, skipped across the room, fetched the bag, then sat back down beside me.

220

'Open it.'

She did, and looked inside. 'Oz! What's this?'

'Fifty thousand of Uncle Sam's dollars,' I told her, 'drawn from Amex to give to Maddy, only she sent Tony Lee, her renegade Triad boyfriend instead. They must have been watching him, for his account got closed off before we got there.'

'We? You mean Mike went with you to that bar, and him in danger there?'

'He insisted, but it wasn't a risk for him. Only one guy in Singapore knows about his Interpol work, and he's on our side. Thank Christ, I might add, because he cleaned up the mess.'

She sat for a while, frowning as she took it all in. 'So Harvey's ex is on the run from these diehards . . .'

'Triads.'

'Why?'

'She took a photograph of their top man, and they found out. His identity's the biggest secret in South East Asia, apparently.'

'Why did she do that?'

'She thought Tony was shagging him. As it turned out, he worked for him.'

'So she's out there, with these desperadoes after her, and you're back here? You're her only hope and you've abandoned her.'

'That's how it looks, but we'd nowhere else to go.'

'Bollocks! There's always somewhere else to go; you're always telling me that. Get out there and find her.'

I smiled at her. There is no greater motivator than my lovely wife. 'I was hoping you'd say that,' I told her.

35

Where do you begin looking for a woman you don't really know who's missing on the other side of the world? At home seemed to me to be a good place to start. Next morning I called Harvey: there was no answer from his mobile, so I had him paged at the Advocates' Library.

'Oz,' he said, slightly breathlessly, when he came on line, 'where are you?'

I told him. 'But I'm empty-handed,' I added.

'She wouldn't co-operate?'

'No, to be fair to her, it's more a case of not being able to. Remember I told you that things had gone sour for her out there?'

'Yes.'

'Well, that was maybe understating it a little. She's got herself mixed up with some very bad people and now she's on the run.'

'Where?' Harvey's a naturally unflappable guy, but this time he was flapping good style. He'd forgotten about photographs, and everything else. I'd guessed right about his reaction: Maddy was a bitch, but for a while she'd been his bitch.

'Her last known location was an island off Malaysia. From there she headed back to the mainland, but that's it.'

'What do these people want from her?'

'Same as you, some photographs, but I don't think they exist any more. Now they just want her.'

'But what are they going to do with her?' He sounded bewildered; this was a man who had spent part of his career prosecuting and occasionally defending a succession of fairly vicious criminals . . . if Sammy Goss hadn't escaped, he might well have been on the list . . . yet he didn't get it.

'They're going to kill her, Harvey.'

'My God! Oz, what can I do? Have you reported this to the police out there?'

'The police know about it, but there's nothing they can do. If she gets out of the region she's got a better chance, but we still need to find her. Once we've done that we can keep her safe . . . or try to.'

'How do we do that?'

'Through the other side of her life. Sooner or later she'll contact someone she knows. Friend, relative, maybe even you. Tell me what you can about her family, her friends, those you can remember at any rate.'

'Her father's dead; his name was Luke Raymond. He was quite an eminent photo-journalist, but he was killed in the Lebanon twenty-five years ago. Madeleine takes her adventurous side from him. Janine, her mother, is the opposite, a vicar's daughter from Uxbridge. I'm still on her Christmas-card list, but I doubt if Madeleine is. There's one sister, Theresa, three years older. She was a career academic, a reader in philosophy at Cambridge when Madeleine and I were married. And there's a younger brother, Trevor, who was in the army last I heard.'

'Did the sister have a husband?'

'No. A wife would be more likely. As for friends . . . Maddy didn't have any close female friends that I knew of. She hung around the theatre company in Edinburgh, at the expense eventually, of our marriage, but you know that. She may have had some there.'

'She met Primavera there; Dawn was with the company at the time.'

'Did she indeed? Yes, I can imagine those two would get on. Things in common.'

I chuckled quietly. 'Shagging actors, you mean?'

'I wouldn't have been so blunt.'

'No, but you're a lawyer: you're trained to bring out responses like that one. Do you have an address for your former mother-in-law, better still a telephone number?'

He had both: he read them out and I noted them on the pad I keep on my desk. 'Will you start with her?'

'Yes. I'll look everywhere, don't worry. I'll even go back to Rosebud.'

'When you find her, what will you do? From what you've said I surmise it's organised crime that's on her tail. How can we protect her from people like that, in the long term?'

'Harvey, right now, I don't have a clue, but that question won't arise till we find her.'

I hung up and looked across at Susie, who had come into my study half-way through the conversation. (I know: it sounds pretentious, a bloke from Fife having a study, but it's my quiet room. I use it to read scripts and to do the sort of business that doesn't allow for kids yelling in your ear.)

'Needle in a haystack, isn't it?' she said.

'I wish it was that easy; you could find that with a big enough magnet. A crumb in a biscuit factory might be a better analogy. And speaking of crumbs . . .'

I turned to my computer and opened the AOL search engine. Two minutes later I had a number for Pitlochry Festival Theatre and three minutes after that a very helpful director had given me the number of the small hotel where Rory Roseberry was living during the run of *Death of a Salesman*. He was there. Good start, I thought.

'Rosebud? Oz Blackstone.'

'Oh, no, fuck off, please.'

'What?'

'I don't want to speak to you, Blackstone. Leave me alone, or I'll . . .' I could hear him searching for a threat. 'I'll complain to Equity.'

'Listen to me quake in my sandals. You're fifty million euros too late for that.'

'Oz, please, leave me alone. First it's you thumping me, now it's this other bloke.'

'What other bloke?'

'Trevor, Maddy's brother. He was waiting for me after the show last night; crazy man. He wanted to know if I had spoken to you about her. When I said I had he beat me up. You should see my face: Makeup won't have a chance with it. I'm out of the run.'

'Have you called the police?'

'What? And have him come back again some time?'

'What did he say, this guy? Anything other than that?'

'He was yelling at me so much I can hardly remember, but this one sticks. As he was kicking me, on the ground, he said, "Putting him on her trail nearly got her killed. He's a fucking hitman for his brother-in-law." Don't tell me what he meant; I don't want to know.'

'Anything else, Rory? Did he say anything else?'

'I don't know. Wait, he said, "And he's next." Yes, that was it. Now please, Oz, get off the line.'

He didn't have to tell me that. I cut the call then redialled the Advocates' Library. 'Page Mr January again, please.'

'I'm sorry, sir,' the operator replied. 'Mr January is unavailable.'

'I spoke to him ten minutes ago. I know he's there.'

'That may be, sir, but he's unavailable.'

'This is his brother-in-law, Oz Blackstone, and it's urgent. Now make him available.'

'Hold, please, sir.'

I held, as patiently as I could. After a minute or so, the operator returned. 'I'm connecting you now, sir.'

'Thank you,' I said. 'Harvey . . .'

'It's not Harvey, I'm afraid,' a smooth Edinburgh voice replied. 'This is the Dean of Faculty. Harvey has just been attacked in the Great Hall while promenading with an instructing solicitor. It only happened five minutes ago but from what I can gather it was completely unprovoked. The man burst into the hall, saw Harvey and went for him.'

'With a weapon?'

'No, his bare hands, but that was bad enough. He was still unconscious when I left him to take your call.'

'And the man?'

'He was restrained by other advocates and eventually by the police. We have officers in attendance in the vicinity of the court all the time, as you can imagine. I don't know anything about him, though.'

'I do. His name's Trevor Raymond and he used to have the same job description as me: Harvey's brother-in-law. You can tell the police that.'

'Thanks, I will. CID are on their way from Gayfield Square.'

'Good, because I'm on my way too.'

The decision was made pretty much there and then: Susie and I were going into the jet-charter business. I told her what had happened, asked her to call Ellie before the Dean or the police did, then tasked Audrey with booking me another Citation flight to Edinburgh. I was in the air by eleven thirty, and in Edinburgh before one, British Summer Time.

By that time Harvey was out of whatever danger he'd been in. He'd been rushed to the Western General, but had come round in the ambulance. The neurologists were satisfied that he'd sustained nothing more sinister than severe concussion. That would wear off in a couple of days, but the broken nose and three cracked ribs would take rather longer to heal. In my relief, I found myself wondering if a Supreme Court judge had ever been installed before while wearing a couple of black eyes.

I'd called Ricky Ross before leaving Cannes. He was waiting for me at the general-aviation terminal and drove me straight to the police headquarters building at Fettes. Ricky still has a lot of clout with Lothian and Borders Police: he'd dropped a word and the case had been taken over by Special Branch.

227

We were met by a guy called Detective Chief Inspector Oliver Coffey; he looked familiar, but I couldn't place him. He assumed that my interest was straightforward.

'Have you got any idea why Raymond should do this?' he asked me. 'Mr January's been divorced from his sister for ten years, and as far as I can gather they've had no contact since then. Is he just a nutter?'

'He may well be, but it's not as simple as that. I'd like you to do me a favour, and let me speak to him alone.'

Coffey whistled like a kettle coming to the boil. 'I don't know if I can do that, Oz. This guy's dangerous.'

'So am I,' I told him. 'After what he did to Harvey, and to a harmless wee actor up in Pitlochry last night, I'd just love him to have a go at me. But chain him to the floor if it makes you happy. I promise I won't touch him.'

The DCI nodded. 'Okay. Since you were once one of us, you can do it. Have you forgotten that you and I were at the police college together?'

I placed him then: Ollie Coffey had been on the same new entrants' course as me at Tulliallan. A couple of years later he'd been selected for an accelerated promotion course and I'd been turned down. That was a close shave, I thought. If they'd picked me I might have wound up interviewing hoodlums in windowless rooms.

Trevor Raymond was around the same age as me, but about three inches shorter and quite a bit lighter. His hair was close-cropped, he had heavy dark eyebrows and a tattoo on each forearm. His left cheek was red and swollen. I guessed that he had resisted arrest, or that one of Harvey's brother advocates had got in a good one.

They hadn't chained him to the floor, but he was in a restraint belt and his ankles were shackled. As I stepped into the room, his eyes lit up with hatred and he tried to stand up.

'I promised not to touch you,' I told him. 'I don't advise you to make me break my word. You might be good but I'm better, you might be tough but I'm tougher, you might be strong but I'm stronger. Those aren't boasts, they're facts. Now, why the vendetta?'

He spat at me, a good-sized gob, but he wound it up so I was able to dodge it.

'Man, they're filming this, and they're angry at you as it is. The police like Harvey; you're lucky you've still got the same number of teeth you woke up with this morning. What did Maddy tell you?'

'Fuck off.'

'Hey, a response! When did she call you?'

'Go and fuck yourself.'

'Are you still in the army?' He glared at me, but stayed silent this time. 'Doesn't matter, Coffey will have found out by now. Either way, you're not any more. But you have had a call from her, yes?'

'When I get out of here I'm going to fuck your wife.'

'I don't think so. One, the way you're going your dick will be withered by the time you get out of here. Two, I employ a better soldier to protect my family than you've ever been. Three, you have got all this fundamentally wrong. Okay, I'm not going to ask you any more questions. I'm going to tell you stuff instead. The last time your sister was seen was on Monday, on an island called Dayang, which is, interestingly, and I will quote this fact to bored listeners for the rest of my life, not far from the island that they used as the fictional Bali Hai in my mother's favourite movie, *South Pacific*.' I'd clocked the camera by this time, top right corner facing me: I winked at it.

'While she was there she killed a man called Sammy Goss. It's technically not correct to say that Sammy was the last person to see her alive, because she shot him in the back of the head as soon as he stepped into the room, so he never saw her. Nobody will ever blame her for that, for Sammy was a very dangerous wee man. So dangerous, in fact, that he killed her boyfriend, Tony Lee, more or less right under my very nose.' I could picture

Coffey and Ross as they listened to this; I nodded towards the watching lens.

'After killing him, she took the boat that he sailed in on, and that's the last I knew of her, until you stuck your oar in. Now I know that she made it to the mainland and on from there. I know you've had a call from her, because last night you showed up in Pitlochry and gave her ex-boyfriend a gratuitous battering just because he admitted having spoken to me about her. Let's say you spent half a day getting there. That tells me she probably called you yesterday morning. All I don't know is where she was at that time. And I need to know, Trevor, because I am the only person who can save her life. I have no idea why she resents me, for I had agreed to give her a lot of money, but I don't care about that. I just want to know where she is, or was yesterday morning.'

He glared back at me. 'I don't know where you dredged all that crap from,' he hissed, 'but the only thing I will ever tell you is . . . fuck off!' I was looking in his eyes as he shouted the last two words of advice, and I knew that he meant it.

I walked behind him and leaned close, then whispered something, so quietly that no mike would have picked it up unless one of us had been wearing it, keeping my face off camera so I couldn't be lip-read. 'A promise. If you ever go near any member of my family again, I'll have you killed.' He twitched; that was all, but it was enough to tell me that he believed me.

I straightened up and walked out of the room, waving goodbye as I closed the door behind me.

'What was that all about?' Coffey asked, when I rejoined him and Ricky.

'The Triads are after Harvey's ex, for reasons which to them seem pretty solid. Nobody outside this room needs to know that, though.'

'What sort of a world are you living in these days, man?' asked Ricky.

I looked at him. 'Listen, I'm supposed to be on my holidays. These things just happen to me.'

'He had a mobile on him when we brought him in,' said Ollie Coffey, thinking like a real policeman. 'If it needs a password we'll never get it from him, but I can access the information on it, one way or another. You guys go for a pint somewhere; I'll join you when I've got it.'

36

In fact we went to the Western General, to check up on Harvey's condition. Ellen was with him when we got there, having left Jonny in charge at St Andrews. He wasn't with anyone: he was awake but dazed, and sedated on top of that. When he spoke, it was nonsense.

At least he knew me when I walked into the small room they had given him. 'Hello, brother-in-law,' he said. 'How are the fish?'

'Fine,' I replied. 'I fed them before I left.' That seemed to satisfy him, for he smiled and settled back into his mountain of pillows. I'd been right about the black eyes. They were well puffy already; in a couple of days they'd be prime shiners.

Our Ellie was less easy to placate. 'What is this all about, Oz? Why should someone attack Harvey like that? He doesn't have any clients with a grudge. And how could it happen in there?'

'Parliament Hall is a public room,' I told her. 'And it wasn't a disgruntled client. It was his first wife's brother.'

'What? Trevor the bloody soldier? What could Harvey possibly have done to upset him?'

I had hoped, against all hope, that Harvey had taken my advice and told Ellie the whole story. But clearly not: he might have faced up to some serious villains in the witness box, but my sister is a different story. He had bottled it and, in the process, put me right in the firing line. 'Actually,' I admitted, 'it's more me who's upset him. He just took it out on Harvey. I'm just not sure why he's gone off like that.'

She took me by the elbow, as she used to when we were kids, and led me into the corridor, then looked me in the eye and said, 'Right, spill.'

It took me a while, but I told her everything, including the bits I'd left out to spare Harvey's feelings. No, not everything: I didn't tell her about Mike Dylan. To my relief, she didn't rant, and she didn't rave. She waited until I was finished, and then she shook her head.

'You two,' she sighed, 'you're just a pair of stupid boys. Okay, so a sleazy tabloid publishes an ancient photo of the new Lord January in his dad's old robes with his cock hanging out. So what? He's not a faggot Aussie actor playing a stud in a TV show, plus, the Supreme Court only acknowledges the existence of the tabloids when they've got one of their editors up before them for contempt, so how can it really harm him? He'll be the laugh of the New Club for a week, and that'll be the end of it. But, no, you and he had to take the whole thing seriously, and you wind up flying half-way round the world to buy the silly bitch off. Have you still got the fifty thousand?'

As a matter of fact I had: it was in the knapsack, over my shoulder, although I wasn't quite sure why.

I decided it was time to mount a counter-offensive, to appeal to her soft side, wherever that might have been hiding. 'We did it for you, you ungrateful hussy. Harvey wanted to spare you the embarrassment.'

It didn't work. 'Why should I be embarrassed?' She snorted. 'Between you and me and anyone else who asks, I'm very proud of my husband's chopper. Big improvement on the last one, I'll tell you. You're lovely lads, but you're silly; I wouldn't have minded that much.'

'Whatever, it's gone way beyond that now, though, Ellie,' I pointed out. 'Even if I hadn't gone out there, she'd still be in deep trouble, and maybe dead by now.'

'Agreed, so why's her brother gone off the deep end at Harvey?'

234

'I'm going to find that out when I trace the bloody woman.'

'You might have a job doing that. She's taken a scunner to you it seems.'

'I'll find her, sis. I'm going to save her bloody life in spite of herself.'

'Well, when you do, tell her to come and see me. Mind you, she might prefer those Triangles to that!'

As she spoke I was looking over her shoulder, at Ollie Coffey who had just turned the corner and was coming towards me. I introduced him to Ellie. 'Have you got this thug well locked up?' she demanded.

'Yes, Mrs January, he's for the court in the morning. I've been checking up on him too. Your husband was right, he was in the army for a while, second lieutenant in the Green Jackets, but he resigned his commission after a few years because he felt he wasn't seeing enough action. Then, believe it or not, he joined the French Foreign Legion, and served there for eight years. Since then he's been a freelance journalist, specialising in military matters. He's popped up once or twice on television and radio news programmes as a quote, defence expert, unquote.'

'Sounds like a fantasist,' I said. 'His old man was an adventurer and died on the job. Like father like son.'

'What's he being charged with?' Ellie asked. 'Attempted murder, I hope.'

'With no weapon used we'd never make that stick. It can only be serious assault for now, but the Lord Advocate's told the Crown Office to take a longer look. Legally speaking the attack happened within the confines of the court.'

'What difference does that make?'

'About five years, depending on the judge.'

'That'll do for starters.' She left us and went back into Harvey's room to send out Ricky Ross.

'I've got something,' said Coffey, when he arrived. 'Raymond's only had one call on his mobile in the last couple of days, yesterday morning as you thought, Oz. It was made from a callbox at the airport in Ho Chi Minh City, Vietnam.'

'She made it out of Malaysia, then, thank Christ. Can we find out where she's going from there?'

'Ouch!' said Coffey. 'That's going to be a bit more difficult. It's going to involve other agencies; I don't know if I can do that.'

'Come on, Ollie,' Ricky cajoled him, 'you're Special Branch, you've got access. The woman's brother's just attacked a judge, and you've got evidence from Oz here that she's been involved with organised crime in the Far East. You've got every reason to try and trace her.'

'He's not a judge.'

'He will be inside a fortnight,' I volunteered.

'In that case, I suppose I can,' he conceded. 'Leave it with me.'

We left it, and Ricky left me, promising to give me any feedback he got from Ollie. I found a pay-phone and called Susie, to reassure her that Harvey was going to be all right, and then I went back to Ellie. We stayed in the tiny ward for half an hour or so, until the consultant came back and told us that we might as well go since the patient would be dozing for the rest of the night. All being well, he promised (meaning if his brain didn't implode during the night), he'd be able to go home some time the following day.

I could have stayed in the Caley, but I'd seen enough of it. Instead I went to Fife with Ellie, to look in on Dad and Mary and give them the positive tidings (I didn't give them any details about the attack: I said it was a random nutcase and that was all), and then to spend the night at her place in St Andrews.

Every time I see my nephews, these days, I see a change in them. Jonny's sixteen, and starting to fill out; he's a big, good-looking boy, with a quiet self-confidence that never threatens to spill over into arrogance. Ellie says he's like me at that age, so I'm glad he's got Harvey around now to steer him along a conventional and responsible path. He seems to be serious about the law as a career; I'd rather see him being a pro golfer, but I hadn't been bold enough to tell his parents that. Colin, the incorrigible imp of mischief that he's been since he was born, has edged into his teens and, without anyone really noticing it, he's quietened down. Of the two, it's Jonny who's the more outgoing now, and Colin who spends much of his time indoors, hunched over a computer. My fear is that he's starting to turn into his father, the boring Alan Sinclair.

Cooking wasn't an option: I told Ellie we were all going out to eat. St Andrews was gearing up for the ritual of the Open Championship the following week, and already the place was full of golfers, journalists and fans. Somehow, though, I used connections to find us a table at the Seafood Restaurant, a relative newcomer to the old grey town, as Alex Hay loved to call it when he was in the BBC commentary box. Ellie was grudgingly impressed, but not half as much as later on, when Seve Ballesteros came across to our table and asked for my autograph. We swapped, and he signed the three other menus as well, plus a fourth for my dad. He still says that Arnold Palmer is the most exciting golfer he's ever seen, but Seve gets my vote every time. Tiger? He's on another planet; at his best he's chilling. It's like watching a trained assassin at work, killing golf courses.

When we got home, the lads turned in. Colin was on the team that would man the main scoreboard at the Open, and Jonny had a caddying job next day, for a young American qualifier who'd come over early to get acclimatised. If they got on, there was the possibility he'd be hired for the championship. Bearing in mind that the previous two Opens had been won by inexperienced American qualifiers, I wished him luck.

Ellie and I sat in the back garden when they were gone, just as we used to in our younger days, each of us clutching a bottle of beer. It was a warm, balmy night by St Andrews standards, and pleasantly cool by mine.

'He's going to be all right, Oz, isn't he?'

'Harvey? Of course he is: advocates are notorious for the thickness of their skulls, and QCs even more so. When they're ready to go to the Bench it would take a road drill to get through one.'

She laughed quietly. When she tones down the volume my sister has a beautiful laugh, just like our mother. 'I'll tell him that. Actually, I meant Jonny.'

'Jonny? Why do you ask that?'

'Ach, he's torn, Oz. He wants to be like Harvey, and to impress him, but he wants to impress you even more. He wants to be like you too.'

'Then send him to drama school, not law school. But better still, get him working on the golf so that in a couple of years he'll be a candidate for a scholarship at an American university. He can study law there, then see what direction he wants to take.'

'Golf?'

'What are you going to do, Ellie? Tell the man what he's going to do with his life? He won't take that, and if you push it, you'll wind up hurting you both.'

'He's a boy still, Oz,' she protested weakly, with the voice of someone who had strained it shouting at the rising tide, ordering it not to come in any further.

I took a sip of my Rolling Rock and looked at her over the neck of the bottle. 'You're talking like a mother, Ellie. He's a man. Legally he can walk out the door tomorrow, get his own place, start a career, start a family. Sure, he's still got some growing up left, but those are his rights now, at his age. You want to help him, then advise him: set out all the options for him, even fucking dentistry, whatever Dad says, and let him make his own choice. Once he's done that, respect it, but while he's making his mind up, impress on him that his final choice shouldn't be what he thinks Harvey or I might like him to do, but what he wants, in his heart.'

'Jesus,' she whispered. 'Where did you acquire wisdom?'

'Through long nights spent talking to Jan's ghost.'

She stared at me. 'Funny, that. Me too.' Of course, Jan was her sister as well; I wished I could tell her, but I know I never can.

238

'Will you be all right, Oz?' she asked suddenly.

It was my turn to stare. 'Hey, that sounds like what the bell-boy's supposed to have said to George Best when he brought him and the latest Miss World room service. "Where did it all go wrong, Georgie?" I thought I was doing all right, thank you very much.'

'Aye, you are, and you wear it well, too; you're gracious. But there's something eating at you.'

'No,' I protested 'I'm fine.'

'You're fine and yet you're not. Are you and Susie okay?'

'Susie and I are perfect. I just . . . I wish I could spend all my time with her and the kids, but the life I'm in doesn't allow for that. I wish I could be there now, but Fate says, "No way." I've spent the last couple of weeks on a familiarisation course of Edinburgh's two hospitals, and chasing around Singapore and Malaysia after an ungrateful fucking cow. I'm not blaming Harvey for that, by the way. If I was in trouble he'd be the first guy I'd go to for help, and I'd get it. But when I'm away I feel unsettled, I feel vulnerable, I feel . . . I can't explain.'

'Try.'

'Okay, in Singapore I met this girl, Marie. She's an actress and she helped me out with something. I liked her, we had a drink, and we had lunch together on Tuesday.'

'And you . . .'

'No.'

'Let me finish. You wanted to but you didn't.'

'Ellie, I can't even admit to myself that I wanted to.'

'But you did, you were attracted to the woman sexually, and maybe it was there for you. You're a man, for God's sake, and your profession exposes you to some of the most beautiful women in the world, and occasionally exposes them to you, from what I've seen of your movies. You shouldn't be ashamed that you wanted to have her. You should be proud that you didn't.'

She got up from her garden recliner, went into the kitchen, and

239

came back with two more Rolling Rocks. 'Go home, Oz. Let the police find the first Mrs January.'

'The police? I was a policeman and I couldn't find my arse with both hands. Mike Dylan was a policeman, and he got shot. Ricky Ross was a policeman and he got slung out for screwing the wife of a murder victim, a prime suspect in a case he was investigating. Maddy January's in trouble because her talent for candid camera photography led her to take a picture of the top man in organised crime in South East Asia. He's been there for years, and their police are so good that they don't know his name or what he looks like. Ellie, if I had your confidence I'd do what you say, but I don't. I'm the best chance this woman's got of staying alive, even if she doesn't know it. If I give up on her and she dies, as she will, Susie will never forgive me, Harvey will never forgive me, and I'll never forgive myself. But you know what frightens me the most?'

'What?'

'Jan will never forgive me.'

'Oz,' our Ellen whispered, 'Jan's gone.'

I found that I was crying softly. 'You may choose to believe that,' I told her, 'but I never will.'

37

I didn't sleep that night: I knew that if I dropped off I'd dream of Jan, and that if I did, waking up would hurt, maybe more than I could handle at that time.

So instead I read a book, *Lethal Intent,* the latest Skinner novel, which Ellie had left for me in the guest room. Eventually the pages swam before my eyes, so I laid it down to be resumed later (I'd buy my own copy next chance I had: as an actor I have this secret belief that sharing books and DVDs is morally wrong) and picked up a notepad and pen from the bedside table.

I began to make notes, and to look for unanswered questions flowing from what had happened in Singapore. When I thought about it, there were only two. Had Sammy Goss's meeting with us in the Crazy Elephant been sheer, blind coincidence? Since I only believe in coincidence when it doesn't matter a damn, that led on to the second question. How the hell had he known that we'd be there?

I thought about that for a while, but I got nowhere near an answer.

After that I just thought, ready to make random notes about oddities as they occurred, but none did . . . until around four thirty in the morning. I found myself looking at a mind picture, looking for something, and being unable to find it. I switched on my mobile, found the entry for Benny Luker, and hit the call key.

'Yes,' he shouted in my ear, over background music that sounded as if it was live.

'It's me,' I said. 'Where the hell are you?'

'The Iridium Jazz Club, on Broadway; Mose Allison's on. The set's just winding up. Hold on and I'll find somewhere quieter if that's possible in here.'

I waited until the music stopped and the background buzz was cut off.

'Okay, I'm in the gents'. What's up? Has she been found?'

'No, but she was in Vietnam on Tuesday. She called her brother from there, and she's seriously pissed off at me, for some reason. He's caused some local difficulty, but that's been dealt with and he'll be going away for a spell.'

'Do you know where she headed from there?'

'No, but Ricky and I have someone working on it, Ollie Coffey, Special Branch.'

'I remember him.'

'Yes, well, try and remember this. When we were in Tony Lee's flat, in his office, we saw a docking station for a palmtop computer, a PDA.'

'Yes, Hewlett Packard manufacture.'

'Did you see the unit itself anywhere?'

As he thought about it, or as I thought he thought about it, I heard a toilet flush. 'Sorry. I took a piss while I'm here. The answer is no, I definitely did not.'

'No, me neither. So, possibilities: maybe Tony had it and Sammy took it after he'd killed him.'

'Maybe, or maybe it was in his car, or in his office.'

'Or maybe Madeleine took it with her. They had a scanner, okay, mostly she used film for photography, but there was an empty folder called "Maddy's pics" on the computer. What can you store on a PDA?'

'Quite a lot: they take standard SD cards. I see where you're going. You think she might have taken some bargaining power along with her.'

'My, my, we do work well as a team. I'll keep you informed if Coffey comes up with anything.'

'Coffey might get his arse kicked, getting involved with this.'

'Knowingly or not, Maddy incited an attack on Scotland's newest judge. He can dress that up as possible terrorism.'

'She's really in bother now, isn't she?'

'Indeed. Go on, get back to old man Mose. Are you on your own, or are you trying to gain ground with your lovely editor?'

'No,' he said. 'Just a friend. Hey, what time is it with you?'

'Going on five.'

I heard his sigh, all the way from the crapper in the Iridium Jazz Club. 'Pal, when this is over, you really must get yourself a life.'

And then he was gone, and I was left to wonder.

38

I went back to Edinburgh with Ellie next morning, but not before I'd gone down to the Old Course with Jonny, to meet his employer for the day, and to walk the first few holes with them. He was a nice lad, and he welcomed the attention; he even welcomed the early-duty photographers who spotted me and focused on us. I apologised, but he told me not to be worried. 'My sponsors will love it,' he said.

Being a youngster, playing with two other young Americans, he had an early time, but that suited me, since I'd been up with the lark; in fact, slightly before the chirpy wee bastard.

I hadn't been alone. 'Who were you calling in the middle of the night?' Jonny asked me, as we strode down the first, after the boss's opening six-iron. He'd asked my nephew what he should hit; like an old pro caddy, the lad just took the club from the bag and handed it to him. 'Leave yourself a full wedge,' he'd said.

'America,' I told him. 'Business.'

'At five in the morning? I'll need to talk to Aunt Susie about you. She needs to get you under control.'

He was dead right. I left them on the fifth tee, at which point Jonny's boss was two under par, and headed back for breakfast.

When we reached the Western General two and a half hours later, Harvey was sitting up in bed. His eyes were blackening up nicely and his cracked ribs meant that he couldn't get comfortable, whatever way he tried, but otherwise he was fine, back to his normal self.

'Well,' he said, greeting us. 'Bloody Trevor, eh? Stupid lad. I just had the Lord President on the phone: he's absolutely livid and is insisting that he be charged with gross contempt. I tried to intercede, but he's adamant' He looked at me. 'Why did he do it, Oz? All to do with Maddy, I expect.'

'Yes, as far as I can see, she's blaming us for disturbing her happy life.'

'Silly bitch. Is there anything more we can do to help her?'

'I've got someone working on it. You forget about it, though, you've got an installation to prepare for, and a practice to wind up.'

'Yes, indeed. The LP told me that the announcement's been accelerated, in view of what happened. It's being made this morning. God knows what Madeleine will do when she reads about it'

I grinned at him; couldn't help it. 'I don't think it's going to be the top item on the news in Ho Chi Minh City, Harvey.'

I left the two of them there, eventually, and went out to Crewe Road to look for a taxi. I had no clear idea where I wanted to go, but finally when one stopped I was forced to it. I decided on Ricky Ross's office and gave the driver his address. Ricky was with a client, but his secretary was happy to lend me a desk and a phone. I began by calling a travel agent to book a scheduled one-way flight to Nice. Eventually he found me one that left at six thirty and got me there at midnight; it meant going to Frankfurt again, but I booked it anyway.

Next I called Alison Goodchild at her office and told her that the threat to Harvey was probably still active, but that if it happened the family reaction was going to be 'So fucking what?' as politely and eloquently as she cared to put it.

Finally I dug out the list of numbers I had acquired over the previous few days and called Janine Raymond, Madeleine's mum. She really did sound like a vicar's daughter, very soft-spoken, very polite and very sorry for Harvey when I explained to her what had happened to him.

She sounded sad, but not surprised. 'My younger children have been a great disappointment to me as adults, Mr Blackstone,' she admitted. 'I rarely see or hear from either of them.'

I didn't tell her how much trouble Maddy was in, but asked when she had last been in touch.

'I had a postcard from Singapore three months ago,' she said. 'Thankfully, Theresa is everything a daughter should be. She calls me every weekend without fail, and we see each other twice every year. It's a pity she's so far away.'

'Where is she, Mrs Raymond?' I asked.

'New Jersey,' she replied. 'She has a chair in philosophy at Princeton University. I go there every Thanksgiving; it's a lovely place, not like you expect America to be.'

I left it at that: if I'd pressed her for a phone number she'd have twigged that I hadn't just called her to tell her the bad news about Trevor.

I was at a loose end, for the first time in a couple of weeks, but fortunately, before I could get up to any mischief, Ross came back from his meeting and announced that he was taking me for an early lunch. I was expecting the Doric Tavern, or the New York Steam Packet, but I must be a good client for he forked out for Oloroso, on the roof of the building at the corner of Castle Street and George Street.

We were able to eat outside: good, in that the weather was kind enough to allow it, but bad, in that it means the mobile-phone reception is full strength. It was like a pop concert up there; however good the food was, it was beginning to get on my tits, till Ricky's cell played a tune that sounded suspiciously like the chorus of 'The Ball o' Kirriemuir'. He laid down a forkful of distressed spinach or some such, and answered its summons.

'Indeed,' he said, then nodded and muttered for about half a minute, until he looked at me. 'Yes, he's here.' He passed the phone across. 'Ollie Coffey.'

'Oz,' said my former colleague. 'I've got some more on the fugitive lady.'

That got my attention. I hadn't really expected him to come up with anything, for he's pretty low down in the food chain of the intelligence community. 'Do tell,' I invited.

'She caught a plane from Ho Chi Minh to Tokyo, about two hours after she called her brother on Wednesday. There, she boarded another flight to Los Angeles, which got her in yesterday morning local time, yesterday evening BST. The only problem is she doesn't appear to have got off. Madeleine January boarded the flight at Narita Airport, but she didn't fill in a US landing card or Customs declaration.'

'So she's got two passports.'

'She must have. Given time, the US immigration service will be able to come up with the name under which she was admitted, but LAX is a hell of a big airport and they don't have a lot of time on their hands.'

'She's gone anyway. That's eighteen hours ago.'

'Yes, but,' DCI Coffey had the air of a man who was desperately pleased with himself, 'about half an hour ago, her brother's cell-phone rang. The detective constable on whose desk it was sat at the time showed remarkable initiative. He answered it, told the female caller that Trevor was in the bog and that he'd left his phone. He told her to call back in ten minutes, then hung up before she had a chance to ask who the hell he was. Okay?'

'Okay.'

'Right, so we then take the phone to Trevor's cell. By this time, he's worked out that his brief had better have something to offer the judge in mitigation, and also, I think, that we're the good guys. So he plays along. He tells her that everything's kosher and he's still in England, and he keeps her on the line so that we can pinpoint the origin of the call ... the fatal weakness of cell-phones, as you probably know. It was made from the Shoreham Hotel, number thirty-three West Fifty-fifth Street, New York City.'

'Yes!' I hissed. 'Ollie, that selection panel was right: they did pick the right guy for the accelerated promotion course. Thanks, mate, the fucking Milky Bars are on me. Plus, you are now owed a big-time favour by a High Court judge, which you can put in the bank for future use. Cheers, mate.'

I closed the phone and tossed it back across the table to Ricky, then fished my own from my pocket. Ten minutes later my Nice flight was cancelled and I was on the two-ten British Airways shuttle to Heathrow, connecting to JFK. I'd brought enough bloody luggage for two nights, maximum, and I was going to New York: happily I also had all my credit cards and fifty thousand in readies, which for some blessed reason I'd brought with me, possibly because Susie's parting words, not entirely in jest, had been 'Don't come back until you've found this woman and got her out of our bloody lives!'

39

It was tight, but Ricky got me to the airport in time; I was the last person to board the flight and got the usual friendly glares from my fellow passengers, but I ignored them all. I called Dylan's mobile from the devil's playground that is Heathrow on the move between terminals.

When he answered, I could hear more background noise. 'Benny, where are you this time?'

'The Carnegie Deli, having a late breakfast.'

'I thought you lived in the Village.'

'I do, but I'm with the friend I told you about. She's staying in the Algonquin.'

'You got a spare room?'

'No, that's why she's in the Algonquin.'

My favourite New York hotel. 'Okay,' I said, 'book me in there too, for tonight, maybe tomorrow as well. Meet me in the Blue Bar at seven thirty.'

'Are you serious?'

'Of course I'm fucking serious. See you later.'

When I called Susie from the departure gate a few minutes later the idea that I might be kidding never crossed her mind. 'You're taking me at my word, aren't you?' she said.

'I always do, love, I always do. But I promise you now: when I get home this time, we're going away. Maybe Los Angeles, maybe Spain, but wherever it is, we're not going to tell anybody, not even family, where the hell we're at.'

The New York flight gave me plenty of thinking time, if I'd

251

been able to take advantage of it, but to be honest my brain was numb. All I could focus on was number thirty-three West Fifty-fifth Street, and whether Maddy January was still there. Eventually, as a distraction, I tried to watch *Star Wars III: Revenge of the Sith,* or *Taking the Pith,* as a perceptive critic christened it. Ten minutes of that and I was asleep.

The immigration queue at JFK can be a real bugger, even when you have a permanent visa like me, but when you travel upstairs in a jumbo, you're first off the plane so I got through quickly. I rated a 'Have a nice day, Mr Blackstone,' from the desk officer. She didn't even ask me about the fifty grand declared on my landing card: she probably thought it was just walk-about money for a movie star. (To some I know, it is.)

There were the usual guys outside touting limos, but they can take you anywhere, and very often anywhere other than the place you want to go, then charge you a few hundred dollars for the privilege. I chose an ordinary Yellow Cab, and the driver had me at number fifty-nine West Forty-fourth in just over half an hour.

Mike had booked me a suite, more than I needed for a short stay, but it was pretty classy so I didn't mind. I dumped my stuff, shaved, and rode the lift down to the Blue Bar. There was a table with a spare Budweiser; Dylan was there, and so was his friend.

'Hi,' she said, her cheeks turning a nice shade of pink beneath the Mediterranean tan she'd acquired.

'Primavera.' I chuckled as I picked up the beer and took a long swig. 'Why am I not surprised?'

'I was bored up in Perthshire.' She pouted. 'I've been here since Tuesday. Our Benny got a hell of a shock when I called him.'

'I'd a notion it was you when he mentioned the Algonquin.' When we were together, Prim and I had a couple of holidays in New York, and we'd stayed there. 'How did you get into the country?' I asked her. 'They're a bit fussy about admitting convicted felons.'

252

'No problem,' she replied cheerfully. 'I lied on the landing card.'

'Imagine,' said Dylan, mournfully. 'I get home midday Wednesday, jetlagged and full of hell, and at five o'clock this one phones me, to be taken out on the town. I'm glad to see you, pal, for lots of reasons.' Then he looked me in the eye, serious all of a sudden. 'Has she surfaced?'

'Right here in good old New York.' I glanced at the Breitling. 'About twelve hours ago, eleven blocks away from here.' I drained the Bud in a second pull. 'Fancy seeing if she's still there?'

'Sounds interesting; I'll go along with it.'

'Me too,' said Prim, 'whatever it is you're talking about.'

'Maddy January,' I told her.

'Then I'm definitely coming.'

'I'm not so sure. She might turn nasty.'

'It won't be anything you two big strong boys can't handle, I'm sure. Come on.' She slid out from behind the table and headed for the door.

'Eh, honey,' I called after her, 'I hate to point this out, but you don't know where we're going.'

We followed her, though.

It was a powerfully warm evening, more humid than Monaco but nothing like Singapore. We started walking, on the look-out for a lit-up taxi but at that time on a Friday evening they can be hard to come by. We'd reached Sixth Avenue and Forty-eighth by the time we spotted one, but by then we were half-way there, so we decided to continue on foot. We strolled on, past Radio City. I was astonished to see that the Moody Blues were scheduled to appear there on the following Thursday. I found myself wondering if they'd written any new stuff since I was five years old. I said as much to Dylan.

'Who the fuck are the Moody Blues?' he muttered. Back from the grave, but still a Philistine.

West Fifty-fifth was as narrow as most of the trans-avenue

streets are in Midtown Manhattan. The Shoreham Hotel wasn't hard to find; its sign hung out over the street and a modern, fairly tasteless steel canopy hung over the entrance. I caught Prim frowning. 'Hey,' she exclaimed, 'we were near here this morning. The Carnegie's just round the corner.'

'Too bad Maddy didn't fancy chicken soup and matzoh balls for breakfast,' I grunted back at her, 'or you might have saved me a trip.'

We went into the bar by mistake before we found the reception desk. When we did, it was staffed by a couple of young ladies who seemed to be doing their best to bristle with efficiency.

'Hi there,' I said, giving them my best smile, 'we're looking for a friend. I believe she may be staying here. The problem is, we're not sure what name she's travelling under. Her Christian name, though, is Madeleine, Maddy for short. You can't miss her: she's tall, looks mid-thirties, although it may say different on her passport, and she has sensational auburn hair, like in the L'Oréal ads.'

The older of the two receptionists, a chubby black girl, nodded. 'From the description, that would be Mrs Lee.' She broke off for a few seconds to refer to a computer terminal. 'Yeah, that's Mrs Madeleine Lee, travelling on a Singapore passport. She was our guest.'

'Was?'

'Yes, sir, I'm afraid she checked out midday.'

'Damn,' I whispered, and then I saw her smile.

'Would you be Mr Blackstone?' she asked. 'The movie star?'

I gave her my Gary Cooper. 'Yup.'

'She left something for you.'

'She did?'

'Yes, sir. She said that if Oz Blackstone came looking for her, I should give you this.' She took a hotel envelope from under the desk and held it out. 'I thought she was maybe a little crazy,' the receptionist confessed, as I took it from her.

'This is New York,' I reminded her. 'It takes a lot to count as crazy here.'

Mike and Prim watched me as I turned my back on the desk and opened Maddy's gift. It was lightly sealed and peeled back at the touch of a finger. There was a single sheet of paper inside, folded twice. It was only rough, a file that most probably had been copied on to a computer, printed, then, I guessed, deleted. It had been done on ordinary paper, not high quality, but I knew what it was, almost before I glanced at it. When I did I saw red robes; that was enough. I refolded it quickly and slid it back into the envelope, then pocketed it.

'What's that about?' Dylan asked.

'It's why I'm here. I think it's a warning to leave her alone.' I looked at the girl behind the counter. 'The chambermaids didn't find a body in her room, did they?'

She stared at me as if I was the crazy one. 'No, Mr Blackstone,' she murmured uncertainly.

'That makes a change,' I told her.

'Another cold trail,' said Mike, grimly.

'Not necessarily.'

I walked through a door to the left of the desk, back out on to the street. What passed for a doorman was on duty there, a guy with a West Indian look, wearing a long jacket and a leather pork-pie hat. 'Were you here at noon?' I asked him.

'Yes, mon,' he drawled, confirming my guess about his origins.

'A woman left here then; striking, tall, with long dark hair.'

'I remember the lady. I got her a cab.'

I gave him twenty bucks, up front: I didn't want him making up a story just to get his hands on it. 'Do you remember where she went?'

'Sure, mon. She asked for Penn Station, that's Thirty-third and Seventh.'

I slipped him another twenty. 'Thanks, mate.' He'd told me where she was going.

40

Dylan ducked out of dinner: he said he was knackered, but I wasn't sure. I reckon he'd been at enough tables with Prim and me.

I told him that if he wanted to be part of the continuing adventure, he should meet me at the Algonquin at ten thirty next morning, with an overnight bag as we'd be going on a trip for a day or two.

'In at the death, eh?' He grinned. 'You don't think I'd miss that, do you? Make it eleven thirty, though. I'm not an early riser these days.'

'Me too,' Prim piped up. 'I'm coming.'

'I know you are,' I told her. 'You might have a part to play in this unfolding drama.'

Dylan headed for the subway, while my good buddy on the door got Prim and me a cab. We went back to the hotel and to the Round Table restaurant. The Oak Room had been our favourite when we had been there before, but there's no cabaret in July, and that's why you go there.

We both knew what we wanted without looking at the menu: lump crab cocktail and spring chicken pot pie, with a bottle of Ruffino Pinot Grigio. The waiter gave us a nod of approval, always a good sign. That was how it worked out.

'Well, Tom's mum,' I said, as the last of the chicken disappeared from her plate; Prim could eat for Scotland. 'How do you feel?'

She looked at me. 'Now I'm properly back in the world?' I

nodded. 'Settled,' she replied. 'Oddly content. I don't know what the rest of my life holds for me, but I don't give a damn because I've got my son and I know he's well loved and looked after even when he's not with me. There's more too.' She laid her hand on mine. 'The way things are, it keeps me involved in your life. I really hated it when I wasn't; that's how I got so bitter and twisted and vengeful. I'm sorry for that, but please, love, don't shut me out again. You can't deny it, we share something, you and I. We've got a bond. We're joined in . . .'

'Wickedness,' I finished it for her. 'You're the bad cherub and I'm the devil.'

'That's a bit hard on both of us.'

'If that were only true, baby. Remember that man in Geneva.'

'That was different: he was trying to kill us.'

'More fool him, then.' Our eyes met and we both smiled . . . wickedly: we were talking about the death of another human, and grinning.

'Hold on, though,' she said, 'we can't be all that bad. We made Tom, after all.'

'That's true. We're going to have to keep a close eye on that boy as he grows up.' I finished the Pinot Grigio.

'What about you and the girl in Singapore?' Prim asked suddenly. 'You were taking a chance, with Mike around.'

'I didn't take any chances. Nothing happened. It's all in Dylan's lurid imagination. I'm giving Marie a part in the movie of his book.'

'He said you had her on the casting couch.'

'He's dreaming.'

'You fancied her a bit, though; admit it.'

'No. I fancied her a lot, but she's a nice, proper girl and nothing happened.'

'My God,' she chuckled, 'am I listening to Oz Blackstone?'

'You are now.'

She looked at me for a while. 'You want to know what I think?' she whispered, as if someone was eavesdropping, although there were no other occupied tables within earshot.

'Would it matter if I said no?'

'Not a bit. I know you love Susie; that's beyond question. But one of the reasons you do is because she's safe, sound, solid, loyal and reliable. Did I say safe? Well, I'll say it again, because that's what you crave the most these days, safety. But in truth, you're going against your nature: you might not be the devil, but you've got some of him in you. You can act the wholesome home boy all you like, my love, and show the world your funny, user-friendly face, but you can't hide the other one from me.'

I said nothing as we walked to the lift to go up to our rooms. But I knew full well that she was right. And so I stopped trying.

41

Next morning, after a deli breakfast in the Stage, just along from the Carnegie on Seventh Avenue, we went for a walk in the park; Central Park, that is. The place used to have a bad reputation, and maybe you still shouldn't venture in too deep after dark, but on a sunny Saturday morning in summer, as Manhattan is rising into wakefulness, it's an absolutely beautiful place to be.

I looked around, and upwards: it's important to look up as you walk at the spectacular skyline that surrounds it, a jagged line of buildings like the Essex House, the Plaza Hotel and, most recently, the towers at Columbus Circle.

I was wearing jeans and my last T-shirt. Prim was in a halter top, her midriff bare, and in a pair of shorts so tight that she couldn't have slid a postage stamp into the pockets. At some point I realised that we were holding hands, and in public too, but I wasn't bothered. It didn't mean anything in the greater scheme of things, and Primavera had hit the nail on the head about that bond between us. I've had three wives, and my relationship with each has been special and unique in its own way.

I found myself telling her the truth that I'd discovered about Jan. I don't know why I did that, for what I was doing was adding to the power that she had over me. Maybe I wanted that. Maybe I needed an excuse for giving in to her and her whims. She wasn't shocked when I told her. All she did was shrug her shoulders and say, 'Mac's a very attractive man, even in his mid-sixties. Forty years ago he could probably have pulled half of Fife if he'd had a mind to. If he was anything like you, he probably did.'

Prim wanted to take a ride in a buggy, but I vetoed that for two reasons. We didn't have time, although we could have kept Dylan waiting, but most of all I had no desire to spend any part of my day staring at a horse's arse, watching it fill the bucket, which, in New York, they tie to its tail. I wonder if that was an election pledge of Mayors Bloomberg or Giuliani: 'Vote for me and I'll keep the streets shit-free.'

We'd both checked out of the hotel when Dylan arrived, and my wardrobe had been swelled by a few items I'd bought in a clothing store on Sixth. They were packed away in a new cabin bag: I may possess a world-record number of small suitcases on wheels, such is the unpredictable nature of my life, but my inherent Fife instinct never allows me to throw anything out while there's another mile left in it.

There were more than a few miles left in the car that the boys from Hertz delivered. It was a Cadillac De Ville, complete with satellite navigation, something I never go without in the US.

'So, where are we heading?' Mike asked, from the back seat.

'Not all that far, actually: we're off for a drive in the country. I'm told that it's very pretty, although I've never been there.'

'Try me with a clue.'

'Have patience, my boy.'

'Since it's in the country, might there be lots of wild geese around?' Prim put in.

'No, but I'm betting that we'll find a pretty bedraggled bird, who's flown a hell of a long way to get there.'

I kept them guessing as we set off, crossing Sixth, Seventh and Eighth, before taking a left turn and heading for the Lincoln Tunnel ramp that headed to New Jersey. I cruised on, letting the navigation system take charge and obeying its commands as it guided me on to I-95, heading for Newark.

I drove slowly, below the speed limit, enjoying the comfort of the Caddy on the frenetic highway. We'd been on the road for around forty-five minutes when I took one exit then another and joined US-1 heading for New Brunswick and Princeton.

'I spoke to Maddy's mother,' I told my companions, finally letting them in on our destination. 'She has an older sister who's a professor at the university down here.'

'And you think that's where she's headed?' Dylan said sceptically.

'This is her last bolt-hole, the way I see it.'

'What about back home to dear old Mum?'

'She's forgotten how to get there, going by what Mrs Raymond said. There's no fatted calf grazing in the garden in Uxbridge, waiting for the chop. Besides, she wasn't in London yesterday, she was in New York.'

We had run out of the urban sprawl of northern New Jersey, and into leafy countryside, the way I had been told it would be. A few months before I'd been invited to take part in a debate organised by one of the university drama clubs. I'd almost accepted, but it fell into a period where a movie schedule might have overrun, and I didn't want to have to withdraw: bad for the image.

After a few miles the car told me to turn off the highway, then take a right on to Washington Road. We drove past the university football stadium on the right and on until I was directed left on to Nassau Street, and immediately left again. We stopped on command, right outside Nassau Hall, the university's main office. Bloody marvellous, these systems, aren't they? Sure, but there's always a downside. We were International Rescue, on the trail of a damsel in distress, but if we'd been the forces of darkness, well, our sinister mission had just been made a lot easier. Nowadays even the Keystone Cops can get where they're going without mishap.

'So this is Ivy League?' said Prim, as she slid out of the front passenger seat into the sunny morning.

'I believe so.' I looked around. It was the leafiest town I'd ever seen in America, all neat brick and clapboard buildings, much more rural than Oxford or Cambridge . . . or Cambridge, Massachusetts, where Harvard, Princeton's greatest rival, is located.

It was also very quiet.

That's when it dawned on my companions that the mastermind who was running the operation had failed to account for the fact that universities tend to be on vacation in July and even more so on any given Saturday. The bloody office was closed, wasn't it?

'So what do we do now, Clouseau?' Dylan growled.

'You're the fucking author, Benny,' I shot back. 'Make something up.'

'Let's go for lunch,' he proposed. 'When we find a place, we'll ask for a telephone directory. That may provide what we mystery writers sometimes call a clue.'

We climbed back into the Cadillac. I didn't bother with the clever system this time. Instead I headed along Nassau Street, until Prim spotted a seafood place called the Blue Point Grill. They were still serving and we were very lucky, the waiter told us, because they had two tables left. They also had a telephone directory, which contained no listings for either 'Raymond, T.' or 'Raymond, Professor'; there was only one and his forename was Norman.

'She may commute,' Prim suggested. 'She may not live anywhere near the campus.'

'No. Her mother definitely said that she comes here for Thanksgiving every year.'

'Why don't you call her and ask for her address?'

'That's a last resort. I don't want to have to explain what's going on to the old lady. She's got enough trouble with her son facing a stretch inside.'

'You could ask him,' Dylan volunteered. 'You know where he is.'

'The last thing Trevor said to me had the word "fuck" in it. I don't imagine he'd react any differently. We'll ask around here before we get to Plan C.'

The food was good, but the information was lousy. They didn't know Theresa Raymond, and if she was anyone important in

Princeton, they were sure they would have. 'Unless she's allergic to seafood,' I said to the waiter.

'I've never met anyone who's allergic to seafood,' he replied.

'Maybe that's because you work in a fish restaurant.'

We left no wiser than we had come in, but Prim had a bright idea. We should split up and go into as many shops as we could until we found someone who knew the Prof, and could point us at her. She volunteered to do the dress shops. Surprise?

We agreed to meet in front of the Blue Point Grill in an hour for an update on progress. I crossed the street and started walking, feeling more than a little daft. I tried a pharmacist first: she was a woman, so she must need . . . things; makeup and stuff . . . and the campus was nearby. They had no clue; I could have asked the people in there for the time and they'd have had trouble. I tried a hardware store: as far as I knew Theresa Raymond lived alone, so she probably handled her own DIY. If she did, she didn't shop there.

I almost walked past the Cloak and Dagger bookstore. In fact, I would have, if I hadn't spotted in the window *Lethal Intent*, the brand new Skinner novel I'd begun at Ellie's. Alongside it a sign, 'signed by the author'. I'd met the guy, when we did the movies of the first two books.

I went inside; the place was neat, and full of well-displayed stock. 'Have I just missed him?' I asked the lady behind the counter, as I handed her the book. She wore a name-tag which identified her as 'Aline Lenaz, proprietor'.

'No,' she admitted. 'These were signed in London. He has been here, though; last year, in fact.' She took a closer look at me. 'Aren't you . . .?'

Instead of replying, I handed her a credit card. 'What brings you to Princeton?' she asked.

I'd taken a punt once before in a bookstore and it had paid off. In my experience, such as it is, the independents stand or fall on the strength of their mailing list. The ones that make it keep in touch with their regulars at every opportunity. There's a place I use in Westwood Village, Los Angeles, and I'm often invited to in-store events there.

'I'm trying to find somebody,' I told her. 'She's the sister of a lady I know, and I promised I'd look her up, but being basically disorganised I've lost the damn address.'

'What's her name?'

'Raymond, Professor Raymond. She teaches philosophy at the university.'

The woman's friendly face lit up. 'Ah, Trey. Theresa Raymond, she lives at seventeen Mimosa Avenue. She's one of my best customers, reads a lot of Sarah Paretsky, Val McDermid, Patricia Cornwell.' She tapped *Lethal Intent* as she bagged it. 'And this guy, too.'

'How do I find her?'

'Easy. You go along Nassau past the main campus, until it becomes Stockton. Then you turn right into Elm Road. Mimosa Avenue is second left.' She handed me a credit-card slip and a pen. 'That's how you find her house,' she said as I signed, 'but you won't find Trey. She's on vacation or, rather, a lecture tour, in India.'

'Damn,' I muttered. 'I should have phoned her. Of course, I don't have the number either, do I?'

'I can give you that.' She took a bookmark, wrote on the back and handed it to me. I thanked her, and took my purchase. I was about to leave when she asked if she could have a photo taken with me to go on a board at the back of the store. Naturally, I agreed. 'Jerry!' she called. A tall slim guy came out of a back office. 'My husband,' Aline said. 'And photographer.'

I was really pleased with myself when I left. The team leader had come up trumps. I walked back towards the Blue Point, and saw Prim standing there waiting for me. 'Mimosa Avenue,' I told her.

'I know. I found her hairdresser.'

We'd have had to wait another half-hour for Dylan, but I

spotted him coming out of a coffee shop and gave him my best piercing whistle. 'Any luck?' I asked, as he drew close.

'Not a bit.'

'Just as well you're with us, then. Come on.'

42

If I'm ever a Princeton academic, and my life has been so strange that I will never discount the possibility, I'll want to live in a place like Mimosa Avenue. It was quiet, it was secluded, it was exactly the sort of place you would want to hide out if you were on the run from a murderous gang . . . and from a movie star.

We sat in the Caddy, parked outside number six, with a clear view of Trey Raymond's place. It was a white two-storey house, the sort of dwelling I'd hire as a location if I was making a movie and needed a home for a model American family. But it was still and silent: nothing was moving, the garage door was closed and there were no toys, or anything else, in the yard.

'And now?' asked Prim. 'We go up and ring the doorbell?'

'That would be a very bad idea,' Dylan, in serious mode once more, told her. 'The last guy who walked in on this lady had a gun placed against the back of his head and his right eye blown out.'

'So? We just sit here? Which one of you two guys is Dumb and which one is Dumber?'

'Neither,' I said. 'This is what we do.' I took out my mobile, checked the signal strength, then keyed in the number Aline had given me. The phone at the other end rang, ten times, unanswered. I disconnected and tried again. The fourth time I called, it was picked up, on the sixth ring.

'Yes? Is that you, Trey?'

'Maddy,' I said, as gently as I could, 'why the fuck are you running from me?'

'You bastard!' she screamed. 'Leave me alone. Come near me and I'll kill you too.'

'I'm not going to come near you if you don't want me to. But I want you to tell me why you're acting like this. We made a deal in Singapore, remember? I'm ready to complete: I've got fifty thousand dollars with me right now, as agreed.'

'Sure,' she snarled. 'And when I show up to meet you, someone else is waiting, your other hired killer.'

'What the fuck are you talking about?'

'What happened to Tony?' she shouted. 'What happened to my husband? Are you telling me he isn't dead?'

'I'd love to be able to tell you that, Maddy, but if I did I'd be lying. Tony was killed in the Next Page, when he turned up to meet me, like you just said. Somebody was waiting for him. If Tony had the film, I guess he took it after he stabbed him.' I heard her sobbing. 'If it's any consolation in the long term, you killed the guy on Dayang.'

'And now the Malaysian police will be after me for murder. Very neat, Oz. If I escape from you, they hang me.'

'The Malaysian police aren't after anyone, Maddy. Sammy Goss had a very quick funeral at sea, well away from where the scuba-divers will ever go. Maddy, think about this: he had a cool box with him, and you know what that was for. Suppose I did want you killed, a huge overreaction by the way. When you consider the size of the threat you pose to my brother-in-law, why the fuck would I want your head? If I'd sent Sammy, I'd have told him to take a photograph of you dead, for Christ's sake. That would have been all the proof I'd have needed. It's the Triads who go in for extravagant gestures.'

I looked at Prim as I spoke. 'Ouch!' she mouthed. 'You'll terrify her.'

I ignored her. 'Why, Maddy? Why would I do that?'

'I saw you with him,' she blurted out. 'I watched you all the way up the hill at Fort Siloso. I watched you, with him and your other heavy. Then they went and hid and you met me

270

on your own. You were showing them what I looked like.'

'Is that why you didn't turn up at the Next Page?'

'No. I trusted you then. It was Tony who didn't. He wouldn't let me go; he insisted on making the trade himself, and he went armed. He sent me on ahead to Dayang, and told me that he'd pick me up from there in a boat and we'd cross to Vietnam.'

'That's five hundred miles.'

'We could have done it in three days. But we didn't, though, did we? Because it wasn't Tony who showed up, it was your man, the little fair-haired guy. I watched him go to Aur, then head across to me in Dayang. When he got close enough I recognised him, and I realised that this wasn't about me photographing some Triad boss, at least not any more. It was about you, taking care of family business.'

I sighed. 'Maddy, everything I know about these guys, and everything I've learned since we met, tells me that you were right to be terrified. You were in huge danger, and you still are. You're right to run, but you're dead wrong to believe you're running from me. I didn't know what Sammy Goss was. I didn't find him, he found me, and I still haven't figured out how or why. I want you to trust me and to meet me again.'

'Where are you?'

'If you come to the window and look to your right, you'll see a car.'

'I'm coming to no fucking window!' she screeched. 'I show myself and I'm picked off. Oz, I promise you, as soon as you step into this house, you or anyone else, I'll kill you. I have another gun, my sister's gun, and I'll shoot the first person who comes near me.'

'Okay, okay, I'm not going to rush you. You're paranoid, woman, but you probably have a right to be. So I'm going to propose something else. I'm going to send someone across, someone you knew when you were in Edinburgh.' I looked at Prim: I'd had a feeling it might come to this. She nodded. 'She won't be armed; given what she's wearing, you'll be able to see

271

that. I want you to let her in, and let her talk to you. She'll be your hostage if you want to look at it that way. She'll even bring the money if you like.'

'I don't want your fucking money!' she snapped. 'I want to stay alive.'

'Then let me do this, and you've got a chance.'

I listened to her breathing. I felt Prim's eyes on me, and Dylan's, but I kept mine fixed on the house, looking for anything, the faintest twitch of a blind or curtain.

'Okay,' Maddy said eventually. 'Send her across. But no tricks, or her brains will be all over the hall.'

I ended the call and turned to Prim. 'She's says she's armed and we have to believe her,' I told her. 'Plus, she's very emotional. If you say no, I'll drive away right now, but I don't know what we do to help her after that.'

'You give me as long as it takes,' she replied. 'While I'm in there, you do not phone again. If either of you gets out of the car, you keep your hands where they can be seen from the house at all times.'

'All of the above,' I murmured.

She squeezed my hand, leaned over and kissed me quickly on the cheek, then opened her door and slid out.

We watched her as she walked away from us, her brown body seeming to glow with health, her hips moving rhythmically, encased within the skin-hugging shorts.

We watched her as she stopped at the door of number seventeen. Almost at once, it opened. 'There's only one place she could possibly be carrying a weapon,' said Dylan, as she stepped inside, with a flash of the crudity for which he had been famous in Scotland, 'but no way could she ever get it out in time.'

43

We waited there for thirty-seven minutes. I know this because I must have checked my watch at least thirty-seven times. My patience control was set at one out of ten, but I managed to keep it in check. After half an hour I stepped out of the car, laying my hands on the roof as Prim had specified. The metal was burning hot, but I didn't care: it gave me something else to think about.

I jumped when my phone rang. I snatched it from my pocket and flipped it open. 'Yes? I snapped.

'Hey,' Susie exclaimed, 'what's with you?'

'Can't talk now, love,' I said. 'We're almost there. I'll call you when it's all sorted.'

It rang again two minutes later, and this time it was Prim, calling from the house. 'Okay,' she whispered. 'Maddy says you can come in, but only you.'

'Sorry, pal,' I said to Mike. 'You're not invited.' He wasn't bothered. He'd started on my book; looking for ideas, I supposed.

I crossed the street quickly and took the steps in front of the house three at a time. Prim opened the door for me. Maddy was in a sitting room to the left of the entrance hall. She bore no resemblance to the assertive, well-groomed woman I'd met on Sentosa Island; even her hair was a mess. A gun lay on a coffee-table, a big Colt automatic, forty-five gauge at least. I'd fired one in a movie, blank rounds. If she'd tried to use it, the recoil would have taken it right out of her hand.

I held up both of mine. 'Hello,' I began. 'I am the Lone Ranger, honest. Tonto's out in the car.'

After everything that had happened to her, she managed a laugh. A weak one, but I took it as something positive, a sign that she didn't feel alone any more.

'What do I do now, Oz?' she asked.

'Whatever I say, would be a good place to begin. I think we should all get out of here. This is a dead end, Maddy, we don't want to be cornered.'

'Where do we go?'

'Anywhere out of Princeton. Pack what stuff you have, and let's move. We can make decisions on the road.'

'Will I be safer?'

'Sure. The Triads may be looking for you, but they're not after me. With me, you're less visible.'

She agreed, and she didn't have a lot to pack. We were heading out of Princeton inside ten minutes. She was going to leave a note for her sister but I vetoed that. Just in case the opposition arrived and broke in (classic security: the key had been under a big flowerpot in the back garden) I didn't want to leave any clue that she'd been there.

I decided against going back to New York. Instead I went back to Highway One and headed south for Trenton, the state capital, less than fifteen miles away. We didn't shop around for a hotel: I spotted a big Marriott, almost on the Delaware River, which at that point divides New Jersey from Pennsylvania. We headed straight there.

We took three rooms; Madeleine wanted Prim to share with her, but there was no way I was bunking with Dylan. I filled out the registration forms, using phoney names (I registered Maddy as Ms April July and the clerk didn't bat an eyelid) and hoping that I wasn't as famous in Trenton as I was in most other places. I paid for two nights up-front, cash.

Once we were settled in, I went out and bought a case of beer from a liquor store I'd seen on the way in. Back in the hotel I called the girls' room; they'd showered by that time, so I went along. I opened a beer, handed it to Maddy and she guzzled it like

274

she'd been dying of thirst. I gave her another; that went the same way. Half-way through the third, there was a knock at the door, and Prim let Dylan in. He'd brought some Miller's; great minds and all that stuff.

'Were you and Tony really married?' I asked, when everyone was relaxed.

Maddy nodded. 'We did it in Singapore. They can be a bit old-fashioned about living together over there. Plus, I loved him.'

'I'm sorry.'

'He was a gangster, Oz,' she said philosophically. 'I suppose danger comes with the job. If he'd bothered to tell me . . .'

'What?'

'I'd probably have stayed with him. As it was, he loved me. He gave up his life trying to protect me.' She started to sob quietly. 'If only I wasn't so pathologically jealous. I had a bad experience with that Australian faggot, Sandy. When Tony started keeping odd hours, I thought the worst . . . and the worst happened, although not as I'd imagined.' She killed her third can. I gave her another. 'Now,' she belched quietly as she tore it open, 'I'm royally fucked. Tony didn't leave me in any doubt about these people. They will keep coming.'

'Then we'll have to stop them,' I said.

She sighed. 'And just how are we going to do that?'

'Good question,' Dylan chipped in.

'If you're writing this book,' I asked him, 'what happens?'

'Fuck knows,' he said wonderfully tactlessly. 'Maddy keeps on running or, like I said in jest a while back, lives with me in New York till the heat's off?'

Madeleine scowled at him: clearly she didn't fancy that idea.

I leaned back against the headboard of Prim's bed. She was reclining beside me, wrapped in a hotel dressing-gown. 'Way I see it,' I took time to kill some beer of my own, 'there's only one thing you can do to break the cycle. You've still got these pics, am I right?' She nodded. 'Stored on a PDA?'

'Clever boy.'

'Then use the power they give you.'

'What do you mean?'

I laughed at her amazing ability to think in everything but a straight line. 'Maddy, why do these people want to kill you? What did Tony tell you? The man you saw with him, the man in the photographs: his identity is unknown to anyone outside his organisation. The Singaporean government has been trying to identify him for years, and shut him down, but they can't because he's too strong, and too clever. At least he was, until you came stumbling into his life.'

'So?'

'So put an end to him. Use the fucking knowledge: give the photographs to the Singapore police.'

She stared at me. So did Dylan: I'd just written a new twist into his book. (By the way, Maddy thought that his name really was Benedict Luker.)

'It's that simple?' she exclaimed.

'Nothing in life is that simple, but it's all you can do unless you fancy sharing Benny's humble loft for the foreseeable future.'

She frowned. 'But I'm in New Jersey,' she murmured. 'I'm not going back to Sing, Oz. I can't do that.'

I shook my head. 'You don't need to,' I told her. 'I'll arrange for Sing to come to you.'

44

By the time Maddy had been convinced, with Prim's help, I have to say, that she had run out of healthy options, it had gone eight thirty. We ordered room-service sandwiches and ate them in virtual silence.

Pretty soon, the effects of the beer started to show on Madeleine. I motioned to Dylan that we should leave the girls to settle down for the night, and led him back to my room. I did a quick calculation and reckoned that it would be mid-morning in Singapore; Sunday morning, granted, but the guy I was planning to call wasn't the type to go off watch, ever.

As we'd done in the Stamford, I put the hotel phone on hands-free mode and dialled Jimmy Tan's mobile number. I'd been wrong: there was no answer. We watched some baseball on TV, then I tried him again an hour later. This time I came up lucky.

'Who this?' he asked suspiciously. The readout on his cell-phone wasn't giving him any clues.

'Oz Blackstone and Benny Luker,' I told him.

'Ah, you guys. You still chase the lady? If you find her tell her from me there no problem with that thing in Malaysia.'

'We have found her, Jimmy.'

His chuckle filled the room. 'There no escape from you bad boys,' he said. 'But so what?'

'So plenty,' Dylan cut in. 'She has something you've been trying to get your hands on for years, and she's ready to hand it over.'

'What she got that I would want?'

'The picture that started all this off: the one of Tony Lee and the Triad chieftain. We assumed that he had burned it with all the rest, and maybe he did, but Maddy made another copy, on computer.' We could hear Tan's gasp.

'You serious?'

'Never more so,' I told him.

'This is great news; I tell the prime minister about this.'

'You don't tell anybody, Jimmy,' Mike insisted, 'until you have the pictures in your hands and until Maddy's well clear of pursuit.'

'Okay, he can wait. Where are you?'

'We're in the US; Trenton, New Jersey. How soon can you get to us?'

'Oz, I never leave South East Asia. I send someone, my most trusted person.'

'Jimmy, we want to deal with you.'

'I send you my right hand. You want me cut off real one, send that as proof?'

I looked at Dylan. He shrugged and nodded. 'Okay,' I conceded. 'What do we do?'

'Where is nearest airport?'

'There's one in here in Trenton,' Dylan volunteered. 'I saw a sign for it as we came into the city.'

'Then that where we meet; you find meeting room in terminal, my person find you, give you letter of introduction from me. You hand over photos and have plane waiting; soon as it's done, you all get hell out of there, you, woman . . .' he paused '. . . and Mr Luker.'

'Why?' I asked.

'Simple precaution, Oz,' Mike said. 'Jimmy doesn't like to admit it, but the Triads are everywhere and there's an outside chance they've penetrated his organisation. If his messenger has been followed, well, we don't want to get caught there. Right, Jimmy?'

'Right,' Tan growled. 'But only very outside chance.'

'We won't risk it, though,' I decided. 'I'll have a private jet on the ground ready to move. When?'

'It long flight, Singapore to eastern seaboard.' He was silent, calculating. 'Sunday morning here now, maybe can't get on a plane tonight. Make it six, Monday evening, USA time.'

'Right; we'll be ready.' I frowned, as if he could see me. 'When you get these photographs, Jimmy, you will shut these people down, won't you?'

'Oz,' he chuckled, 'they not know what hit them.'

45

The waiting, again. Tom Petty and the Heartbreakers were singing in my brain all that night and all through Sunday. Maddy never left her room, and she was never left alone either. The security bolt was on all night and during the day either Mike or I was always with her.

I left all the arrangements until the Monday morning as a tiny piece of extra security. They didn't take long to make. I booked a twelve-seater Gulfstream jet, to be on the ground and fuelled up by five thirty, ready to take off on command, destination Newark, ready to connect with a British Airways flight to Heathrow for Mrs Primavera Blackstone, Ms Madeleine January and me, and with the train to Penn Station for Mr Benedict Luker.

The terminal building at Trenton Mercer Airport is very small, they told me, but they did have a VIP room which they'd be happy to prepare for the private use of my party and me prior to our flight.

The charter company wanted passenger names in advance: a TSA requirement, they said. I gave them mine, Prim's and Benny's, and they didn't quibble over the fourth member of the group, Doe, Jane, Ms.

When all that was done, I left Mike guarding our charge and took my ex-wife for a walk, a tour of the State Capitol building, an impressive pile, which is, they say, the second oldest in the US. Neither of us was really interested, though: there were things, I sensed, that we wanted, no, needed, to say to each other, but they'd take more time than we had available.

That's the trouble with the really important things, and time. Too often, there isn't enough of it; too often, it's the wrong moment. That, of course, just ain't true. For matters important enough, there's always enough time; there's never a wrong moment.

But, as it was, we wiled away a couple of hours, looking at old stones in silence, until it was time to gather the team and get the show on the road.

I drove us the short distance to the airport in the rental car. I'd arranged for Hertz to collect it. It was five forty when we arrived, were greeted by the airport manager and shown into our private room. As he left us, Madeleine stepped up to me. She kissed my cheek, and slipped a small square envelope into the breast pocket of my shirt. 'Just a little card,' she whispered, 'to say sorry and thanks for everything.'

We sat on our hands for the next twenty minutes. I'd set the alarm on my watch for six exactly. Everybody jumped when it went off.

Two more minutes went by, before we heard a soft knock on the door. I went across, opened it, and almost cried out in my surprise. Standing there in a silk dress with a slit up the side, a bag over her shoulder and her letter of introduction clutched in her hand was Marie Lin. 'What the hell?' I gasped.

'My father sent me,' she said. 'He trusts nobody in the world more than me.'

46

When I stood aside to allow her into the room, I could see the flash of astonishment in Mike's eyes, but he controlled it well, and didn't let it transfer to his mouth.

She insisted that I read her letter of introduction, and I went along with it. The notepaper bore the embossed crest of the Government of Singapore.

Dear Oz [it began],
Allow me to introduce formally my daughter, Tan May Wee, who is my emissary in this matter. I apologise if this has come as a surprise to you, but I ask you to accept that when one's father is head of the security police it is wise to pursue one's profession under an assumed name.

Marie is indeed an aspiring actress, and she was very honoured to make your acquaintance in Singapore, although she was unaware, until I told her of the incident in the Next Page, that you had made mine.

She is a good, brave woman, and you may trust her to complete our mission properly and to return the material safely to me, so that use may be made of it.
Yours truly
Jimmy

When I'd finished, I passed it to Mike; he read it in turn, unsmiling, then put it back into its envelope and handed it back to me.

'Okay,' I said to Maddy. 'This is Marie, the agent of the Singapore security service, and she's here to take charge of your pictures. So, hand them over and let's get the hell out of here.'

She looked at me, almost gratefully, then reached into her bag, removed an HP personal organiser, a state-of-the-art model, and handed it over. 'Go to "Home" then "Pictures" if you want to see them,' she offered.

'My father said I must not look at them,' Marie told her, 'for my own safety.' She switched off the palmtop and removed the memory card from its slot. 'They are stored here?' Maddy nodded. 'Then that will be sufficient.' She handed back the wee silver computer.

'Good,' I said. 'Now, come on. Let's board the jet.'

A second door in the VIP room led directly on to the tarmac. I opened it, and found the co-pilot waiting outside. 'If you'll come with me,' he said. He was a big, beefy lad with a blond crew-cut. His ID said he was called Scott, and he looked as if, at some point in his college career, he could have been a pretty effective nose tackle.

Mike took each of the girls by the elbow and steered them after the officer towards the Gulfstream, which was parked only thirty yards away. They wheeled their luggage and his was slung over his shoulder. I waited in the doorway with Marie. 'I want to thank you for this,' I told her, 'and your father. You've saved a woman's life here.'

She looked at me as she had as she disappeared down the escalator at the Clarke Quay MRT station, the last time I'd seen her. 'Then thank me,' she whispered. 'Stay behind with me for a while. I know you well enough now.'

I felt a tiny shudder run through me. I almost turned and walked away, as I bloody well should have done. Instead I looked at her, or maybe the devil in me looked at her. Again, I almost turned away, and then I heard inside my head a voice, crystal clear, a voice I'd known all my life: Jan's voice, my sister's voice, my soul-mate's voice.

'*You can trust this girl,*' it said. '*You can trust her with your life.*'

I turned and looked towards the plane. The other three were on board, and Scott was standing at the top of the steps. 'Go on without me,' I shouted to him. 'I've changed my mind. I'll drive the hire car back to New York.'

'Very good, sir,' he called back, then stepped inside and closed the door behind him.

A few seconds later the plane began its taxi. As it pulled away, the last thing I saw was Prim's face, framed in a small round window. I could see mischief in her eyes; I could almost hear her chuckle.

47

I drove us back to the hotel and checked in again. If the desk clerk was surprised, he didn't say so, even when I checked in under a different false name than the one I'd used before. I suppose that in Trenton, New Jersey, they see many things.

Marie began to undress as soon as I closed the door. I watched her as she slipped her shoulders out of the silk dress and let it fall to the floor. I watched her as she slipped off her thong with her thumbs.

And then it was my turn.

I made love to her slowly, very gently, taking my time, as I sensed she wanted. She winced a little when I entered her, and I realised she was a virgin, only the second I'd ever been with. I held nothing back; I gave her the best I could. Maybe here I should lie to you, and say that it was magical: yes, maybe I should, but it wasn't. It was just all right, for me at least, although she wouldn't have known if it had been cannon-fire, she'd nothing to set me against.

I told her it had been wonderful, though; well, you do, don't you, if there's anything of the gentleman about you? After a while, we did it again, and this time, Marie contributed more, although I could tell that she was making it up as she went along, trying to please me as best she could.

About ten minutes before ten, she got up. 'I have to go downstairs,' she said, as she headed for the bathroom. 'I need things for morning. There's a pharmacy across the street.'

'I'll go,' I volunteered. 'You stay here.'

She smiled at me. 'Don't be silly. You can't shop for what woman needs.'

I watched her again, as she dressed this time. It didn't take long. When she was ready she picked up her bag and stepped through the door, closing it behind her.

I lay there for a while, still naked, wondering what the hell I'd done, and where it was going, if anywhere. I think I began to feel ashamed, but as it turned out I didn't have time to dwell on it.

To divert my thoughts, I picked up the television remote and switched it on. The hotel menu popped up on screen; I pushed a number at random and found myself watching more bloody baseball. I moved on to the next channel.

'Blackstone.' My name came out at me; I was watching the local CBS station and they were talking about me. 'I repeat,' said the announcer, 'our breaking news story. English movie star Oz Blackstone is believed to have died tonight when a private jet crashed in a New Jersey swamp, *en route* for Newark Airport.

'He was one of four passengers on the chartered Gulfstream when it came down. Emergency services report that so far five bodies have been recovered, those of the two pilots, the flight attendant, a woman as yet unnamed, and the promising New York mystery writer, Mr Benedict Luker. Police and fire-fighters are still searching for the remains of Mr Blackstone and of his former wife, Mrs Primavera Blackstone, the sister of Oscar-nominated Dawn Phillips, wife of Miles Grayson. More news and pictures on this story as it develops.'

48

I suppose I knew then that Marie wasn't coming back. In fact, I guess I knew everything, although it was quite a while before I was able to lie down, quietly and with something approaching rationality, and put all of the pieces together.

At that moment, though, I was struck down, numb with grief. Primavera was dead. I could have stayed behind for another night in Trenton with her, rather than with Marie. I had been thinking about that in the State Capitol building, and so had she. If either of us had come out with it, said what we were thinking, given voice to our unquenchable lust for each other, then Marie would have been catching the plane back to her father, and Prim would be alive today.

And Maddy was dead: I'd gone to all that trouble to save her life, I'd thought I'd triumphed, but after all my efforts to save her from the gangsters she was still stone dead, crisped in a swamp in New Jersey that had been a Mafia dumping ground for decades. That's a fine irony for you, Blackstone, is it not?

Dylan? Yes, he was dead too, but he'd been fucking dead for years.

The television was still droning on: they had moved on to the day's death toll in Iraq, but I had my own casualty list to grieve over. I forced myself into action. I got up, showered and dressed. Then a horrible thought struck me. I snatched up my cell-phone and called Susie.

It was Conrad Kent who answered. 'I'm sorry,' he said, before I'd had a chance to speak, 'Mrs Blackstone is not taking calls.'

The media jackals were gnawing at my corpse already. 'Shut up,' I shouted at my assistant. 'This is Oz. I wasn't on that fucking plane. Now put me on to my wife.'

It took me a while to calm Susie down. It took me a minute or so to believe truly that it was me speaking to her. Christ, I was so fucked up in my head that I wasn't even a hundred per cent sure myself.

'What happened?' she asked, when she could speak properly.

'The plane must have been sabotaged, somehow. It was flying Maddy to safety but the Triads got to it.'

'So they killed her, after all.'

'Yes, but she wasn't the target,' I told her, even as the first significant part of the truth hit me, clear and ringing as a bell. 'Mike was.'

49

The rest of it didn't even begin to come together until I made it back to New York, driving, dangerously, through the fog that seemed to have spread inside my head. Everything was instinctive. I don't remember anything about the journey. The navigation system was switched off, but I made it on my personal auto-pilot, just heading north and taking signs as they came up.

I must have been burning rubber for it was just after midnight when I drove out of the Lincoln Tunnel and on to Manhattan. I dumped the car in a Hertz drop-off location somewhere in the Forties, shoved the keys and papers at the receiving clerk without a word, took my bags and almost stumbled into the night. I was headed anywhere but towards the Algonquin: I wanted never to go back there, ever again. Still I don't, and I won't.

I walked across to Broadway, then headed south. It was early Monday morning and the city was as quiet as it ever gets, so quiet that some idiot tried to mug me. He was standing in a doorway just past Thirty-eighth; as I passed he pointed a gun at me and told me to give him my wallet. I looked at him, and considered his options. He didn't look drug-crazy enough or scared enough to shoot me, so I snatched the pistol from him, pushed him back deeper into the doorway and beat him bloody, then shoved the barrel up his arse. I'm speaking literally here, folks. I told him, although I doubt if he was hearing anything, that if I turned and saw him crawling out on to the street I'd come back and pull the trigger, then I carried on in my aimless way.

Finally it dawned on me that I'd better get off the street before

I killed somebody, so I checked myself into a hotel on West Thirty-second, just past the Empire. It wasn't much better than a flophouse, and they gave me a room next to the lift-shaft. I don't even remember now what it was called, but it had four walls and a roof, and that was all I wanted. As I lay there in the dark, the shock began to wear off. I began to come to terms (whatever the hell that actually means) with my grief, and I revisited it with a vengeance.

I cried for a while, for quite a while, for Primavera and for the times we had shared together, the good, the bad, the thrilling, the exciting, the downright scary. I cried for the love we had made, and for Tom. Soon I was going to have to tell him that he'd never see his mother again, other than in dreams. I'd try to find the positive side for him, though, when he was old enough, that he'd always see her young and beautiful, and that he wouldn't have to watch her dynamism fade, and her body weaken and wither with age. I never saw that in my mother. I'd never see it with Jan, and I'd never see it with Prim.

It's a terrible curse, being married to me: it's as if you seal your fate when you sign the contract. I have been married three times and two of my wives have died prematurely, at the cold emotionless hand of Fate. Now I live my life in a constant state of fear for Susie, and with the dread that she might carry it too. I've found myself wondering whether I should leave her, for her own good, to try to protect her. But that didn't do Primavera any good, did it?

I thought of all these things as I cried myself out, and then I began to think of what had brought them about, and I began to see more of the truth, beyond that first flash that I'd revealed to Susie.

First and foremost, I knew for sure that Sammy Goss hadn't met us by accident: he'd been sent. Someone had noted my arrival in Sing, someone who knew all about Maddy January, and made the connection with me. Once Goss had latched on to me he hadn't let go.

Only it had been more complicated than that. Something

unexpected had happened. Someone entirely unlooked-for had turned up, and changed some people's priorities.

I knew all these things: they followed a logical and inescapable pattern, yet it was all theory, all fucking Sherlock stuff, with no hard evidence, no reinforced concrete proof.

And yet there was, and I nearly threw it away.

I forced myself upright at eight fifteen next morning. The water pressure in the shower above my bath, its enamel worn almost through by countless thousands of feet, was so poor that it took me ten minutes to do the job according to my standards. I didn't bother to shave: I wasn't ready to look at myself in the mirror.

Back in the bedroom, I took a fresh shirt from my bag. When I had removed it from its wrapping, I picked up the one I had worn the day before, meaning to stuff it into the polythene and toss it all in the waste. But as I crumpled it in my hand, my fingers closed on the forgotten envelope in the pocket, Maddy January's parting thank-you card.

I took it out and opened it. It was inscribed as she had said, but with it there was something else: another tiny square SD disk. 'As a token of good faith,' she had added, 'and maybe a little insurance.'

50

As I stared at it, I felt as if someone had switched me back on. I had purpose again; I had things to do.

The first of those involved breakfast. Somehow I'd managed to skip lunch the day before, and I was starving. I checked out of the dosshouse and took a cab to Seventh and Fifty-fifth. They were between rush-hours in the Carnegie Deli, so I was afforded the luxury of a table on my own. I demolished a Woody Allen (lotsa corned beef, plus lotsa pastrami) and a side order of cinnamon toast, and I was on my second coffee refill when I was aware of a guy peering at me. He wore a white apron; it was too pristine for him to have been a cook, so I guessed that he had to be the owner. 'Hey,' he asked hoarsely, 'ain't you Oz Blackstone?'

I ran my hand over my heavy stubble. 'So the beard didn't fool you.'

'Buddy, you're supposed to be dead. It says so in the *Daily News.*'

'Shit, and I felt fine when I woke up this morning.'

He chuckled. 'Yeah, maybe I should be careful what I believe. They ran another story about a guy found semi-conscious on Broadway with a Smith and Wesson up his ass. I didn't swallow that one, though. No, you maybe don't look so great, Oz, but I reckon you're alive. Tell you what, buddy, how about proving it by sending me a picture for the wall?' (I forgot to mention that the Carnegie is decorated with the autographed photographs of thousands of celebrities who've eaten there over the years.)

'I'll do that,' I promised.

'Great. When you do, be sure to put today's date on it.'

When I'd mopped up the last of the maple syrup with the last of the cinnamon toast, and paid at the counter on the way out, I caught another cab. I'd done some telephone-directory research at the hotel so I was able to ask the driver to take me straight to the British Consulate General, on Third Avenue at East Fifty-first.

I walked in off the street, and asked to see the Consul General and the Press Officer, in that order. The counter clerk looked at me sceptically until I handed over my passport: that got her attention, big-time. I was shown straight in to see the boss.

I kept my story simple.

- I had never been on the plane; I had decided at the last minute to drive the rental back to New York, so I hadn't been aware of the tragedy until I'd been approached in the Carnegie.
- I'd thought the guy was joking until I bought a *Daily News*.
- I had just bought the rights to Benedict Luker's novel, and we had been in Trenton to look at a possible location.
- Primavera had met Luker in Monaco when we had closed the deal, and had subsequently arranged to visit him in New York.
- Ms January was her friend and, coincidentally, was the ex-wife of my brother-in-law, who had just been appointed a judge by Her Majesty the Queen.

The last part really sealed it; obviously, the cops in New Jersey wanted to talk to me, but the Consul General insisted that they do so on what was legally British soil. An assistant Chief of something and another senior officer came to Third Avenue at half past midday and took a formal statement. They were clued up enough to ask me about Marie; I was ready for that, and told them that I was considering her for a role in the movie of *Blue Star Falling* (true) and that the meeting had been arranged to suit my schedule (lie, more or less).

Once they were done, they asked me if I would identify the bodies of Dylan and Maddy . . . they still hadn't found Prim. I was able to do so from photographs they had brought with them: they'd been banged about, obviously, but not too badly burned because of the swamp, so they'd been made recognisable. I nodded, mute, as I was shown each one.

They asked me who would be handling the funeral arrangements. I told them that Ms January's mother lived in England but that she had a sister in Princeton, who could be contacted in India through the university. I added that, as far as I knew, Benedict Luker had no next of kin and that I would take care of his needs.

As soon as they had left, the Consul General authorised the Press Officer to issue a statement announcing my miraculous escape, and recounting most of the story I'd told him and the cops. He offered me lunch, too, but I was still full of Woody Allen and cinnamon toast, so I passed on that. But I did ask him for his secretary's help in getting me out of the country; within half an hour she had me booked on the six thirty out of JFK, connecting to Nice and getting me home well in time for lunch the next day.

51

They gave me the full diplomatic treatment on both sides of the Atlantic. I never saw Customs or Immigration at JFK or 'Eefrow and, better still, I never saw any journalists.

The evil hour was only postponed, though: there was no protection in Nice, and I have never been happier to be met by a minder. Conrad, ever efficient, had hired extra security; just as well, because the airport staff couldn't have come close to coping. This was the Cannes Film Festival and Grand Prix week rolled into one and trebled. And all for poor, poor, pitiful me.

It was easier in Monaco: the Prince had ordered the police to guard my privacy while I recovered from the terrible shock I'd had.

I had another thing to recover from too. I had to tell Susie exactly why I'd missed the plane. I may be pretty good at manipulating the truth, but not when she's around. She didn't take it well. For a while I thought that the curse of being married to Oz had struck again, but eventually she told me that she'd rather have me, in her words, 'with a stain on your record and by my side than sat spotless up on a cloud playing a fucking harp'.

She went on to add that there can be very few people in history who could claim that their dick saved their life. Even so, I don't think that she's quite forgiven me; maybe she never will.

The kids didn't understand any of what had happened, thank JC, and won't for a while. Tom knows his mother won't be coming back, and he's making of that what a four-year-old can. Being brutal about it, he hadn't seen much of her for a year, so it would have been worse for him if it had been Susie or me who'd been put out to the pasture in the sky.

A week later, I was back in New York, with Susie. Benedict Luker's cremation was private; there were only five of us there, the two of us, his publisher, his editor and her secretary. The lovely editor was heartbroken. I reckon old Benny had been right: he might well have been on there.

The memorial service we held for Prim in Auchterarder, ten days after that, was an altogether different matter. David and Dawn Phillips were the chief mourners, of course, but Tom Blackstone was there too, with his dad, and Bruce Grayson, Prim's nephew, with his. They tell me that there were four hundred people outside the jam-packed church, listening as the service was relayed on speakers.

David asked me to do a eulogy for his daughter. I was touched, and agreed, of course. When I considered what I would say, I found myself remembering the last time Prim and I had really talked to each other, in the Algonquin, our favourite hotel in New York. And this is how it turned out.

'If you're the sort of person who looks at life through rose-coloured spectacles, you'd have seen Primavera Phillips as a conventional angel, clad in white. But if you were to take them off, then paradoxically, you'd have seen her still angelic, but maybe clad in a different colour, for Prim had some of the fallen one in her too, or at least she tried to make it appear so.

'She's touched my life in more ways than I can explain. I know this: from the moment I met her, I became a different person, a deeper person, a stronger person. A better person? Others can decide that. But without Primavera, I wouldn't have become what I am, whatever that might be, however you people see me as I stand here, unable to read my carefully drafted script for the tears in my eyes.

'She's touched your lives too, with the sheer excitement of being around her, with her mischief, with her devilment, but never with her badness, for despite all the things she saw and did . . . and there have been a few which I could not possibly recount to you, not here in this place, nor in any other . . . there was none of that in her. In spite of herself, in reality she was a wholly good person, and if she'd have liked to have been bad, well, she never quite made it, however hard she tried.

'We're not having a funeral today, because we have no body to commit, although we retain the hope that one day we might be able to do her that final honour. Still, where Prim rests right now, she shares that place with the likes of the fictional Luca Brasi, and maybe the real Jimmy Hoffa, and a few more similar characters. I find comfort in the knowledge that, in her wholeheartedly perverse way, she might like that idea.

'Yes, she played the game of life with all her great heart, and usually she won. She and I may not have played it too well together, not all the time, but when we were good we were great and when we were less than good, what the hell? We still managed to make Tom. He'll go down as her crowning achievement, and I promise you and her, I'll make damn sure that her spirit burns on in him.

'It was Kitty Wells who sang that it wasn't God who made honky-tonk angels. I reckon that in at least one case old Kitty was wrong. So long, Primavera, from me, from our boy and from all of us who love you and who will never forget you.'

I heard them applaud in the church, and outside, but by that time I couldn't see a single fucking thing.

52

Before all that came to pass, though, I did something else.

As soon as I'd tired the kids out playing with them, and that took a long time, I went off to my study, alone, and locked the door. My digital camera was in a drawer of my desk, where it usually resides because I always forget to take the bloody thing when I go on a trip. I took it out, connected it to my computer with a USB lead, then replaced the memory card with the one Maddy January had slipped to me.

I opened the software, and retrieved the images it held. There were only two. There was Harvey . . . or Hard-on, as I would call him ever afterwards when we were alone . . . in his father's red robe and wig with a cigarette in one hand, a can of the inevitable Irn Bru in the other, and an erection as big as his smile.

And then there was the other. Shot through a window and amplified, it was a back view of someone whom I knew had to be Tony Lee, his head slightly bowed as if in supplication. Facing him solemnly across a table was a man whose face I'd come to know well during our very brief acquaintance: Jimmy Tan.

In the background, beyond him, there was someone else: her face wasn't quite recognisable, but I knew her body and who she was too.

It had all clicked into place before that: the photo was just confirmation of what I'd known since Marie had left me in Trenton. Jimmy, the head of island security, had been aware of Maddy January's background, and he'd known of her connection to me. When he saw my name show up on what was probably his routine list of VIP arrivals, he put two and two together and came up with the correct number, or one that was near enough to the mark. Until Dylan told him the truth in the Next Page, he may have thought that she had sent for me to help her, but that didn't matter. Jimmy had put us together and that was enough.

He'd sent his tame Scots hitman to intercept me. I guessed that he'd staked out the hotel and had simply followed our taxi to the Crazy Elephant. Casually, during that first Saturday evening, Sammy had given me the tip to go to the Esplanade, and there Marie had been waiting to point me to Tony Lee.

He'd been a marked man himself, of course. He had to die with his wife, yet they knew he'd never betray her, and with him dead, how would they find her? Answer: by recruiting an unwitting mug like me to lead them to her.

But then, as I told you earlier, the simple game had changed, and had become much more complex.

First, Lee had been smarter than they had anticipated, sending Maddy out of Singapore and turning up to meet me himself. (He'd been right: if she'd gone to the Next Page, she'd have died there.)

Then Tan had been called in, not to bail me out of a nasty situation but directly by his old acquaintance Martin Dyer, the insider agent who'd gone down in flames in a shoot-out in Bangkok, of which Tan, the Triad chieftain, had known in advance, but had been unable, or maybe even unwilling, so devious was he, to prevent.

From that point, his prime objective had been to kill Dylan, the Interpol plant who had wrecked a Triad drug empire, and cost the lives of many men, but to do so in a way that nobody would ever uncover, by making him appear to be collateral damage in the death of Maddy January.

And in my death.

I had no doubt then and still have none, that Marie's mission had been to see me on to that plane with the rest. But she had failed her father: she'd been unable to watch me go on board to die so she'd offered herself to make me stay with her in Trenton. Yet she almost failed. I would have died, I would have gone with them, had it not been for that voice in my head.

Jan's message made me stay with her; I truly believe that Jan saved my life, from wherever she is now. You think I'm crazy? Tough shit.

How had Jimmy Tan reacted when he found out about his daughter's weakness, I wondered? With indifference, I guessed. In his great secret life, who was I, and what could I prove?

He was right, every step of the way, and I'd shown him to be so when I'd fed the cops a fable in New York. As always, Jimmy Tan had won. He was still the most important man in Singapore, and maybe in the whole of South East Asia, and nobody knew, outside the highest strata of his Triad clan.

Jimmy Tan was a wise and cunning man, and he understood this. All knowledge is power, and that is demonstrably true. But there is one form that bestows supreme power on those who hold it, and that is knowledge of which no other living person is aware that its bearer is possessed.

I wiped the images, both of them, from the card.

53

It's our plan now to winter in Los Angeles, every year. We'll hire tutors for the kids to keep their education up to scratch, but I will not be parted from my family, ever. Where I go they go, and my schedule will be arranged to 'make it so', as Captain Picard always said.

I am now consumed by the need to be there to protect Susie all the time. It would be seen by others, if they knew about it, as quite manic. But that's the way it is. The curse of being my wife is real and only I can keep it at bay by being around her wherever she is. As a result I've begun to acquire a reputation in the business for being very choosy about the projects I accept. Interestingly, that doesn't bother Roscoe Brown at all: he says it makes directors all the more anxious to cast me, whatever my price.

Five months have gone by since all that stuff happened.

Prim's body is still missing, but okay, so is Jimmy Hoffa's.

Miles and I accelerated the *Blue Star Falling* project, and we've just finished shooting on a sound stage in Hollywood. The part involving a Chinese girl was changed to Caucasian: we hired an emerging pop starlet to play it. I had fun being Benny Luker's *alter ego;* it was eerie but I enjoyed it. And, after all, who was better qualified to play him?

Incidentally, there was a reason for our haste. When Benedict Luker's will was read, it was discovered that the bastard had named me as his executor, and that he had left all his growing wealth and contractual rights to the mother of a deceased Scottish policeman, one Detective Inspector Michael Dylan.

I'd just viewed the rushes of the final scenes in the movie, a couple of days ago, when Conrad and Audrey Kent came back from a fortnight's well-earned holiday. They'd been to the part of Thailand that wasn't wrecked by the tsunami. It was a bonus from me, in addition to a substantial sum deposited for them in a Swiss bank account.

As he went to dump his case in their quarters, Conrad passed by my office. 'There's the newspaper you asked for, sir,' he said, laying it on my desk.

It was a copy of the *Straits Times,* three days old, and one story filled half of the front page. I glanced at it.

Singapore is in a state of shock [it began] *in the aftermath of the assassination of the island's security chief, Superintendent of Police 'Jimmy' Tan Keng Seng.*

Mr Tan (57) was gunned down with his daughter, Tan May Wee (25), in the bungalow they shared. She was a promising actress who used the stage name Marie Lin. Two men, believed to have been bodyguards, were also found dead at the scene.

In a statement, the Police Minister, a long-time friend of Mr Tan, said that the killings were clearly the work of terrorists. He vowed that Singapore would not be intimidated.

And so on, and so on; those fundamentalists are everybloody-where, are they not?

I tossed the paper aside.

All knowledge is power, especially when the other guy isn't in on it. Isn't that right, Primavera?

The end?